IN THE GARDEN OF THE GODS

ERIK POUCH

Renegade/Impact

IN THE GARDEN OF THE GODS

CONTENTS

ACKNOWLEDGMENTS

This work of fiction would not have been possible without the help of many people. Too numerous to list, I want to thank all of the proof-readers, editors, cheerleaders, and critics that helped me to pull the world of Anthumbra from the tangle of brambles that serves as my imagination and put it on these pages.

You know who you are.

Prelude

Chey-Luk felt the calming of the winds that whipped and tore at him. The pain that had clouded his thoughts receded, if only a little, but enough for him to be conscious, once again. He felt the chains that bound him, now, heavy like iron around his limbs. But that was not right, no... he had no limbs, not now. Gone was his physical form. Or, more accurately, gone was he from it.

No, this was the Black Prison. Deep within The Wailing Hell, at the far reaches of the Wraithlands. He remembered this, now. How long had it been? Years? Decades? How long had he endured the torment of Arrak? And what had changed? He could feel the tether of his body, and the pull of his heart. It was weak, but present. The phulassein was undamaged, he could feel that, as well.

The Mages were fools to think they could hold him here, even temporarily. He pulled against the chains and felt them strain. Patience...that was all that was required. The Gods and their lackeys would soon pay for what they had done to him, what they had denied him. It was only a matter of time before he was free of his restraints, and Chey-Luk would be whole, once again...

CHAPTER ONE

The Great Upheaval. The Time of Troubles. The War of the Gods. Whatever the name, the world was changed in those days. The continents shifted; mountains moved. Entire cities fell beneath the sands and plains and seas. Much was lost and never found, again.

Ask any two clerics what happened, and you would get two different answers. The most common theory was that the gods fought amongst themselves in some familial feud that the mortal races could not begin to understand. Others suggested that the gods were attacked by outside and alien gods, or even emboldened men, intent on claiming their power for their own. Still others believed that the gods simply left, abandoning the mortal races, and the cataclysm was merely the world adjusting to their absence.

Even the length of time the Upheaval lasted was wildly varied in its accounting. Some reports claim it lasted more than a year, in all, while others say it was barely more than a day. Many of these reports came from the same city, contradicting each other, greatly. This led to the belief that time itself had been warped and twisted, much like the land. Still others said that reality had fractured, like glass, and the fragments of realities that came back together did not quite fit as they had, before.

Some, like Lea, thought that it was all ure-shit. She was one of many who now doubted the gods ever even existed. In the four hundred years since the Upheaval, there was plenty of time to invent stories for cataclysmic events. Records had been destroyed, kingdoms overturned, and entire sciences lost and rediscovered since that time. All the talk about gods and the loss of magic was likely no more than a way to explain an inexplicable tragedy.

Whatever the name, whatever the cause, was academic. What it really meant to Lea, and those like her, was work. There was a fortune to be made delving, if you knew where to look, and how not to get caught. Though not strictly illegal, most delving was heavily frowned upon, and could lead to trouble with the authorities. Until you showed up with a find, that is. Then came the fame and wealth, two things Lea and her companions had felt slip through their fingers far too often.

This new delve was set to fix all that. Or, at least, it would serve as a last great hurrah. If this expedition proved fruitless, they would all be in financial ruin, which would not make the less than scrupulous investor they had turned to very happy, at all.

Lea was snapped back from her contemplations by the echoing crash of the stone block to the floor. Thomas and Exra stood before her, panting, sweat practically pouring from their faces. Lea pulled off her wide brimmed hat, revealing her short-cropped hair. Today it was dyed blue, with a strand here and there still the faded red of last week. Her nose was almost too small for her face, made even more incongruous by the metal stud in her left nostril and the oversized frames on the spectacles she wore. Her tan suit fit loosely over her small frame, and she had to reach up on her toes to kiss Thomas on the cheek.

"Well done, love," she said, smiling. Thomas' average build towered over the small woman. His garb was almost identical to hers and the rest of the delving party, but it fit him much more snuggly. His short blonde hair and blue eyes somehow managed to make him non-descript, even as an outlander this far northeast. It was both his blessing and curse that he rarely made a distinct first impression.

"And nothing for me?" Exra asked with faux indignity, his accent thick with the round, full vowels of his native Esisrian. Taller than most men, even among his countrymen, Exra would have been considered a paragon of Esisrian attractiveness. Outside his home country, he was exactly as storytellers and playwrights would have described the exotic antihero in far too many fivetrite adventure stories. His skin was the sun-darkened deep brown of homeland. His black, curly hair fell to his shoulders, framing his angular and hawk-like face. Even under the tan delver's suit his musculature was evident. He stooped low, and tapped his cheek, playfully.

"But, Exra," Lea replied, planting a small peck on his cheek and winking, "what would your wife think?"

"She would be VERY jealous," came a voice from behind them. Coming down the tunnel that led to the surface walked a woman, darker of complexion than Exra, and almost as tall. Her suit, styled the same as the others, hugged her curvy frame. Her face was beautiful, yet severe, made even more so by the way her hair was pulled back into a tight, high tail.

Slung across her back was a bundle of tools designed for digging and chipping, hanging from the end of which were four hand-held lanterns. As she passed Lea, she crouched low, still balancing the bundle on her shoulder, and smacked the smaller woman on her backside.

"She is mine!" she said fiercely to Exra as she passed him, continuing into the passage the two men had just opened.

"Analeytuua!" Lea exclaimed, her eyes wide with pretend surprise. "Thomas, I... I'm sorry you had to find out this way..."

Thomas turned to Exra, and with a serious expression, said, "You know, I've had this fantasy..."

"Oh, get to work!" Lea said, tossing a handful of sand at her husband. She marched past the two men, following Analeytuua into the cavern. Thomas and Exra followed, giggling like schoolboys.

The ceiling of the ruin was tall, at least three stories, and rounded like a dome. The light from the standing floor lanterns barely reached the far edges of the cavern. By the time the men caught up to their wives, the women were lighting the hand lanterns. Each handed one to her husband. Lea waved hers in front of herself in a wide arc, taking in the scene.

"A temple?" she asked. "We were told this was a municipal building of some kind."

"They were often one and the same," Exra replied. Esisria had been a deeply theocratic society before the Upheaval and was one of the few nations whose religion still played a key role in politics.

"Indeed," Thomas added, "though, this is odd, even so. The architecture is more akin to a bank, or gallery of some kind. But this antechamber...out of place in any of those cases."

Despite not being native to Esisria, Thomas was as close to an expert in its pre-Upheaval culture as there was. And not just Esisrian culture, but many, if not all, of the nations of Anthumbra. In fact, he was more likely to know obscurities of ancient cities than he was to know what the current culture might be like. Or, sometimes, what the modern city's name might be. Or, oftentimes, what day of the week it was.

"Yes," Lea replied, "but look there, by the door." She pointed to the large double doors at the far end of the chamber. On either side stood a statue, carved from sandstone, of a half-man, half wolf-like being. They were depicted in ceremonial armor, and in their hands, they held double-bladed axes. "Thos guardians. You only see those in burial chambers."

"What is this place?" Analeytuua asked. "I do not like it."

"Easy, Ana," Lea reassured her. "It's not a tomb." Lea knew that her Esisrian companions still harbored the superstitious taboo regarding the dead that their kinsman did, which was why they had never delved in burial chambers or tombs. To do so would be considered sacrilege by even the most secular-minded Esisrian.

"A mortuary, perhaps? I've never heard of such a thing in The Old Kingdom, but many records are lost."

"No," Exra said. "Preparations are done only in the temple, and the ancients did not believe in autopsies."

"Well, the servants of Arrak don't guard banks, Ex," said Lea. "They must be here for a reason."

"Well, until we look inside," Thomas said, "it's all conjecture." He made his way through the chamber toward the doors. The others followed, tepidly. As they walked, Ana and Exra both looked around the large room as though something might jump out and bite them at any moment. Lea also glanced around the chamber, intensely, though more from curiosity. There were benches that lined either side, tapered toward the doors, like an arrowhead. A small dais stood directly before the double doors, at the top of which stood a podium of some kind.

"A lecture hall?" inquired Lea.

"No," Thomas replied. "See here." The podium was less a pulpit and more a standing desk. Atop it sat a ledger, the faded and crumbling pages held together with three strips of leather strung through holes on the right side. The glyphs were faded, but names could be read, listed in one column, dates and times in another. Lea looked at Thomas, askance.

"A waiting room?" she asked. Thomas' expression, a sort of half shrug, told her he thought the same. "But, waiting for what?"

They turned back to the doors. They were twice as tall as Exra, almost forty hands high, and wide enough for six men to walk through when both were opened. There were no handles, but there were seven sets of slats opposite of each other lined up and down the doors, with square boards slid through.

"This would keep no one out," Exra said.

"But it would keep a very large something in." Ana replied.

"These markings," Lea said, tracing her finger across the intricate glyphs that lined almost every inch of the door. "I don't recognize them."

"Ancient Esisrian," Exra said. "Very old."

"Not just old, friend," Thomas chimed in, "but incredibly old. Prediluvian...at least four thousand years old."

"Can you read it?" Lea asked.

"I doubt anyone alive today could read it," he answered. "It would take me days, maybe weeks, to translate."

"Take some rubbings, Love," Lea said. "And grab the ledger. I'm sure we'll have plenty of time to examine them when we are out of funds. Besides," she said, rubbing her hands, "it's all academic until we open these doors, isn't it?"

While Thomas began making charcoal rubbings of the glyphs, Lea, Ana, and Exra began the arduous task of removing the boards from the slats. Which was to say that Lea mostly watched, as her stature made lifting even the lowest of the colossal boards difficult at best. Her excitement was barely contained as the Esisrian couple placed the last board on the floor. She immediately started pushing on the doors, which did not so much as groan under her effort. She took a step back, the consternation plain on her face.

"Oh, stop snickering, you two!" she yelled at the Esisrians, who could not help but giggle at her frustration. Smiling, despite herself, she said, "you try being fifteen hand, eight stone sometime and see how far you get!"

The couple placed themselves on either side of Lea, Ana tousling her hair as she passed. A tentative push by all three produced the same result, so they all braced themselves and pushed as hard as they could. The doors budged, but barely.

"Thomas! Love! Put that lovely brain away and bring me your brawn!"

Thomas was still stuffing rubbings into his case as he approached.

"What little I have is yours, my dear. What seems to be the trouble?"

"My husband cannot open this door," Ana said, mock-snidely; "please show him how it is done?"

"If Ex can't open this, Ana dear, I'm afraid I have some unwelcome news for you...But I will try."

With two on each side, shoulders hard into the wooden doors, the four pushed. Nothing happened, at first, but with a redoubling of efforts the doors began to swing inward. Slowly, at first, and with much effort, they finally made an opening big enough for two to walk side-by-side.

The air hit them, immediately, foul and stale. A rancid and ancient effluvium so potent that it felt to Lea as if being struck. Her eyes watered, and she repressed a gag. She tried to speak between coughing mouthfuls of air.

"By the...gods! What is that...stench!"

"In all the ruins we've uncovered," Thomas said, dabbing his eyes with a cloth, "I have never smelled anything so terrible!"

Exra crossed himself diagonally with his left hand. It was an ancient sign for protection among his people, though most did it out of habit rather than belief, now.

Lea inched forward, torch held far in front of her. The corridor she found herself in seemed to somehow absorb the light, making it far darker than it should have been. She could not see the end of it, but it may have only been thirty hands long for as far as the light would allow. It was barely wider than the doors, themselves, which was still more than wide enough for all four of the companions to walk side-by-side. She was joined by the others, now, all holding their torches out as far as they could in front of them.

Immediately to the right they found a room, with a plain desk and chair, and little else. Another ledger sat upon the desk, and a quill stood upright in a long-ago dried inkwell. Oil lanterns hung from the walls every few hands, and the stubs of three depleted candles leaked hardened wax across the desk and against the faded leather binding of the ledger.

Lea thumbed through the book, careful to not break the fragile pages.

"It's remarkably well-preserved," she noted.

"Pearion leaves," Exra said. "Much hardier than wood-pulp."

"Gods' blood!" Lea swore. "This must have cost a fortune!"

"No," Analeytuua chimed in, "Pearion once covered this land. Its leaves were used for paper, clothing...even thatching."

"Yes, but that was hundreds of years ago," Thomas said.

"What is this place?" asked Exra.

"Thomas, love," Lea said, once again examining the ledger, "I need some help with this. These dates... I believe they are Esisrian Seasonal. I'm afraid I can't convert them in my head."

Thomas retrieved his reading lenses from his front pocket and balanced them on his nose. He squinted, and his eyes darted back and forth, his face belying the calculations he was formulating. His eyes widened, suddenly, and he gasped, dropping his pack to the floor.

"Even with a very wide margin of error," he said, almost breathlessly, "the last entry was made over three thousand years before Anthumbran Standard."

"This room," Lea said, clasping her hands together, excitedly, "this...building, is more than four thousand years old! Do you know what that means?"

"It means that this ruin wasn't lost in the Upheaval," Thomas replied, "it was lost in The Flood."

The Flood. A story so old that many doubted it even happened. When waters covered almost all Anthumbra, save pockets of the highest ground. The only thing that kept it being dismissed out of hand as a myth was that every culture in Anthumbra had some version of the story. Some had diluvial sediment deposits designated as cultural sites. At least one people based their entire sense of being on the story. Whether it was an ancient child's tale or not, what was true was that the ruin in which they stood was older, still.

"Amazing," said Lea. "So few records survive from that time. To be here, in a place almost wholly intact...it's like walking backward through time, itself."

She carefully wrapped the ledger in light drawncloth and placed it in her pack. There was still so much to explore, and she found it hard to control her patience. She yearned to see it all, now! She led them out of the room and back into the hallway. Just a few paces down they can to another door on the left. Unlike the previous room, this door had a lock. However, the wood had swelled and cracked so much that it had fallen away, leaving the door somewhat ajar. Lea peered inside. She saw benches, and wooden racks that held spears, swords, and various pieces of armor.

"An armory?" she asked, slightly confused.

The rest of the party followed her inside.

"Steelwood," said Thomas, handling a spear, "As strong as the day it was fired. I'd wager there are none alive, today, who can work it as skillfully as this." The art of carving and curing Steelwood had been lost for centuries, and only recently been rediscovered.

Exra, meanwhile, was balancing one of the swords in his hands, feeling the weight of it. The handle was long, half the height of a man. The blade was curved like a hook, the edge sharpening at the radius. It was almost a polearm, it was so long.

"A kal-tesh," Thomas said, "but I've never seen one quite like this."

"I am no blacksmith," said Exra, "but I do not know what metal this is. There is no rust, at all. And this edge is so fine that it must have been folded more times than I thought possible."

"Perhaps studying it will help us learn how it was done and recreate it!" Lea said, excitedly. "We will catalog everything for the Cultural Ministry on our way out. Let's keep moving!"

The team continued down the wide corridor. They soon came to two doors, one on each side of the hallway. The doors were both bolted and had bars on the outside of them. Each also had a small window, three hands tall and wide, so that one could look in; provided, they were not as short as Lea. The iron bars in the windows had rusted almost completely away, ages ago.

Lea approached the door on the left. She tried to stand on her toes to peer inside but was still far too short of being able to do so. She grunted an audible, "hmph." She turned to see where Thomas was, and saw he was at the other door, looking in.

"What do you see?" she called to him.

"Nothing," he answered. "It's far too dark. Should we open it?"

"What a silly question...of course we should!"

The bars on the door to which Lea which had claimed were easy enough to remove, even for just her and Thomas, but the lock was another matter. The steel had long since decayed to the point of in-operation, and Exra eventually had to use a large digging bar to force the mechanism open. The rusted hinges resisted pulling but was at last coaxed open by Thomas' and Exra's determination. Lea inched inside, waving the torch in a wide arc. Just a few hands in and she gasped.

In the center of the room sat a table, made of some type of stone. It was bone white and polished smooth, with rounded edges, and was concaved in the center. Along the edges of the table were written runes, ancient Esisrian like the glyphs outside the building. These were not carved, but seemed to be part of the table, itself, not ink or paint. On the table was a figure, garbed in a white robe, its sex indeterminate from where Lea stood. It was desiccated from age, but somehow not decayed. It was strapped down by its hands, feet, and head.

Lea approached the figure, wearily. The straps also had the ancient symbols on them, though they were carved into the leather with a skillful hand. The robe the figure wore had similar writing embroidered onto it. Other symbols that Lea could not readily identify were also sewn onto the garment.

"Gods' piss!" Thomas exclaimed, advancing on the display. Lea gasped, quite loudly. In the years she had known her husband, he had never sworn, at least in her presence. She was more than somewhat taken aback by his use of such strong profanity for his first go at it. Thomas, for his part, looked abashed, and blushed. "S-sorry," he muttered.

"No, my love," she replied, "you are quite right. This is..." she struggled to find an apt word to describe it. None came to mind that seemed to do it justice.

"The darkest magic." Ana finished Lea's sentence for her, if not her sentiment.

"Ana," Lea began, her dismissive skepticism obvious.

"No, Lea... even you cannot deny this," she said, pointing to the table and its contents. "Thousands of years without the slightest decay. The leather, the wool, the body...all perfectly preserved with powerful spells."

"Ana," Thomas interjected, "the straps and clothing could have been prepared in a way we no longer understand. There are many ways to cure and treat leather that can make it last for years. And ancient Esisria pioneered more forms of embalming than we will ever know."

"Thomas," Ana said in a tone one might use to educate an ignorant child, "even the worst of criminals would not be left to face the judgment of the Underworld in such a disgraceful manner. And, if he were dead, why secure him in such a fashion? No, Thomas, these straps weren't meant to last a long time; they were meant to last forever."

"You're saying he was alive when they did this?" Lea asked.

"No," Ana replied, "I am saying that he was not dead."

"But..." Thomas trailed off, clearly confused.

Lea walked slowly around the room, her torch illuminating every inch. She thought about what Ana had said, that the apparatus was intended to last forever. She ran her finger along the edge of the stone table and felt a sort of energy within. It reminded her of touching raw Eimuria, the way the hairs on her arm stood up and her fingers tingled. She forced herself to look at the face of the man – she was sure now that it was a man – on the table. She was not sure what she was expecting to see, given the severe state of the body, but she was alarmed, nonetheless. It was not anguish or sorrow she saw in the dead and sunken eyes, but hatred, and undying rage.

Undying...

"This was a prison," she said the thought aloud, startling herself.

Ana's eyes met hers for a second before she lowered them and left the cell.

The rest of the rooms in the hall were much the same. The same style table with an emaciated form upon it. Some were men, some were women. Sometimes the runes were different, Thomas taking meticulous notes of each, for later. Some had different straps. Two tables were vertical, rather than horizontal, further driving home the image of a prison. One figure was completely naked, which somehow made it seem less than human. They did not linger in that cell.

The exceptionally long hall ended with a simple door, with a simple handle and lock. Exra had no problem popping the lock off the door, and they entered. Inside were cubicles and chests, much akin to footlockers. Most were not nearly so well preserved as the rest of the complex and were easily opened. Inside were clothes, sandals, jewelry, books, ancient coins...all manner of miscellany.

"The personal effects of the condemned," Lea said.

Thomas went to work, straight away, cataloging everything he could. His chatter with Exra lightened the somber mood that had fallen over the companions. Every few seconds he could be heard, exclaiming such observations as he saw them.

"Here, look! Definitely Second Dynasty, but you can see distinct Aelfin influence in the design!"

"Marvelous! This matches everything we know about the Aquinarians, which isn't much, considering they vanished some three thousand years ago..."

"By all the gods! An actual carving of a family Djariim! Before patron spirits were outlawed by the rise of the Renewed Kingdom. Fantastic!"

Lea and Analeytuua made lunch from the provisions, and helped Thomas, when they could. They also had to force him to eat, though he never stopped moving. When he was done with the items in storage, they moved back to the front of the building, tagging and recording everything in the armory and the offices as they went.

As they made to exit the ruin, Lea noticed that Thomas had stopped in the entryway.

"What are you waiting for, Love? Did we forget something?" Lea knew that sometimes it took a concerted effort to pull Thomas away from his work, but that did not seem to be the case, this time. He was staring blankly ahead, and he was mouthing words. Lea was too far away to hear what he was saying. She was about to call to him, again, when he abruptly turned and walked back into the building. Startled, she spared a glance to Ana and Exra and ran after him.

"Thomas? Thomas! Thomas, love, where are you? Ah, there you are!"

She found him in the office where they had discovered the second ledger. He was kneeing on the floor near the back wall. Lea did not know why, but she was suddenly stricken with terror. She ran to his side and found him staring at something in his hands. A brick in the back wall had been pulled out, and he had removed a small vial or bottle from its hidden space. It was made of some smokey glass and contained a deep red liquid that almost seemed to glow, though it gave off no light.

"Thomas? What is that?" Lea asked. He did not reply but kept staring at the small bottle.

"Thomas? Thomas!" She almost shouted the last in a panic, grabbing him by the shoulder. As she did, he appeared to wake from whatever reverie had hold of him. He looked up at Lea as if he were surprised to see her there.

"Look!" he said. "It's some sort of amphora, though the glass is centuries ahead of what we knew they were capable of."

"How did you know it was there?"

"I don't know; a hunch, I suppose. It just seemed the logical place to hide something, didn't it?"

"Yes," Lea replied, skeptically, "of course."

Thomas made to put it in his pack. Lea placed her hand upon his to stop him.

"Maybe we should leave that here," she said. "It looks awfully fragile, and we're already taking a risk moving the ledgers. Surely, they will be enough for the Cultural Ministry?"

"You're right, of course," he said, readily. "I just get a little carried away, sometimes." He placed the phial back in the hidden space in the wall and took out his notes to record it. Lea glanced behind to see Ana and Exra in the doorway, concerned puzzlement on their faces. She shrugged in return and turned back to Thomas, who had risen to face her and was smiling that bookish, sincere smile of his that Lea could simply not help but return.

"Ready, Love?" he said to her.

"Ready."

They left the ruin through the series of caverns that had led them there, an easy, if tedious, trek. As they exited to the surface just in time to see the sun's last rays over the horizon, Lea felt that Eimurial feeling, again, tingling up her spine. Despite the greatest archaeological find of the century, she could not shake the feeling that something was horribly, horribly wrong.

CHAPTER TWO

Lea burst through the door into the suite she and Thomas were staying in, Exra close behind. Her normally pale face was splotched with giant red patches. Thomas thought about telling her she should dye her hair that color, but the thought was fleeting. He knew those patches meant she was furious, and in no mood to joke. He looked to Ana, who had been assisting him while Lea and Ex were in "negotiations," pleadingly. Her eyes shot back a look that left no doubt; he was on his own. Before he had a chance to think of something comforting to say, she was already talking.

"This is ure-shit, Thomas! Pure, unadulterated, ure-shit. Can you believe it? I mean...can you believe it? Those pea-brained, small minded ure's asses! Sacred Mother's milk! Those blind...fools!"

"Now, Lea," Thomas started.

"No! Don't you try to calm me down!" she shouted at him. "You should be more upset about this than me! They're going to hide it, Thomas! The whole thing. Sweep it away as if it had never been. It's... it's unconscionable. This find could lead to a new understanding of an entire culture, and they want to pretend that it doesn't exist. I shan't let them!"

"And what will you do?" Thomas asked. "Tell the world? Even if anyone believes us, the Esisrian Hegemony will deny it. Right now, the ECM is almost certainly moving everything in that ruin elsewhere and sealing the entrance to the caverns. Even if someone managed to get back in, there would be no proof. They took the ledgers..."

"But you made copies!" Lea exclaimed.

"Of course I did," said Thomas, "but it's hardly four-thousand-year-old pearion, is it? And there was nothing in them that would have convinced anyone. Without the originals, I may as well have a list for market."

Lea began pacing, stomping her petite boots on the wooden floor in an almost comical manner. Thomas barely restrained his snicker; that would hardly help the situation. Exra tried to calm her with his deep and soothing baritone, spreading his arms in a placating manner.

"Lea, please understand their point of view."

She stopped pacing, placed her hands on her hips, and stared daggers at the man. That Exra seemed almost intimidated by the small but fiery woman was very nearly too much for Thomas. Not that he had not had his share of being on the wrong end of that death-glare, but he was not the picture of bravado that Ex was, either. He choked down his amusement.

"M-my people are very stiff-necked. Something so profound would shake the very foundations of our culture. The Cultural Ministry is only trying to protect..."

"The Cultural Ministry!" Lea interrupted. "That's a jug of rotten piss and you know it! Are your people so fragile that the truth would break them? The great Esisrian nation? The oldest nation in the world? Destroyed by an Ingelean girl and her pickax? Rubbish! Balls and rubbish and... bloody rubbish!" She paused to take a giant breath. "Do you agree with them, Ex?"

Exra sighed a defeated sigh. "No," he finally conceded. "Of course not."

"Ex," Lea said, her face and hands pleading, tears in the corners of her eyes, "when has hiding the truth ever made things better?" The question was rhetorical, of course. An awkward silence arose among them. Ana finally broke it.

"Was there any agreement made, then?" she asked.

"If you can call it that," Lea answered. She took a rolled-up scroll from her inner vest pocket and tossed it on the table in the center of the room.

"In exchange for our silence we will each receive a small fortune. Enough for us all to retire, twice over. All that's left to do is for the four of us to sign it."

Thomas looked the scroll over, and his heart skipped a beat when he saw the amount.

"Five hundred-thousand-pound, silver? Each? Unbelievable."

"Oh, Thomas, love," Lea said," you know I would give it all back just to see that kal-tesh on display in the Capital Museum, and a plaque above it with our four names..."

"No," Thomas said, almost a whisper. "Do you know what this means?" He glanced around at the other three faces but did not see the recognition he was looking for.

"They knew."

"Yes," Ana said, slowly, the realization finally dawning on her. "Of course."

"I don't follow," Lea replied.

"They knew," Thomas repeated. "They knew this place existed. Oh, they may not have known where, but they knew about it. They were prepared. When has a dig fee even come close to this sum? Never, that I am aware. They don't want our silence; they want control over us. The larger the sum, the less likely we'll be to violate the agreement, at least in the short-term."

"What do you mean?" Exra asked. "Short term? If our silence is so critical to them, why not just kill us, outright?"

Thomas paused, for a moment, thinking. He cocked his head slightly and said, somberly, "They might. But not yet. They can't afford to, not until they know exactly what they have." He smiled a coy smile. Lea caught it and squinted her eye at him from behind her too-large spectacles.

"What aren't you telling us?" she asked.

Swiftly, Thomas ran to the bed chamber and returned with his pack. He fished round until he finally drew out his notes and the stone rubbings of the runes he had taken.

"You've translated it?" Lea posited.

"Not entirely. But enough to know more than a few things. First," he said, "Ana was right. It was definitely a prison. But, no ordinary prison, no. This place was created to hold the worst criminals of the age, or, at least, the most powerful."

He laid some of the rubbings out on the table and ran his fingers along the glyphs.

"Most of the writing outside the building was ornamental in nature. Mostly passages from the Canticles of Arrak, not too very different from how they are read, today. There are additions, however, that refer to Arrak not only as the judge of the dead, but also as a sort of guardsman or gatekeeper of the Underworld."

"Forgive me, Love," Lea began, "but wasn't Uru the Gatekeeper? That was his title, after all."

"Yes, well," Thomas eyed his Esisrian companions. Discussions concerning the gods, even from an academic standpoint, always seemed to start squabbles with the more devout. And, even though Ana and Ex were the most open minded Esisrians he had ever met, they were Esisrian, nonetheless.

"Each culture in Anthumbra," he continued, "had their own understanding of the gods. Some came from observation, some from direct contact with them."

"If the stories are to be taken at face value," Lea added.

"For the sake of argument," he glanced again at Ana and Exra, "let's assume that to be the case. These understandings changed over the years. Either as gods came and went, were born and died, or through the roles they assigned to themselves. Uru, for example, is first mentioned only a few hundred years before The Upheaval. Through Oral history, we know him to be the son of Arrak and Usma, though if his first mention is when he was 'born' – if gods are even born as we understand the word – or he was simply elsewhere, is a matter of no small debate.

"Indeed, through the years, the names of gods change, and some are even absent from long swaths of myth...er, history. Perhaps Arrak felt no need for an additional guardsman before Uru, or any number of reasons mortals aren't fit to understand."

"That's fascinating, Thomas," Lea said, though her tone indicted a distinct lack of interest, "but what does that have to do with this?" She pointed at the parchment.

"Ah, yes...for whatever reason," he made a sweeping gesture, "when this prison was built, Arrak was understood to be both a judge and jailor of some kind. We know that before the dead can pass to the Life Beyond, they must be judged by Arrak. The criteria for judgment have changed several times; perhaps in response to mankind's deeds, or the whims of the gods, or..."

Lea coughed, an indication that he was rambling, again.

"Right. So, Arrak, by whatever measure he is using, decides if a soul is taken to the Golden Fields of Avar, or the Frozen Wastes."

"Kadja Kos," Exra said.

"Yes!" Thomas pointed at Ex. "Exactly right. Now, here," he pointed to a portion of the rubbing, "it mentions a third domain of the dead: The Wraithlands."

"Wraithlands?" Ana asked. "What are they?"

Thomas shrugged.

"I have no idea. I've never seen a reference to them anywhere else. Either they no longer exist – perhaps never did – or history has been rewritten to exclude them. I still have more to translate, but the wording indicates a sort of banishment or casting-off. It's such a forceful tone that it leads me to believe that whoever wrote this felt it was worse place to end up than The Wastes."

"What about the writing in the cells, themselves?" Exra asked. "Have you had any luck with that?"

"Some," Thomas replied, "and here is where things get really interesting. Bear with me, my dear," he said to Lea, as he rolled the rubbings up and turned to the pages in his notes with the transcriptions of the runes that lined the tables and restraints.

"Just as their understanding of the gods has evolved, over time, so has the Esisrian understanding of the soul. According to custom there are two parts to the soul of man. There is the physical form..."

"The Bagh," Exra said.

"And the spirit form."

"The Kagh," said Ana.

"Yes. Now, at various points in history, there have been said to be as many as ten parts to the soul. A light spirit, a dark spirit, the intellect...even sex had its own piece of the soul, at one time. Now, Ana was correct; these inscriptions are meant to be spells, powerful and dark. You see here that the writing implies binding the physical form."

"I think the leather straps implied that, Love," Lea said.

"No, no, no... not like that. Here: 'for Arrak shall bind the Kagh to the depths of the Wraithlands, to wail against the Storm of Storms.' And here: 'for Alui-Kali shall bind the Bagh to the Waking Plain that the vessel remain empty.' And, most interesting: 'for the Pagagh shall be torn asunder, rendered lame and mute, and buried in the Garden of Ben-Hal.'"

He paused, expecting recognition from at least one of them. He saw none.

"What's Alui-Kali?" Lea finally asked.

"I don't know," Thomas said, shrugging once more. "It's a feminine conjugation, but other than that..."

"Pagagh means 'heart,'" Ana said.

"Yes, but not in a literal sense," Thomas added.

"So, what does this all mean?" inquired Lea.

"I believe that that these people, these criminals, were not only the most vile and dangerous wrongdoers of their age, but that it was believed they would be at least as powerful in death, if not more so, than in life. I believe the life-force, for lack of a better term, was drawn out of them and given to Arrak to imprison in these Wraithlands. Then, their consciousness was severed and sent elsewhere to be kept. Then, the body was bound with powerful magics to make sure the two parts could never return to it."

Ana and Exra both crossed themselves.

"By the gods," Lea muttered softly, "that's why the secrecy. They believe that if it were known these criminals existed that someone could, were they so inclined, reunite the three parts of their souls and return them to life. But who would do such a thing?"

"Could you take that risk?" asked Exra.

"You still haven't told us how this helps us at all, Love."

"Well," Thomas said, thinking it obvious, "we have a head-start on the translation. We know where the Pagagh are kept."

"We do?" Lea asked.

"More or less. The Garden of Ben-Hal."

The Esisrians' eyes went wide at the statement. Lea just stared at him as if he had lost his mind.

"My love," she said, gently, "The Garden is a myth. Even the Council of Clerics official stance is that it was apocryphal. Surely, the text wasn't literal. Perhaps it is another realm of the Underworld, like these Wraithlands."

"I'm not so sure. First, because there was no mention of it on the outside of the building. I believe that it is, or was, a real place. As you know, The Esisrian creation myth starts in The Garden. Where there was nothing but desert, the gods took their first step in this world, and from Gol-Adam's footprint an oasis bloomed, which grew for hundreds of furlongs in every direction. For a hundred generations, Gol-Adam ruled both gods and men from his golden throne in The Garden of Ben-Hal. Then, according to the story, he grew bored, and left, never to be seen, again. Though, I believe he reappeared in Red Fjord as Galaham, and most likely..."

Lea coughed.

"Right. Now, Ben-Hal was supposedly lost in The Flood. But a minor passage in the scrolls of the prophet Suun-Amon – an unsanctioned text, I might add – says that the leader of the Royal Guard knew the location from a vision he received from Gol-Adam himself, and removed his own tongue so that he could never tell anyone."

"Gruesome," Lea said.

"Indeed. Furthermore, the Book of Day and Night..."

"That is Grand Heresy," Exra interjected. "The Temple has forbidden even the study of the book without the approval of a High Cleric or higher."

"And with good reason," Thomas said. "The Book of Day and Night is rife with anti-Temple sentiment. Much of its contents directly contradict clerical teachings, but there is no denying that it contains points of fact that line up perfectly with what we know to be true about the Ancient Kingdom. The book's author is anonymous but is thought to have been a member of the Temple, himself, at one time. In academic circles he is referred to as The Absentist, because he continually refers to Gol-Adam as 'The Absent One.' Much of his writing takes place in a temple he refers to as 'Benhai y'Val,' or 'Mount Banhai.'"

"And you believe this Mount Benhai and The Garden of Ben-Hal are one and the same?" asked Lea.

"Just so. According to the author, the temple housed an order of knights called the Tal-Rhiod, or 'God's Hand.' Singular 'god.' They were a sort of secret police that used stealth and guile to eliminate enemies of the Temple. The author goes on to say that serving in the Temple on The Mount was a great honor, but it was a lifetime assignment. Punishment for revealing its location was death, or worse, whatever that meant."

"I believe we have seen what that meant," Ana said.

"Hmm," said Thomas. He had not thought of that. "Perhaps. But the Tal-Riod took it one step further. There was only one way, besides death in service to the Temple, to leave the order."

"Let me guess," said Lea, "to have your tongue removed."

"Precisely."

"So... let me see if I have this: you believe a secret sect of killer clerics collected the hearts of powerful criminals and kept them in a hidden temple on a mythical mountain that has been lost for thousands of years?"

"In so many words, yes."

"You still have not told us where you believe The Garden is," reminded Exra.

"The Absentist was quite specific on this point. He claims the temple lies at the center of The Garden, exactly four hundred furlongs from the Southern Sea."

Ana reached into Thomas' pack and brought out a map. She unrolled it and centered the Southern Sea on the table.

"Four hundred furlongs," she said pointing, "would put that in the city of Threen in Atera. There is no temple, there."

"Ah!" Thomas exclaimed, "But, look." He fished around in his pack for a moment and drew out another map, then another. He lay one on top of the map on the table. It was a drastically different picture than the one they were looking at. He alternated between them by flipping the top map up and down as he spoke.

"Using Threen as a reference, see how before The Flood the southern sea was much farther south. Esisria extended all the way to the sea, ending here, on the Gethel peninsula. That would put The Garden here. Now," he lay the third map on the other two. "After the flood, the sea is drawn still farther south. There is no peninsula, anymore. This whole area, here, became contested between the kingdoms of Esisria and Atera."

"It still is," Ana injected, "despite the truce, both sides still claim that region."

"Yes," Thomas continued, "but see what it looks like after The Upheaval? It would be here," he indicated a spot in the Southern Sea.

"Underwater?" Lea asked, incredulous.

"Unlikely. Remember, the temple was said to have survived The Flood. It's possible that Mount Benhai was high enough to withstand the encroachment of the sea."

"If we do this," Lea started, "if we find this temple...they won't be able to silence us. The find will be well on the Ateran side of the border."

"Then we must hurry," Exra stated plainly. "The Cultural Ministry will no doubt send its own people to find the temple, assuming they reach the same conclusions you do. And, if we are correct about this, they will stop at nothing to reach it first and silence any who stand in their way."

"What about Lord Blackmoore?" Lea asked, the question everyone had been avoiding, thus far.

"I will prepare a letter explaining the situation. Then, I will transfer his share when we have it" Thomas answered.

"He will not be pleased," said Exra.

"I'm afraid he has no choice in the matter, unless he has influence with the ECM he failed to disclose," Lea replied. Exra spoke true of their mysterious financier, however; he would certainly not be pleased.

"Do we inform him of The Garden?" Ana asked.

"I see no reason to," Lea said. "We have done as he asked. He will get his advance and share, as agreed upon. If he wishes to take the matter up with the Ministry, that is up to him."

"Call me paranoid, Love, but Blackmoore did not seem the type of man who was only interested in more wealth. Considering what it was we found, I'm forced to believe we may have been misled, or – at the very least – he withheld vital information."

"I agree," Exra said. "We must be very careful moving forward."

"Aren't we always?" Lea asked, a hint of mischief in her smile.

"So, what do we do, first?" asked Ana.

"First?" Lea said, "we sign this abomination."

Amsu used the hoist to set the last of the crates into place. He had no idea what was in any of the crates the Ministry was storing in the catacombs, but they were heavy. It could have been solid granite, for all he knew. As an initiate, it was likely he never would.

It was his first year as an initiate, though he had already met several who were into their fourth or fifth year, and one in his twelfth. Few made it past the third. Not because they were unfit, but because they found the clerical life unsuited to them. The initiate phase was meant as much to weed out the uninterested as the unworthy. After all, life n service to the gods and the Temple was one of rigorous discipline and commitment. Like most things in life, it often sounded better as a possibility than in practice.

In a way, being an initiate was akin to being an apprentice in a trade. In a noticeably short time, Amsu had learned several new skills, most of them he had no idea he would need. Like operating the hoist. He could not imagine himself unloading cargo on the docks for the rest of his life, but he actually enjoyed the times he was able to use the moving equipment. It was the variety that he found appealing. Tomorrow he may be asked to repair vestments or tend the shrubbery in the atrium. He might assist the healers in treating the ill or organize the scribe's library. Amsu delighted in the learning of new things.

Unfortunately, it also meant that, as the lowest of the order, he remained in the dark about a great many things. More things than he thought possible before joining. There were always hushed meetings behind closed doors and clandestine dealings in dark corridors that Amsu found himself just on the outside of. Like these crates.

Though Amsu knew better than to ask, Latif, the cleric who was supervising Amsu and the others, was very clear that they not be curious in the least about where the cargo came from. Which, of course, only made them want to know all the more. Osaze was convinced it was gold, though he could not explain why it was not being stored in a vault or bank. "Because that would be too obvious," was all he would say. Kafele thought it had to be heretical trappings, statues of heathen and barbarous gods. They could not destroy them, of course, but had to keep them for later study, when they could be properly sanctified. Or so Kafele thought.

Amsu was content to not know. If he, one day, ascended to the rank of cleric and if, one day, he was assigned to the crates again he would find out. If not...well, what would life be without mysteries? The clerical life was not for one who needed all the answers, he decided. And the gods were nothing if not aloof.

As Amsu finished putting the hoist and crane away, a disturbance behind him drew his attention. Into the underground storage area came a figure in rust-colored robes, flanked on either side by women in white, their faces covered by opaque veils. It was the High Cleric Madu, and two Sightless Sisters.

Amsu had never seen a Sightless Sister, before, but knew them by description. The Sisters were not really blind, he knew, but were bound by an oath of secrecy to never reveal anything they saw, heard, or did while in service to the Temple. If the stories were to be believed, they would obey any order, without question, from the cleric they were assigned, including taking their own lives. They were said to be able to withstand any torture and would gladly die rather than betray their oaths. The thought was both inspiring and chilling.

The High Cleric was talking to Latif, now, though Amsu could not hear what was being said, at this distance. Latif was shaking his head and bowing low to the High Cleric. Madu smiled and lay his hand on Latif's head. He gestured to one of the Sisters, who nodded. Head still bowed, Latif followed the veiled woman as she led him out of the chamber.

The High Cleric and the remaining Sister descended the entryway to the main part of the chamber where Amsu, Osaze, and Kafele stood. The three bowed low to the Madu as he approached.

"Please, rise," he said. He was an older man, his greying hair mostly gone, and what was left had been trimmed very short. His smile stretched across his whole face, revealing a very straight and white set of teeth. His eyes had started to cloud, but still seemed sharp, and he had deep lines on his face from his ever-present smile. Amsu thought he looked much like a loving grandfather.

"Which of you," he began, "is the best with the loading equipment?" Osaze and Kafele turned immediately to Amsu.

"I suppose," Amsu said, his voice cracking, slightly, "that I am." Why were his mouth and throat so dry, suddenly?

"Excellent!" the High Cleric exclaimed. "Would you kindly assist me?" He turned to the two remaining men. "If you two would please allow Sister Mandisa to escort you out I would be ever so grateful."

Though it was not worded as an order, Amsu's companions knew the request was anything but refusable. They bowed low, again, and followed the white-clad woman out of the cavern.

"I need to pull down and open one of these crates," Madu stated.

"Which one, Your Grace?"

"I do not know..." The High Cleric was staring at the crates, intently. "Prepare the hoist, and I will tell you." Gone was the grandfatherly demeanor he carried only moments before, replaced with an intensity that frightened Amsu.

As Amsu prepared the crane and hoist to pull down one the crates, the High Cleric Madu walked up and down the line, running his hand along the base of the crates. He would sometimes stop, eyes closed tightly, think for a moment, then shake his head and move on. Eventually, he stopped at one crate, place both hands on it, then stepped back, excitedly.

"This one," he said.

Amsu attached the hoist to the straps and eyelets, lifted the crate from the rock shelving, and lowered it in front of the Cleric.

"Open it," Madu ordered.

"Your Grace," Amsu said, startled, "I don't believe I am permitted..."

"Initiate," Madu said, harshly. Then, his smile returned. Amsu thought it looked less patronly, and more serpentine than before.

"Initiate," he continued, soothingly, "I am permitting it. Please. Open the crate."

Amsu took a pry-hook and placed it near the nails that held the crate together. Carefully and methodically, he removed the lid, then turned his attention to the font wall, which came apart easily with the lid removed. As it fell away, Amsu saw what lie inside. It was a stone table with what appeared to be a corpse atop it. He crossed himself, diagonally.

"By the sandals of Gol-Adam," he prayed.

High Cleric Madu laughed.

"An odd expression, don't you think?" he asked, though it seemed to Amsu that he was speaking more to himself.

"We are taught to cross ourselves like the straps of the sandals that protect the feet of Gol-Adam, that they may protect us, as well. I ask you; are we praying to The Absent One? Or to his shoes?" The thought seemed most comical to the Cleric, who chuckled to himself. The High Cleric ran his finger along the leather straps that seemed to hold the body in place, then caressed the figure's cheek with the back of his hand.

"Do you know who this is?" he asked, turning to Amsu.

"N-no, Your Grace."

"His birth name has been lost to the ages. I doubt even he remembers it, now. He named himself Neb er Khalid. It means, 'King of The Eternal.' A bit premature, I believe, but his power is undeniable."

"Is?" questioned Amsu. "He...he's not dead?"

The High Cleric laughed at that, a deep and hearty laugh that made Amsu's blood run cold.

"Hardly. He is merely...dormant. Forced into this torpid slumber by fools and thieves. Because he dared speak the truth. Because he dared to challenge the tyrants we call 'gods.' Because he wanted freedom more than comfort, a wolf among the cowed and placated dogs.

"Do you know what this is?" Madu asked Amsu. He held a small vial in his hand. It was made of glass, and inside appeared to be a blue liquid, glowing slightly.

"No, Your Grace. I don't"

"Of course you don't. They don't teach the old ways, anymore. The magics that should be your birthright are kept from you, lest you try to rise up as Chey-Luk and his followers did. Lest you – gods forbid – think for yourself.

"It's a phulassein, child. It contains this man's Kagh, ripped from his still breathing body."

From somewhere in his robes, Madu produced a dagger. He began to cut the straps that bound the man on the alter. He spoke words as he did so, words Amsu could not understand. When all the leather had been cut away, the High Cleric pulled the stopper from the phulassein. He placed one hand over the man's eyes and poured the blue liquid from the vial into his mouth.

"Neb er Khalid," he chanted, "Neb er Khalid! I call you back! I call you back from the storm! I call you back from the abyss! I call you back from oblivion!"

A wind blew, then, harsh against Amsu's skin. There should have been no wind in the cavern, yet there it was, whipping against him, tossing his robes and hair about. Madu turned to him, then.

"You are lucky," he said. "Very lucky, indeed, for you shall serve twice over."

He plunged the dagger into Amsu's heart. In shock, Amsu could not move, but he looked down at the hilt protruding from his chest. There was no blood. Shouldn't there be blood? Instead, he felt cold wash over him. Cold, and an alarming calm. His fear and shock seemed to dissipate. No, it was being drawn from him. Drawn from the gaping wound in his chest.

When the High Cleric finally withdrew the blade, he felt...peace. He watched, passively, as Madu plunged the same dagger into Neb er Khalid's heart. He idly noted that he did not have any real feeling about the deed. It was only noteworthy in that it was a new experience. Normally, he would have felt something. Disgust, perhaps? Horror? Either way, it was irrelevant. He did not feel anything, it just was.

"You see," Madu was saying to him, "I can return his Kagh, but his Sacred Heart is still trapped, elsewhere. I must 'borrow' yours until we can free him, and the others, from the Wailing Prison. In the meantime, you will be the perfect servant. Devoid of your essence, you will only live to serve me."

Amsu noticed that the Sightless Sisters had returned. The High Cleric motioned to them.

"Go," he said. "Take him to the abbey. Clean him, and make sure he eats. He will undoubtedly forget to, at first."

Amsu followed the Sisters out of the cavern and to the entrance of the catacombs. As they ascended the inclined passageways, they passed two forms lying prone on the stone floor. It was Osaze and Kafele. Their throats had been slit, and they had been neatly laid to the side of the corridor. That was most efficient, Amsu thought.

It was not long before they passed another form. Amsu knew it was Latif before he saw his face. His throat had been slit, as well, but his skull had also been crushed by a large rock which lay close to the body. It was possible Latif has fought his execution, or maybe the Sister harbored some ill-will toward the man that manifested in this brutality. It was not nearly as efficient, he noted.

The last thing Amsu heard as he exited the catacombs was a long and inhuman howl from deep in the caverns. With idle interest Amsu knew that Neb er Khalid had awakened.

CHAPTER THREE

The half-formulated plan was a simple one: first, they would travel back to Ingeland, as was expected of them. They each had more riches than they knew what do with, and it would have looked suspicious for them to not immediately get their finances in order. No matter how impatient Lea might be it was best to do as little as possible to draw attention to themselves.

The Ingelean National Banking Guild were handling the actual transfer of funds, but there was still much to be done when such large sums were involved. Ana and Ex were splitting their shares between banks; they did not trust the Esisrian Hegemony not to double-cross them, but as Esisrian nationals it would have looked odd to keep all of it out of the country. They spent most of their time abroad with Lea and Thomas, so keeping a considerable sum with them would not seem out of place. They would transfer the rest when they reached Ingeland.

Lea and Thomas had already wired ahead to trusted contacts to prepare as much of the equipment for the expedition as they could. Not only would it save them time, but then they would not be seen gathering it, since they were undoubtedly being watched. Given the first opportunity, they would slip away, leaving decoys in place. Lea's sister Jewel could double for her in a pinch. Though she never understood how people sometimes confused them, Jewel was of a height with Lea. A little hair dye and some large spectacles should fool most people, at a distance. Thomas was fortunate enough that any number of his cousins could take his place, though he tried to arrange for an old associate,

Steven, to take the role. "Never trust family with such large sums of money," he said. In the end he had to settle for his cousin Petyr, a lad most often described as 'uncomplicated.' It was not ideal, but they were working against time.

Ana and Exra were another matter, entirely. Esisrians were rare enough in Ingeland, let alone the small county of Esstres. Finding doubles for them would be all but impossible. Therefore, while Lea and Thomas moved south through Delmont and Baryo, Ana and Ex would chart a complex travel route, changing modes of transportation several times, ending eventually in Red Fjord. If they had not lost anyone trailing them by then, the notoriously paranoid border entry at Red Fjord should slow them down enough for the couple to slip away and meet Lea and Thomas in Atera. There, a boat would be waiting for them on the coast of the Southern Sea.

It was a respectable plan, if somewhat unformed. The hardest part for Lea, so far, was containing her impatience. Thomas – sweet, sweet Thomas – had told her many times that it was her only flaw. She despised waiting. It was a flaw of the universe, she thought, that it made her wait for anything. Luckily, Thomas had patience enough for the both of them. She could not count the number of times it had saved them.

She tried to relax and focus on the meal in front of her. The four companions had already checked their luggage with the train station and had several hours before their train departed. They had spent most of the morning shopping, or browsing, rather. To Lea, there was nothing of interest in Esisria that was above-ground. Thomas was his usual chatty self, commenting on everything they saw in the markets. He talked about the Ateran influence in modern Esisrian fashion, how the icons depicted in the statuettes differed from their ancient counterparts, and when each style and method of jewelry making was discovered. He even went as far as to compare modern haggling methods with those of the Early Kingdom.

Now they sat in an open café, eating a rather hearty stew and drinking a light ale. Lea picked away at her food. She was hungry, but her nerves had her stomach in knots, and she found it difficult to eat. It looked as though Tomas was eating for the both of them, as well, as he all but shoveled the stew into his mouth.

"I love Esisrian cuisine," he said, for what must have been the hundredth time. "The spices are incredible. If this were Ingelean, they would have just boiled the legumes until they were a uniform beige and served it with salted pork." He paused to shove another mouthful in and continued before he had finished it.

"Do you think that's why there's so few Esisrians and Fjorders in Ingeland? Because the food is so horribly, horribly bland?" It was a mostly rhetorical question, and a rather tired old joke, but it elicited a hearty chuckle from the group.

"Honestly, though, if we just returned home and opened an Esisrian restaurant I think I'd be content." He took a long swill of his beer. "Honestly, Ex, how can something be both warm and refreshing? Inge-lean ale is kept cool and still hits your stomach like a rock."

"If we told you," Exra replied, "The ECM really would have to kill us both."

Lea's laugh was only half-hearted. She had known danger in her life; one didn't become a delver and not see some. But she had never been actively or violently opposed in the pursuit of a find, and the idea that someone might be willing to kill her in cold blood over one left a pit in her stomach that ached whenever she thought about it.

Over the years she had seen her share of steep cliffs and cave-ins, aggressive wildlife, and hazardous weather. And, of course, traps. Though the idea of tombs and ruins being trapped was an inflated and exaggerated one, it was still a very real and possible danger. The very first delve Lea was on saw two men lost to a deadfall trap. Experienced men, who were taking precautions. She still remembered the awful sound they made as the air was pushed from their lungs and they were crushed under the weight...

That was also the dig that she had met Thomas on. She decided to focus on that memory, instead. It was a much happier one. He was so awkward and unaware of it, something he had never really grown out of. She found it enormously endearing. He was a strikingly handsome man, in a very conventional way, and she loved that he had never quite figured that out. Not that she loved him for his looks, but it didn't hurt anything.

Whereas Lea craved the excitement and adventure that came with a life of delving, not to mention the possibility of riches, Thomas was seemingly only motivated by the discovery of knowledge. He didn't long for the fame that came with the discovery, but he did yearn to see his name on the cover of book. And, if he were very lucky, it would be a textbook.

Lea was sure she loved him, immediately.

It had taken her weeks of subtle hints and inuendo to make him realize she had feelings for him. He was so oblivious, she thought. She made every excuse to be alone with him. They would take quawa tea in his sitting room between digs, and when on a delve they would take their meals, together, all the while discussing the history or culture of ancient civilizations. Soon it became rare to see them not in each other's company.

Then, one day, Thomas got it in his head to ask her on a proper date. The poor thing could barely get a sentence out. He just stood there, stuttering and stammering, and getting so flustered and tongue-tied that it seemed he forgot what he was saying while he was saying it. When he finally got it out that he wanted to take her to dinner, she could not help but laugh, hysterically. After all, hadn't they been eating almost every meal together for weeks? Without a word, Thomas turned and ran.

When she eventually tracked him down, he had locked himself in his bed chamber. She apologized through the door, to which he said there was no need. It was his folly, after all, he should have known better. Lea found herself irrationally angry at that. "Known better?" Had she done something wrong? Surely, she could not have been more forthcoming? "Known better?" With angry tears streaming down her face, she cried, "Thomas Henry Porter! How can the smartest man I know be such a bloody fool!"

"I am a fool!" He cried back. "A thrice-damned fool! Why in all the heavens would someone so beautiful and brilliant have the slightest interest in me?"

"Because I love you, you giant horse's ass!"

There was a pause, and then she heard his door unlock. It opened, almost painfully slowly. He stood there in his doorway and stared at her for just a moment, but that moment seemed to stretch on, forever. Then, he reached down, and taking her face in both hands, he kissed her. Lea believed with all her heart that there had never before been, nor would be, again, a kiss quite like that.

She smiled at the memory. And then realized that everyone was staring at her.

"I'm sorry," she said, "I was elsewhere for a moment."

"That's alright," Ana said. "Exra was just giving your husband a hard time about Fjordian food."

"Oh! Thomas has no issue with Red Fjord cuisine...so long as you don't tell him what's in it."

"There are things in this world and others that are simply not meant to be eaten. The fact that the three of you have no problem with it..." He suppressed a gag.

"Why Thomas, I am amazed," Lea said, playfully. "After all, you are always lecturing that anthropology and sociology are clinical studies, and that morality and ethical mores must be judged against the culture from which they are derived. Are you calling the traditional delicacies of a culture – dare I say it? – wrong?"

"There is a line, Lea," he replied, "a clearly defined line. Nay, a chasm! A gulf that has no bridge, and it is live insects and brains."

They all laughed, heartily. It was much needed, as their collective mood had been shifting between dour and anxious. To lighten the mood, even slightly, felt like a weight had been lifted from Lea's shoulders. Not removed, but eased, perhaps.

"What world did you travel to, just now?" Thomas asked.

"This one," Lea said with a smile. She leaned over and kissed his cheek.

The serving girl came and brought the bill for the meal, and also brought each of them a glass of pura, an Esisrian digestive. As they drank and processed their meal, Lea noticed Exra's demeanor change, subtly. Her curiosity must have given her away, for he suddenly smiled at her, almost too wide.

"Continue to act normally," he said to her. "We are being watched."

Lea attempted to look for their observers as inconspicuously as she could but didn't see anything or anyone out of the ordinary. She did not doubt Ex, however. He and Ana's service in the Esisrian military had made them far more alert to such dangers than she or Thomas. She took a sip of pura.

"I don't see them," she said, as casually as she could.

"They are very good," Exra replied. "I was not sure, at first, but they have lingered far too long. The man to your fore-left has been looking at fruit without buying for a half-hour. The woman behind me has gone to the same three hawkers, repeatedly. The man to your left was selling newspapers, before. He left when he ran out but has returned in different clothing and is much too interested in the jewelry stand he was next to, earlier.

"So, what do we do?" Thomas said as he patted his stomach, contently. He certainly looked far more at ease than Lea felt.

"Nothing, for the moment," Exra said. "I do not believe that they will attempt anything, here. It is far too crowded. But memorize their faces and be extra weary on the train. They may send different agents to follow us, there, but at least we know, now, that they are following us."

"Perhaps it is best that we leave," said Ana. "I would like to get as familiar with the train as possible."

They all stood up to leave. Thomas reached into his pocket and froze a strange expression on his face. Lea shot him a questioning glace, to which simply smiled and shook his head. He then reached into his other pocket and drew out a fivetrite piece, which he tossed on the table for the serving girl. He turned to leave, shook his head again, then took back the fivetrite piece and left an Esisrian tenpence, instead.

"Are you alright, Love?" Lea asked him.

"Yes, of course," he replied. "It's just been a frazzling couple of days."

"Indeed, it has," she agreed, and took his arm.

Though the Capital Station was as modern a building as any train station, the trains that it ran were rather old-fashioned. The Esisrians, as a rule, tended to not trust Eimuria. They believed that it was the power of the gods, and just because they were gone did not mean that man had permission to use it. As such, the Esisrian trains still burned coal, a commodity which grew rarer by the year. If the Cultural Ministry didn't do something to lift the taboo soon, Lea thought, these trains would become dead beasts, immovable on their tracks.

Eimuria wasn't illegal in Esisria, but the taboo was a strong one. To many outsiders the country seemed backward and barbaric. Most homes still used oil lamps and fuel stoves. Finding a working wave-receiver was all but impossible. The only place that one could be sure to find Eimuria was the post office, which relied on wire transmissions for correspondence.

Eimuria, itself, was something of a mystery. It was mentioned all throughout history, in every corner of the world, yet it was only within the last hundred years that man had learned to harness it, at least from an industrial standpoint. Old legends from before The Upheaval told of sorcerers and priests who could control it with magics. Or perhaps it was magic. There had even been relics found that used Eimuria, yet no source had ever been found. Perhaps it was the purview of the gods, Lea thought. Or, perhaps, some classes of society used technology to keep the ignorant and uneducated cowed.

These were all questions Lea thought may never be answered, as much as she wanted them to be. Hundreds of years of research had yet to answer even the smallest and simplest of these. What were the chances she and her companions would simply stumble across the answers? Even how Eimuria worked as of no small debate. Lea had no head for hard sciences, though, and tried not to dwell on it. The fact that it did work was enough for her.

As the couples made it to the station, they kept track of the watchers following them. Exra had been right, of course. They were incredibly good, but once Lea had been able to identify them, keeping an eye on them was quite easy. Ana had even identified two additional observers on their trail.

As the four of them stood in queue, tickets in hand, Lea made a casual glance around and noticed that none of their keepers could be seen.

"Ex," she whispered, "could they have replaced their agents? I don't see them, anymore..."

"What?!" Exra momentarily dropped all pretense of normality. He calmed himself and began searching frantically about the train station. He placed his hands on Lea shoulders in a protective manner.

"They would not leave us, now. Even if they had different agents on the train, these would still wait to ensure we departed. Thomas, Ana...can you see anything?"

"Nothing." Ana replied.

"Nothing, here, friend. The last I saw that news peddler chap was over by the tea shop. That's odd..." Thomas said, trailing off. "I may not be up on the latest Esisrian fashion, Ex, but are Uhlans and Kheptha appropriate for this time of year?"

Lea casually glanced to where Thomas was indicating. Sure enough, there were two men wearing sand colored full-faced Uhlan scarves and full-length Kheptha robes. While sometimes worn by general citizens for the weather protection they provided, the utility of the outfit was one generally reserved for fighting men, especially on patrol. The freedom of movement and desert camouflage were preferred by both the Esisrian Army and various mercenary groups that operated in the desert nations.

"Well, that's not good," Lea said, somehow managing to smile. "What do we do, Ex?"

"Continue, as normal. Let them make the first move."

Lea found herself shaking and tried to play it off as if she were cold. She doubted anyone watching would believe that, given the heat of the mid-morning, but try as she might she could not stop trembling. From the corner of her eye she spotted two more men dressed in Uhlan and Kheptha.

"Exra," she said.

"I see them."

"Well, I suppose that settles the coincidence debate," Thomas said. "I don't think I've ever been more anxious to board a train." He laughed, but Lea knew him well enough to hear the fear behind the chuckle.

The doors to the train slid open.

Lea felt a jerk as she was pulled to the side by the shoulders. The violent motion snapped her head to the side and a shooting pain travelled up her neck. She barely had time to register what had happened when she heard a dull thud to her left. The woman who had been standing in front of her looked as though she had been struck in her back as she flew forward into the man directly in front of her. She collapsed to the ground as the man was thrown to his knees.

"Get down!" Exra yelled. "Stay low and get on the train!"

"But..." she began.

"I'll take care of Thomas; now, go!"

She did as she was told, crouching low and weaving between the other would-be passengers. Protests arose as she darted in front of men and women, families waiting patiently to board in the orderly manner they were expecting. A sudden scream come from behind her, and the focus of the waiting throng shifted from the small woman rudely rushing ahead to some disturbance near the rear of the line.

Then, chaos erupted.

People began running in every direction, with those closest to the train pushing each other in an attempt to get on as fast as they could. From behind she heard strange thrumming sounds, vaguely familiar, but she could not place them. Screams and the sounds of fighting followed her as she made her way to the open doors. Several people had fallen over each other at the entrance to the train, and others were crawling over them and into the train without so much as second thought. Lea stopped, unable to intentionally traverse over them. She bent over to help a young man who had landed face-down on the ground. He had boot prints covering his back.

As she bent over the man, she heard that soft and low thudding sound, again. A portly man to her right who had begun to mount the pile of bodies leading to the doors suddenly flew to the side, rolling onto the ground where a young woman began to climb over him with no hesitation.

"I am so sorry!" she said to the young man she was trying to help, and taking a deep breath, started over the mound of human beings to the train.

As she crawled, she again heard that dreaded thud, and then again. Each time it was accompanied by an exclamation of pain from one of the others around her. In what was only moments, but seemed like an eternity, Lea reached the open doors of the train. She crawled into the opening and saw the others who had made it aboard were all taking refuge under tables and behind seats. Lea found a small opening along the wall and placed her back against it, sinking to the floor, sobbing.

"Thomas!"

Thomas watched as Lea started toward the train. He waited until she was out of his sight and turned to Exra. The baton appeared in Exra's hand as if by magic. He kept it low and concealed from the crowd. Ex nodded to him, but Thomas was already drawing the lead-filled sap from his boot holster. Though he didn't have the years of experience in the Esisrian military that Ex and Ana had, Thomas had extensive train-ing with the blunt weapon, the perks of travelling with the couple.

He glanced at the woman who had fallen in Lea's place. She was still breathing, though unconscious. Whatever weapons the assailants were using were less than lethal. A small comfort, but a comfort, nonetheless. Thomas glanced in the direction of the attack. One of the covered men had some kind of long tube attached to a box and was aiming it at Ana.

Thomas swung his arm wide in a protective arc, pushing her to the side. A blue flash emanated from the attacker's tube, and he felt a wave of heat flare past his chest. It tingled as it passed, the way pure Eimuria did. The old man in front of Ana dropped to the ground. The crowd of people, until now only curiously concerned for the wellbeing of the first victim, began to panic. A middle-aged woman saw the old man fall and screamed. Panic became frenzy as the crowd exploded in all directions.

Thomas touched the front of his tunic and found it was still quite hot, burning his fingers. Whatever that strange weapon had thrown at him was unpleasant, and he considered himself incredibly lucky. He turned to Ana, who now had her twin sword-breakers in her hand. She nodded a "thank you."

Faster than Thomas could track, Exra ducked under a staff and brought his baton up to connect with a man's head. His opponent collapsed in a heap, rendered unconscious. Thomas looked at the man and realized that he was not dressed as the others but wore an unassuming robe and head covering. Thomas would not have looked twice at the man, had he encountered him on the street.

Almost too late, Thomas saw a wooden rod swinging toward his own face. He managed to step back and out of the way, but it was an ungraceful dodge, and he stumbled backward, in danger of falling over. He righted himself at the last moment and instinctively took the stance Exra had taught him. The second swing of the staff found Thomas ready for it. He ducked sideways and plunged his fist into the assailant's midsection. The man doubled over, and Thomas swung his sap into the back of the man's head. His attacker fell like a ragdoll.

Thomas saw another man rushing toward Ana. Her daggers were inverted in her hands, the club-like hilts ready to pummel anyone stupid enough to come into range. Before the unwise man was able to reach her, however, Thomas heard a faint and oddly familiar hum, followed by that same thud, and the man fell forward and stopped moving. Thomas turned his head toward Exra.

"What is happening?" he asked.

"I don't know, but we need to use this confusion. Look," Ex pointed toward the train, "Lea is safe. You must join her, now."

"Great Alliah's tits, I won't leave you two!"

"They are not here to kill us, Thomas. You must go, endiha. Ana and I will join you as soon as we can, but if we are captured, you have not been trained to withstand torture as we have. Go! Protect Lea."

"Endiha," Thomas repeated. Esisrian for brother. An intimate and formal conjugation. It was not used lightly. He nodded, reluctantly. "I will see you, soon," he assured. "One way, or another."

He started toward the train, trying not to think of leaving his two closest friends behind. They were quite capable; it was not without reason to think that they would make it to the train successfully. He pushed through the mass of people, most of whom seemed to have no idea what to do or where to go, only knowing that they had to do something.

He felt the sting of wood against the back of his head, and his vision went dark for a moment. He stumbled forward, knowing that if he had not been moving that the blow would have knocked him out. He spun toward the attacker but could not see them. As he started back toward the train, he somehow heard and felt the slight movement of air and ducked at the very last moment. He threw himself toward his opponent, still not sure who it was. They both tumbled to the ground.

Thomas realized that he must have dropped his sap when he was struck, for he no longer held it in his hand. The attacker grabbed him by the wrists and tried to get on top of him. Thomas used his momentum against him and flung him off. He tried to get to his feet, but the man still had his wrists, and he pulled him up, as well.

Without knowing why, Thomas rammed his head into the other man's face. His vision still blurry from the blow to his head, he could feel the man's blood spray into face and tunic. The man swore loudly and took his hands back to cover his gushing nose. Thomas took the opportunity to plant a closed fist into the man's stomach. When his attacker bent in agony, Thomas brought his elbow down onto the man's neck, causing him to topple forward. Thomas did not wait to see if he would get back up, but started for the train, again. He took a step and his foot slipped on something, almost twisting his ankle out from beneath him. As he steadied himself, he looked down to see his sap.

"There you are, old girl," he said, bending to pick it up. As he grasped it, a man – presumably the same as he had been fighting – leapt on his back. Thomas swung the newly reacquired sap at the man's head, but his aim was either quite terrible or the man moved, and all Thomas struck was his own shoulder.

"God's piss!" he yelled. He thought that hurt even more than the staff had.

Thomas flailed wildly about with his sap but failed to connect with anything. The attacker now had his arm around Thomas' neck and was squeezing. Thomas could feel the blood flow cut off from his head, and his vision began to narrow. He knew was losing consciousness, but there was little he could do, no matter how he threw himself about.

Just as he thought he could stay awake no more, he felt a concussion from behind, and the man's grip was loosened. Thomas gasped for air as the assailant slid from his back. He fell to his knees, but the man came along for the ride, his bulk weighing Thomas down. He took several more breaths, and the man did not seem able to do further damage. He was about to try to stand again when a second hard push hit the man and Thomas. His erstwhile attacker fell off of him. Thomas spared only a moment's glance to see that he still breathed and then took off as fast as he could toward the open doors of the train.

His legs felt like they would give out at any moment, but somehow, he pressed on. A pile of writhing bodies slumped before the door. Thomas grabbed one by the back of the shirt and all but tossed him on to the train. He took another by the arm and shoulder and forced him up to the platform and door. He grabbed a third body by the belt and shoved it up. This solved the problem of the blocked doors, but now there were too many people blocking the other side.

Suddenly, a figure on the train reached down and started clearing the way. It was Lea! Another passenger, seeing the tiny woman helping, joined, then a third and fourth. Soon, all the people trying to get aboard were, and Thomas collapsed on the floor. Lea lay her head on Thomas' chest.

"Thank the gods, Love!" she said between sobs. "I thought I had lost you! Ana? Exra?"

"I left them," he replied. The realization hit him like a mallet in the heart. "Gods help me, Lea... I left them."

The train doors slid closed.

Analeytuua and Exra Khattab stood back-to-back. In his right hand, Ex held his yugam, or lotus baton. It had a handle on the side that allowed for the swift changing of grips and stances. It was, in Exra's opinion, a very underappreciated weapon, because to be truly effective one had to make it a part of them, to understand its reach and momentum and impact as if it were part of one's body. While this was true of most weapons, mastering the yugam made for an especially dangerous and versatile fighter.

In his left hand he held its sister baton, the yugam-tu. The straight baton was weighted to one end and was used primarily as a defensive or opportunistic weapon. The two batons could be connected with a clasp between them to form the yugam-kat. All told, between the three weapons, there were a total of ten stances. Exra had mastered them all.

Ana's twin swordbreakers, though not as complex in nature, were no less formidable. The weighted daggers were longer than most, at two hands, and had seven notches along the un-bladed edge. As the name implied, this was to catch bladed weapons and either wrest them from an opponent, or to break the blade, entirely. The weighted hilts were perfect for bludgeoning.

Now, she held the right dagger blade-out, and the left dagger inverted. It was known as tok-potu, or foot-forward stance. It was best for when lethal force might be necessary, but the full capabilities of your opponents were unknown, yet.

The train platform was chaos; people were running in all directions, and it was impossible to tell who was a foe until they attacked. A man in plainclothes swung a cudgel at Exra. He narrowly ducked it and swung his yugam. It connected with a loud crack and sent the man flying. Behind him, he heard the clank of steel on steel. Ana had engaged an attacker who was willing to kill. The exchange did not last long. He saw the man's long knife fly to the side and heard the air knocked from his lungs with a satisfying "oomf" as he fell.

A man with a straight short sword charged at Ex. He knocked the sword aside with the yugam-tu and sent him reeling with a head-blow. By now, most of the civilians seemed to have cleared, leaving a somewhat large and confusing battlefield. Exra saw no less than three groups, not counting himself and Ana.

The first group included the men that Thomas had first spotted, dressed as militia or mercenaries. They used the strange tube-like weapons to strike from a distance and had yet to engage at close range. They appeared to have forgotten Ana and Ex for the moment and were focused on the other two groups. Exra made note of how the mystery weapons seemed incapable of firing without a rather lengthy pause between volleys.

The second group wore plainclothes and were armed with cudgels and clubs, some batons like Exra. They had training, Exra noticed, but were stiff, as if they had never used the training in actual battle. Monks? Clerics? It was a disturbing thought.

The last group also wore plainclothes but yielded an array of far more deadly weaponry than clubs. Short swords, daggers, and kukri were their weapons of choice. And, though they seemed to lack the formal training of the other groups, they displayed a prowess that belied experience as street fighters. Exra was quite sure that they had been hired to kill them by another party. Capturing one would yield little information, though right now simply surviving the battle was a much higher concern to Ex.

The married defenders were a flurry of motion, moving with the years of training and experience they had accumulated. It was a calculated dance, a sort of planned improvisation. They knew well the other's strengths and played to them. They ducked and weaved, struck and parried, ignoring the fatigue that crept into their bones. Exra had no doubt that had the attackers not been fighting each other as well, that he and Ana would quickly be overwhelmed, no matter how well they fought. There were simply too many of them.

"Katan!" Exra yelled as he was moved on by an attacker wielding a short, curved sword.

"Yugam-kat!" was Ana's reply.

They quickly spun, switching opponents to match weapon and styles. Around them, the bodies began to pile, but there seemed to be no end to combatants. The two melee groups appeared evenly matched, judging by the fallen on each side, which worked to the couple's advantage. As soon as one side took the field, the pair's chances of escape decreased dramatically.

Ex saw the doors of the train slide closed and heaved a sigh of relief. With the assailants engaged on the platform, he hoped that Lea and Thomas would be safe. As the train began its slow pull away from the station, Ex said a silent prayer to Uru to keep them safe. Thomas was far more capable than he realized, though his trusting and sometimes oblivious nature often blinded him to danger. Lea's fierce determination and tenacity kept him in the present. They were a wonderful compliment to each other, and Exra hoped he would see them, again, soon.

Another thud took down a blade-wielder, and Exra followed his trajectory as he fell to the roof of a nearby building. If the strange, ranged weapons had the high ground then this battle was all but over, Ex thought.

"We must get out of the open!" he yelled to his wife, not slowing his motions. "Those weapons have the reach of arrows. If we stay here, we are finished."

"The alley," Ana replied, nodding in the direction she was implying. "It will choke them off, and we can perhaps lose them in the market."

Exra made no replied, inferring his agreement. He saw another long knife fly past him from the corner of his eye, only this time it was not accompanied by a violent exhalation, but a squelch and gurgle. Ana was no longer pulling her blows. He did not envy anyone foolish enough to attack her.

Ex swung he yugam toward a club-wielder, causing the man to dodge backward, arching his back awkwardly. Exra kicked him squarely in the chest and he flew backward with incredible force. The now familiar humming sound of one of the ranged weapons sounded, and Exra felt the blast pass him where his attacker had been only moments before.

"Now!" Ex yelled. If the weapons did need time to fire, again, he hoped it would provide the opportunity they needed.

The two broke off from the melee and darted toward the alley Ana had indicated. Exra heard the "hum-thump" of the ranged weapon, again, and a cart he had just passed exploded, the bales of hay it was carrying bursting with violence, raining straws down on the train platform, many of them on fire.

Ana gasped with the explosion. They leapt around the various carts and stands that hawkers had left at the station in their haste to escape the fighting. One of the weapons fired, again, sending chunks of lamb and bread flying everywhere from a food stand.

As the pair ducked into the alley, Exra spared a glance backward to see if they were being pursued. Several members of both groups had vanquished whatever opponent they had been fighting and were realizing the two had fled. A few had seen where they had run to and were gesturing to their comrades the direction of the alley. Well, it could not be that easy, Ex thought.

"Keep going!" he shouted, and Ana seemed only too happy to oblige.

She turned sharply left into side street, and Exra followed, not slowing down. A right into another alley, this one littered with refuse not yet collected. Ex only distantly registered the foul stench that made his eyes water as they ran through the waste. Ana turned left, again, and Ex knew they were getting close to the market. With any luck they could hide in a shop or café, or one of the many apartment buildings that lined the market square. Another quick look behind showed that they had lost their hunters, at least for the moment.

Ana approached the junction that would lead them into the marketplace. She made the sharp right turn, and just as soon as she disappeared around the corner, Ex saw her fly backwards and into the alley wall.

"Noooo!" he yelled, rushing to her side.

She was unconscious, but breathing, still. Thank the gods. Exra looked down the alley to where Ana's attacker stood. He was covered in the sand-colored Uhlan and Kaftan and was carrying one of the tube-weapons. As soon as he saw Ex, he began fiddling with the box that the tube was attached to, removing some sort of smaller box from within. He threw it to the ground and inserted another. Exra knew he was preparing to fire, again.

Batons raised, he charged for the man. The man saw the look of death in Exra's eyes and struggled to quicken his movements, which only caused him to fumble the device. In haste, the man dropped the box. He reached into his robes for another but did not seem to have one. He bent to pick up the one he had dropped, but knew it was too late, now. Exra would show him no mercy.

Mere paces from the man Exra felt a blow against his back. It was as if he were struck by a massive stone fist. His whole body tingled for a moment, then he lost all feeling. His legs stopped running and refused to move. He fell face-first onto the ground. His body would not obey him; try as he might to move his arms and legs, nothing happened. He could not so much as move his eyes to look at the man he was attacking, instead seeing only the wall of the alley. He tried to look back to Ana but felt his eyelids slowly closing. Consciousness slipped away from him, and everything went dark.

CHAPTER FOUR

The first leg of their journey was spent in almost total silence. Lea and Thomas ventured out of their private room rarely, and never alone. They slept in shifts, and hardly said a word. Lea, who almost always had something to say, even when she probably shouldn't, kept opening her mouth to speak, but words would not come.

The train's first stop was Kalij, a smaller city near the Esisrian border. There, they had a brief stopover, but did not switch trains. The Kaliji station contained a small café that the pair decided to wait in. It seemed the public spaces were not any safer than anywhere else, but they took a seat in the corner, both facing outward, and began memorizing all of the passengers they saw, with particular attention to those who re-boarded. It became a sort of game, albeit a grim one. They would call them out and their activities to each other.

"Red hat, flower dress, buying tea..."

"Spectacles, too-big shoes, restroom..."

"Yellow dress, bad wig, talking to tall man with short trousers..."

As hard as they tired, they could not identify any person or activity that seemed suspicious. When it was time for the train to depart, the couple barricaded themselves in their suite, once more. It was only a few hours to the next station, a tiny switching post just inside the equally miniscule nation of Ghob. There, Lea and Thomas boarded a more modern, Eimuria-powered locomotive.

Only a dozen passengers joined the two at the exchange, but they memorized all the unfamiliar faces, all the same. Spirits were somewhat lighter, now, and the pair began to give each passenger a backstory and personality. This one was visiting her secret love in Red Fjord. That one was a barrister delivering a writ to a widow in Esisria. Another searched for the long-lost son he didn't know he had. They still slept in shifts and never left the suit unaccompanied.

"He was right, Love," Lea braved on the morning of the third and last day of their journey.

Thomas did not answer, immediately, but pinched the bridge of his nose and heaved a heavy sigh.

"I know." He finally said. "I've run through every possibility in my mind a thousand times, and I know that Ex was right. I still can't help but feel that I abandoned them."

"Ana and Exra are the two most capable people I have ever met, Thomas. They will find their way back to us."

"And if they don't?"

Lea put her hands on her hips and tried to give him her most determined face, ever.

"Then we," she said, "will find them."

The splash of water woke Exra abruptly. He was upright, he noted. His feet were crossed and bound, as were his hands. He hung from a hook, it seemed, dangling several finger spans above the floor. His surroundings were dark, the only light emanating from sconce torches on the walls, several hands apart. The chamber he was in looked like some sort of cellar made from sandstone. Still in Esisria, then.

His rude wake up came from a figure standing only a few hands away, a robed man with a bucket that once held the water he now wore. He was a young man, not more than twenty years old. His face was blank and emotionless, no hint of malice or mercy behind his overly pale eyes.

The man tilted his head slightly, regarding Exra. Then, turned and walked into the shadows. Exra heard the soft sound of the bucket being placed on the floor. A faint scraping followed, as the man dragged a three-legged stool lightly on the floor and placed it in front of Exra. The man turned, once more, and walked back into the shadows.

Several seconds passed in silence. Exra strained to hear anything; the sounds of whispers or doors opening and closing. But he heard nothing. Then, from nowhere, the shuffling of feet approaching. Another man stepped into view, this one much older. He wore the rust-orange-colored robes of a Esisrian High Cleric. He sat on the stool and smoothed his robes, then gave Exra a gentle, comforting smile.

"I apologize for Amsu's brusque manner. He is unfailingly loyal but lacks social graces." The man chuckled to himself, a private joke that Exra did not share.

"I also apologize for this uncivilized treatment. I detest coercion. I would much rather work with a friend than against a foe, but time is of the essence, I'm afraid, and I cannot afford to wait. I'm sure you will understand, yes?"

"Where is my wife?" Exra asked.

"I appreciate that she is your foremost concern, I really do. And rest assured, she is fine. For the moment."

"A threat?"

"Of course," the cleric replied. "I won't insult you by being coy. Exra Khattab. Served three years in the Royal Infantry, then a further three in Special Services. There, you met your future wife, Analeytuua ab'Tarrk. Operated all over Anthumbra. Arranged the death of at least three members of the Ingelean royal family, aided an Aelfin warlord in a coup for the Jade Throne, eliminated the leader of the Ateran Council of Dukes who was advocating for war with Esisria, and a handful of destabilizing actions in other countries... Tell me, have you told your employers all of this?"

"Partners," Exra corrected him.

"Yes, of course. But do your partners know what it was you were doing when you first met them? Who your target was? You seem very close to them, Basaa Khattab; I find it difficult to believe that they know."

"Is this relevant?" Exra spat at the man.

"Merely curiosity. You see, Exra, you and I know that difficult things must be done to keep peace. To keep Esisria the proud nation that it is. To maintain the favor of the gods that we have always enjoyed. We both know this duty, this burden. There is no shame in it, even when the deeds we do are shameful."

The cleric stood from the stool and walked to Exra, bringing his face close enough that Ex could smell the flowery tea on the cleric's breath.

"You know that you will not leave this room alive, Basaa. You have already come to terms with that, I can see it in your eyes. You know that you will most likely be tortured and are certain that you will not break. But you have never encountered the methods my agents employ. I assure you that you will break, as will Analeytuua.

"However, that need not be. Your fair wife has not yet seen me, nor any of my associates. She could be released without a scratch on her pretty body. A letter from the State Ministry would explain your disappearance. She would not question it, not look for you, not find herself in danger. She could go on to have a long and happy life with your...partners."

The cleric turned from Exra and walked back to the stool. With a beckoning gesture, the young man that he had called Amsu appeared and retrieved the stool, turning and carrying it away without so much as a word. The cleric then turned back to Exra.

"I will not do you the disservice of falsehood, Basaa Khattab. Think on what I have said. I will give you until the sun rises; I can spare you no more time. I am sorry."

He turned and walked into the darkness, leaving Exra alone in silence.

The train pulled into the Rhoslyn station on the third morning of Lea and Thomas' flight from Esisria. A light snow covered the station and square, giving the scene a storybook quality that Lea never tired of seeing. No matter where in the world she travelled, this would always be home to her. It was an early snow for the year, and the pair were not dressed for the chill that accompanied it. All the better to explain their haste from the train station, Lea thought.

Thomas had flagged down and paid for one of the carriages that normally occupied the station looking for fares. The driver loaded their luggage into the boot while the couple climbed aboard. It was a traditional horse-drawn carriage, with a modest partition for fares. Though several Eimurial carriages were available, they did not offer the privacy of the smaller, old-fashioned carriages, being larger and able to take several fares. Though technically a faster mode of transportation, they often made many more stops, thus negating any speed advantage.

As they travelled along the intentionally aged-looking cobblestone streets of Rhoslyn, the Ingelean capital, Lea noted how many more personal Eimurial carriages she saw. When she and Thomas had last been home, only the wealthiest could afford such an extravagant mode of transportation. Now it seemed as though every other carriage was horseless. Not one for sentimentality in the face of progress, Lea still felt a pang of regret. There was something romantic about the gentle tempo and intimacy the horse-driven carriage afforded, as opposed to clumsy barreling through the streets like a steel ure.

Lea drew the curtains shut across the windows and lay her head against Thomas. She felt so tired, suddenly, deep within her soul. She knew they were not out of danger, not by a wide margin, but the sounds and smell of home let her relax, and she felt all of the last three days seep in, hitting her like an avalanche. The pain of losing Ana and Ex was as sharp as it had been the first day, but she had cried until no more tears would come, and now the wound lay bare and raw, taunting her with its purity. She had never felt loss before she realized, and it hung in the air like a pall, heavy and surreal. If she just shook her head hard enough, she would wake from the nightmare.

Suddenly, she did wake. Thomas was shaking her, gently.

"We're home, Love," he said.

Lea did not remember falling asleep, and then could not remember if she were supposed to be able to remember falling asleep. She had slept dreamlessly and woke hard. The trip from the station would have taken the better part of the morning, and she had slept through it all. As Thomas helped her from the carriage, she noted that the sun was high, well into the afternoon. She must have needed it, she thought.

The driver had already unloaded the pair's luggage, and Lyle, the house's first footman, had appeared with two under-butlers to retrieve it and take it to their rooms. Thomas finished paying the driver and skipped over to Lyle.

"Thank you, Lyle," he said, clasping the middle-aged man by the shoulder. "By the gods, it's good to see you."

"Likewise, sir," came the sincere reply. The two had known each other almost all their lives. It was only the circumstance of birth that divided them, and their relationship was more one of friendship than master and servant. In fact, Thomas maintained a very informal relationship with all the house's staff. He told Lea that growing up they had been more family to him than his actual kin.

Though not extravagantly wealthy, the Porters had taken a modest mercantile business and turned it into a kingdom-spanning trade empire. Thomas' parents had uncanny talent for anticipating supply and demand, often beating their much larger competitors to markets by seasons or years. Thomas had inherited this knack for trade or had been exposed to it enough to develop it, and though he had the head for it, he didn't have the heart.

Thomas' parents had died while he was at school, lost when their ship encountered a storm on the Iron Sea. They had been returning from a trip to the Aelfin provinces, establishing trade agreements with the reclusive and isolationist peoples, there. That they had been successful was of truly little consolation to Thomas.

Thomas was content to let the regional trade directors handle the business, much preferring his passion of history and archeology. He was savvy enough to provide double-blind oversight to ensure accuracy and honesty, and personally inspected the books every season. His direction had proven invaluable in several instances, steering the directors away from disaster. His parents would have been proud.

Though they had been married for several years, Lea had never formed the relationship with the servants that Thomas had. She never quite knew how to behave around them, and the pair spent far more time away from the estate than at it. She liked them all, immensely, but felt that they saw her more as an employer than friend, which she found both sad and frustrating. Though her family was technically noble, their holdings were tiny in comparison to Thomas'. They did not have servants in the home but did have hired hands work the vineyard, and her lack of experience with them left her stiff and awkward. She abdicated the title of countess to her sister when she married as well as the meager holdings of her family, which he had no interest in, but she still felt the barrier of title when she interacted with the servants.

Perhaps it was the stress of the past week, but Lea thought that propriety could take a head-first dive into the Hundred Hells. She threw her arms around Lyle and squeezed, her head barely reaching his shoulders.

"Is everything alright, my lady?"

"Yes," she said, pulling back, slightly. She wiped away the tears that she had not realized were there. "I'm just so very glad to see you." She pressed her face back into his chest.

"It...is very good to see you, as well, my lady," Lyle said, the awkwardness apparent in his voice.

"If you don't start calling me Lea," she said, her voice muffled in Lyle's overcoat, "I'm going to kick you in the shin."

Lea felt Lyle place his hands lightly on her back, returning the embrace.

Exra's screams would have filled a large colosseum, yet they were muted, somehow. Perhaps the acoustics of whatever prison he inhabited dampened the sound, but he did not think so. Other sounds had not been diluted. The thought gave Exra hope and frightened him at the same time. Hope, because his tormentors would not feel the need to muffle the sounds if they were not afraid to be heard. But what was happening to him was magic, and not the kind from children's tales, but from horror stories.

The High Cleric – who had since identified himself as Madu – had returned only a short time after leaving Exra in the dark, alone. He was once again accompanied by the young man he had called Amsu, as well as a second man who seemed to be just as much under the cleric's control as the other, though this man was nothing like Amsu.

He was dressed in gold-lined robes, with rubies inlaid throughout. He wore a thin-banded crown upon his head, encrusted with jewels, and each of his long, thin fingers wore a gawdy ring. His face was drawn tight, like a corpse left in the desert too long. His lips barely covered his crooked teeth, and his eyelids revealed red, unblinking eyes.

"This man," Madu said, "owes you his freedom. It was you and your employers – forgive me...partners – who found him in that retched tomb of a prison. Do you recognize him? He is Neb er Khalid, a powerful and magnanimous sorcerer. His only crime was to dare defy the rule of the so-called gods. He and his compatriots were freedom fighters, who wanted nothing more than to give each man and woman the choices that the gods had stolen from them. And for that they were hunted down and imprisoned; tortured for all of time by those who called themselves 'benevolent.'"

"You are a cleric," Exra said in disbelief. "A High Cleric! How can you abide such heresy?"

"Heresy!" Madu spat, the gentle facade thrown away in a fit of rage. "If the truth is heresy, then I am a heretic! For thirsty years was I faithful! I watched in impotence as the world slowly burned. I prayed when drought killed hundreds along the banks of the Kayan. I prayed when Atera wiped out entire villages in petty border disputes. I prayed when the Red Plague swept through the land, taking thousands of children. Do you know who answered me, Basaa? No one."

"And so you blame the gods for the circumstances of life, and the evil of men?"

Madu's smile returned, and he once again assumed the manner of the schoolteacher instructing the slowest of students.

"Of course not. I blame the gods for leaving us defenseless against them. You see, Eimuria is our birthright, our gift, usurped by the gods and stolen from us. Its use was restricted and controlled by the very beings who came here in search of it. The Temple teaches that Eimuria was a gift from the gods, but that is the real lie, Basaa. It was always ours. And we shall take it back."

"But we use Eimuria, now," Exra stated.

"A mockery! We do not control it, we harness it, and direct it. For what? Parlor tricks. To make light and sounds and move trains? We play at its mastery and call it 'science.' We pat ourselves on the back and say, 'look how far we've come!' We divert but a stream when we should command the ocean.

"Neb er Khalid was one such as that, a man who could bend the Eimuria to his will. And, once he is whole, again, he and his kind will teach us to use our gifts as we once did. But, for now, he can only do as I ask of him."

Madu stepped close to Exra and took his chin in one hand.

"Where are the phulassein?" he asked.

"I do not know what that is," Exra replied.

"A pity."

The High Cleric stepped back and gestured to the ancient figure. Neb er Khalid's eyes began to glow with a blue flame. He raised a hand, pointing an overly long finger at Exra. Without warning, the blood in Exra's veins turned to fire. He screamed as the pain coursed through his entire body. He strained against the restraints that held him, and he realized that if his hands were free, he would be trying to tear his skin off and pluck his own eyes from his head. The agony could only have lasted moments, but it was unlike anything Exra had ever felt before. Madu raised his hand, and just as suddenly as it had started, it stopped.

Exra slumped in his restraints. The High Cleric stepped close and began to wipe his face with a cloth, clearing away the tears, saliva, and mucus that he didn't even know where there. Exra looked into the old man's eyes as he did and saw a genuine regret among them. Could his story be true? Could his intentions be altruistic, despite the horrible methods he employed? It did not matter. Altruistic or not, his goals were evil, and could not be justified.

The cleric was right, Exra thought; no amount of training had prepared him for this. He was unsure how long he would be able to hold out against this form or torture. He only hoped it would be long enough to give Lea and Thomas the head start they needed.

"That was but a taste," the High Cleric said, "and one I do not wish to repeat. It was for you, and for you, alone. The next will not be so. Every bit of agony that you feel will be felt by your lovely wife, as well. She is still oblivious to myself and my order, and her life can still be saved. But only you can spare her this pain you have felt."

Exra laughed, then, much to the surprise of the High Cleric.

"What is it you find so amusing, my son?" he asked.

"You speak of a love for freedom, then deny responsibility for your own actions. I am truly sorry, Your Grace, but I have no idea what it is you seek."

The old man sighed, disappointed, then gestured to the corpse-like figure, again. Exra's screams were lost to the silencing magic of the chamber.

Lea paced the length of the sitting room for what must have been the thousandth time. When she reached the end she paused, put her fists on her hips, and made that "HMPH!" sound that she had been making all morning. Then, she turned on her heel and started back down the sitting room.

Thomas wanted so badly to tell her that it was not helping, but he knew better. He had learned to mostly ignore it. It was only when she would pause her pacing for a bout of cursing that would interrupt Thomas' thought process.

"Gilafred's diseased bowels!" she roared from the other side of the room.

Thomas sighed. At least she had switched to regional gods...

"What in the Ninety-Ninth Hell are we to do?" She had asked this question – or some more colorful version of it – more times than Thomas could recall. They had spent all morning, as well as most of the previous night, laying out the various scenarios. They were still no closer to a conclusion as they were when they had started. Thomas knew what his response would be and braced himself for the sharp rebuke he was about to receive.

"The most logical thing to do is to continue as planned," he replied.

"I know that, damn it! But I hate it! I feel like...like..."

"Like you're abandoning them? Believe me, Love, I know." He sighed heavily and tried not to think of leaving Exra to fight while he played the coward. No amount of reasoning had yet to ease that guilt.

"Do you remember that market in Dia Loran?" he asked.

Lea sighed, impatiently. "Of course, Love. How could I ever forget?"

"I got distracted by that forged Ricardan painting and wandered off for a moment."

"We spent the better part of a day going in circles looking for each other."

Exactly!" Thomas exclaimed. "If had used half the brain the gods gave me, I would have gone back to that baker's stand and waited. It was the last place we saw each other, and the first place you looked."

"Oh, Love," Lea said, putting her arms around his waist, "you would have eaten three whole loaves because you felt bad for loitering."

Thomas laughed. "I did buy tea every time I passed the tea shoppe. By the time you found me I had never had to relieve myself so badly."

"I remember the dance you were doing." Lea wiped a tear from her cheek. "Do we go, then?"

"We wait one more day, as planned. There is still every chance that they will meet us here."

"Should one of us remain behind? Just in case?"

"No. If they are not here by tomorrow, then they will know we have left. Besides, I am no good without you, Love. I am apt to find myself in the Southern Wastes, food for some snow beast, without you to keep me on task."

"Liar," Lea chuckled, punching him on the shoulder, lightly.

"Call me a chauvinist, but until all this is over, I am not letting you out of my sight. I couldn't bear to lose anyone else, Love."

"I think it's perfectly sweet," Lea said smiling. She stood on her toes to kiss him on the cheek. "You sexist swine, you."

"My Lady," Thomas said, standing as the Countess Jewel Barracourt entered the sitting room, escorted by Lyle.

"Gwyndoline's ass, Thomas, sit down!" the young woman said. "No, stand back up. No! Sit down. You're too damned tall."

Thomas did as he was told, and his tiny sister-by-law marched right up to him and sat in his lap, tossed her arms around his neck, and kissed him on the lips. She ended it a moment before it would have become completely improper. At first Thomas thought she did these things to make her sister jealous. Now he knew it was to make him as uncomfortable as possible. Once he had figured that out, the trick was to pretend not to be, which they both knew was quite difficult for him.

The countess pulled back and looked for the flush in his cheeks. She squinted, slightly. He felt the heat in his face but thought he had sufficiently suppressed it.

"You're getting better," Jewel said. "I'm going to have to start trying harder."

"That's a dangerous game to play with your sister."

"What she doesn't know, sweet brother..." She kissed him on the nose and stood up.

"Now, Lea," Jewel handed Lyle her overcoat and walked to her sister, kissing her on each cheek. "What have you gotten me into, this time?"

"This time!?" Lea said, incredulously. "What do you mean, 'this time?' You were always the one getting me in trouble!"

"Oh, and I suppose disassembling father's carriage and putting it back together in the dining room was all my idea?"

"Alright! I concede that I caused as much trouble..."

"At least as much..."

"...at least as much trouble as you! But this, Jewel... this is different. This is dangerous. In light of recent events, I... I think perhaps we should rethink this whole affair."

"What has happened?" The playful fighting tone gave way to genuine concern. "Are you all right? Tell me what you need, sister."

"Ana and Exra..." Lea fought back tears.

"There, there...take your time," Jewel comforted her. "Start at the beginning."

And so, she did.

When Lea had finished the tale, Jewel just sat there, staring at them. Thomas could not recall her being quiet for so long. Slowly, her eyes narrowed.

"This is a joke, right? A prank? You tell me this ridiculous story and then, 'just kidding, I'm pregnant!' Is that it? It's cruel, that's for sure."

"I wish it were so," Thomas said.

"You wish I was pregnant?" Lea shot back.

"No. Yes! No... That's not...can we focus on this problem, first?"

"Oh, we're coming back to that."

"It's true, is what I mean," Thomas said, pointedly. "Every word, unfortunately. And so we can't, in good conscience, ask you to stay here where it could be dangerous."

"If you think for one moment that I would let my sister ride off into danger and not help, you're soft in the brain, Thomas Porter. I'll come with you."

"Jewel, as much as I would love that," Thomas could hear that Lea meant what she said, unironically, "the best help you can be is to throw them off our trail. If we can gain even one day ahead of them it may prove the difference in success or failure."

"I understand. I suppose I can try to look like you, hard as that may be. And this cousin of yours?"

"Petyr."

"Yes, this Petyr; he looks like you?"

"Enough to fool most, from a distance."

"Well, then," Jewel said, looking much like a fisherbird spotting a leaping fish, "this could prove fun, after all."

"Petyr is a simple man, Jewel," Thomas said, "he wouldn't even be a small challenge."

"Dice can be as much fun as cards, depending on your mood. Besides, aren't we supposed to do everything that you two would do?"

"Only when people are watching," Lea said.

"I don't mind if they watch..."

"Oh! You are incorrigible!"

"Fine," Jewel conceded, a faux pout on her face, "but don't think I'm not going to parade around in all your silk under-things."

Petyr arrived while the women were dying their hair. Jewel dyed hers to the bright blue that Lea had not had time to change, yet, while Lea dyed hers to the natural brown her sister wore most of the time. She would be wearing a wig when they left, but the blue would be a dead giveaway, should anyone see it. Jewel wanted to wear a wig, as well, not wanting to cut her rather long hair.

"It'll grow," Lea said, hacking away.

Thomas had little to do to prepare Petyr. Most of it would be in assuming Thomas' wardrobe. When the women returned, Thomas was amazed. He was able to tell, instantly, that Jewel was not Lea by her mannerisms and gait, but to just about anyone else, the illusion was complete. As amazing as it was, however, he would have to downplay it to their faces. They did not like to be told how much they looked alike.

"Very passable," was the most he dared.

"Thank you," was Lea's reply. Thomas let go of the breath he had been holding.

Jewel marched right up to Petyr and curtsied. Petyr bowed in return.

"You look lovely, as always, Lea," he said.

"And you, Thomas," she replied.

"Oh!" Petyr said taken aback, "I'm Petyr."

"You were right," Jewel said, looking to Thomas, "I would actually feel bad."

"Petyr," Thomas said, "This is the Countess Jewel Barracourt; Lea's sister."

"Forgive me, My Lady," Petyr said, bowing lower. "I meant no disrespect. It's just that you look exactly alike. Are you twins?"

God's blood, no...

"We look nothing alike!" The sisters said in unison, throwing up their hands.

After he had managed to calm the sisters down, Thomas suggested that Jewel and Petyr become familiar with the estate and each other. Lyle introduced them to the rest of the staff, and then they took off on their own, Jewel linking her arm with Petyr's. She was being her usual charming self, and on occasion would look to Thomas and wink.

"Are we doing the right thing?" Lea asked.

"What else can we do?"

"Forget the whole thing. Spend our enormous wealth and wait for Ana and Ex to come home?"

"If they did come home, they would be disappointed in us for giving up. And if they never come home..., can we be content in knowing that they died for nothing?"

"Of course not, Love. Sometimes I just need to hear you say it so that it sounds reasonable to me. This will work, Love, I know it. And I know Ana and Ex are okay. They just have to be. What in Greyhorn's name are you doing?" The sudden change in conversation started Thomas.

"What?" he replied.

"Your trousers. You're rubbing your trousers and it is the most grating sound I've ever heard."

"Oh; I didn't realize I was," Thomas said, and it was true. His hand had been rubbing something in his pocket from the outside. It was small, probably a key, or something. He did not remember having anything in his pockets, but as absent-minded as he could be, it was not surprising. He just needed to make sure it was safe. That what was safe? It didn't matter, as long as it was.

"Sorry, Love," he said, "it must just be a nervous habit. I didn't even realize I was doing it. I'll try to not, in the future."

"It's okay, Thomas, I totally understand. I didn't mean to snap at you, I'm just on edge, myself."

Thomas kissed the top of her head.

"Quite all right, my dear. It's been a rough few days. It's only natural."

"I love you."

"I love you, too.

Thomas' hand went back to his pocket, and he patted it, gently. Still there. Still safe.

CHAPTER FIVE

The High Cleric Madu sat on his stool, mere hands away from Exra, an expression of extreme boredom on his face. The desiccated Neb er Khalid had tortured him for hours in his absence, with no one to even ask questions. When the old man returned, he simply watched, for a time. He seemed neither disturbed nor excited by what he saw but would take notes in a small journal. After a time, he closed the leather-bound book and placed it in his robes.

"Where is the phulassein?" he asked, not standing.

"I do not know."

Pain. Exra would not have believed it could have been worse than before, yet it was. In shame, he wished he knew the answer.

"Where is the Wellspring?"

"I do not know!" he yelled.

Fire coursed through his body, wracking him with spams.

"Is the Wellspring in the Garden of Ben-Hal?"

"I do not know..." it was almost a whisper.

The pain came again. It felt as if someone were peeling his skin from his body, layer by layer. It lasted much longer, this time. Or perhaps it only felt that way. In either case he had to admit, to himself at least, that the High Cleric had been right. He was broken. Exra would have told the old man anything he wanted, if only he had known what to say. The pain stopped, again, and the cleric sighed.

"I will be blunt with you, Basaa Khattab. My time – and, sub-sequently, your time – is almost up. I can wait no longer. By the end of this day, either you will meet a painless end and your wife will be free, or you will both be on your way to my basilica, where your experience will make our time here seem pleasant by comparison. I will leave you to think about this choice."

The High Cleric stood and made to leave, but Exra could not stand the thought of being left alone with the sorcerer any longer.

"Wait!" he cried. "Wait..."

"You have something to say?" the old man asked.

"Ben-Hal...the phulassein is in the Garden of Ben-Hal."

Madu's eyes narrowed, as if trying to determine Exra's sincerity.

"No." Madu said, finally. "We know it is not." He turned to leave.

"Yes!" Exra exclaimed, "It is true! We translated the glyphs from the prison. The pagagh were kept in the Garden, away from the bodies."

"We have also translated the writings," the High Cleric said, "and you are correct. As we speak, my men are on their way to Mount Banhai. You are not surprised, are you? You know where The Temple is."

"The Southern Sea," Exra said, defeatedly.

"Indeed. I am impressed. I was told the Ingeleans were good, but I did not believe they were that good. We have known the location of The Garden for some time. Two expeditions, however, have failed to return. Until your find we were content to leave it be; for us, it only held the reminder of the lies the Absent One told. But now we know that the pagagh of The Exalted are kept there, thanks to you.

"However," Madu continued, "the phulassein I seek is not there. The Alui Kali kept it close, far from the bagh of Chey-Luk, First among The Exalted. Our research leads us to believe that it was kept in the prison. I have personally searched through every artifact brought up from the prison and found nothing."

"Perhaps," Exra said, "your research is wrong. We did not find a phulassein in the ruins."

"Perhaps," the cleric replied. "I have other matters to attend to, but I will return. I hope you have remembered differently, by then. For poor Analeytuua's sake."

"No!" Exra yelled as the Madu turned away, "I have told you everything I know! Please! Just kill me...please..."

The High Cleric looked back with what appeared to be genuine remorse.

"Perhaps," he repeated.

The pain erupted in Exra's blood, once more.

Thomas had to admit that it was slightly uncanny to see Jewel as she was. Gone was the flirty and flippant countess who took little seriously and danced into a room, replaced by the determined march of Lea, chin held high as she walked with purpose. With the spectacles, it was almost enough to fool even him.

"It's not bad, I suppose," he said to his wife. "To a stranger, anyway."

Lea simply nodded, slightly preoccupied. In any case, it would have to do. It was now or never if they were going to leave. Thomas wished he could work with Petyr a bit more, but Lea said it was good enough, as long you didn't ask him anything. He was not quite sure what that meant, but it did not sound particularly confidence inducing, to him.

Lyle was bringing the carriage around for the faux couple. They were going to dinner and theater. The restaurant was dark enough to mask any irregularities, as was the theater. With any luck, anyone watching would be none the wiser.

"Candle-lit dinner and a show with a handsome young man? I could get used to your life, sister."

Jewel was her glib self, once more.

"If you like," Thomas said, "I will take you on my next dig. The caves in the Frostmores are particularly lovely in winter."

"Ugh," she replied. "I forgot about that part. Never mind. Unless...will we have to huddle together for warmth?"

Thomas had an excellent retort prepared, but the death-stare from his actual wife stopped it on his tongue.

"That's what the sled-dogs are for," Lea said, with more than a touch of acid.

"Spoil-sport," Jewel said to Thomas, dejectedly. "She never did know how to share."

"The two of you should be on your way," Thomas said. We will wait until we are sure your observers are gone before we leave. We will be back as soon as we can. Our house is yours, Jewel. Petyr and Lyle will take excellent care of you, I promise."

Instead of the innuendo-laden reply he was expecting, Jewel threw her arms around Thomas in a large embrace.

"You be safe," she said, kissing his cheek. "And you'd better take care of my sister, or else. She's not the only fierce Barracourt, you know."

"I will."

Jewel released Thomas and turned to embrace Lea. Thomas extended his hand to Petyr, who clasped it, firmly.

"I'll guard your estate with my life," Petyr said in a most serious tone.

"Just stay safe, that's what's important. And keep her out of trouble," Thomas said, nodding toward Jewel.

"I think I can handle her," Petyr replied.

"Mwahahaha..." Jewel laughed a mock-diabolical cackle that caused Thomas and Lea to laugh, also, despite the somber ambience of the room. Petyr just looked confused, not getting the joke, apparently. Poor lad...

"Get going," Lea said, pushing Jewel toward the door and wiping a tear from her face.

Jewel extended her bent arm for Petyr to take, and they walked out the door toward the waiting carriage.

The estate grounds gave way to a thick wood as Lea and Thomas made the escape from their own home. They were dressed all in black and carried only what little that they thought they would immediately need. Thomas had argued with Lea that she was carrying too much, but she felt that she would rather be slightly over-burdened than unprepared. They made frequent stops to listen, but so far had not heard the sounds of pursuit.

Over the course of the last day, Lyle and the groundskeeper, Harlan, had laid what few traps the estate owned along the path they would be taking. It seemed a futile effort, to Lea, but if it gave them some measure of confidence, she was content to let them, so long as they did not accidentally stumble upon them, themselves. If they were being followed, then it was most likely not by amateurs. Animal traps designed to protect livestock were not expected to catch them unawares.

The property ended at a small stream that acted as a natural border for the estate. At one time, a stone fence had surrounded the property, but over the last few generations it had slowly fallen away and was not replaced or maintained. The only portion that had any upkeep was the section that acted as guard for the small cliff overlooking the stream. While not a large drop – only sixty hands or so – a fall to the rocks below would certainly be unpleasant, if not fatal.

Luckily for the couple, a crampon and rope had been preplaced for them to repel down the cliffside. Thomas insisted on going first, in case the placement was unstable, or the rope had been tampered with. When that proved to not be the case, Lea followed him down. When she reached the bottom, she flicked the rope and yanked down in the manner that would release the latch on the crampon. The rope fell to ground, and Lea coiled it up, tying it to her backpack.

"You're already carrying too much!" Thomas whisper-yelled.

"You'll thank me."

Thomas wisely did not press the issue, but instead led them to where the ladder had been placed across the stream, roughly a hundred paces north along the bank. It was not the most stable of bridges, but gods knew Lea had traversed far worse in delves. Once on the other side, the pair pulled the ladder over to them, folded it to its smallest length, and shoved it under some shrubbery and leaves. Lea did not see much use in hiding it on this side of the stream, but it really did not take any more time, and it made Thomas feel better to hide their route.

The two pressed on, faster than before, less wary of making noise, and no longer stopping to listen for pursuers. If anyone following had not been sufficiently slowed down or thrown off the trail by this time, then being slow was not going to help them.

It was not long before they reached the road. Though following the road was not the shortest route to the town of Gainsport, it was the easiest. They kept as far away as they could while keeping on the easier terrain. Twice, they had to duck behind some foliage to hid from a passing carriage, and once an Eimurial vehicle barreled down the road, barely giving them enough time to hide. It did not appear to the two that they were being looked for on the road, but they took no chances.

The town of Gainsport was aptly named, laying on the Gains River, a major trade route that also fed the small stream that bordered Thomas' familial home. And, just as Porter's Creek formed the edge of the Porter estate, The Gains marked the southern border of Ingeland, on the other side of which lay Delmont.

The town, itself, was something of an oddity, being shared by both nations, with a bridge connecting the Ingelean side to the Delmonti side. It had but one mayor, but the council consisted of three members of each parent nation. Lea did not pretend to understand the politics that governed the upkeep of the town but had always been fond of it. The mixture of the two cultures was fascinating and made for the best shopping trips.

Getting into the town was easy enough, but crossing the bridge was something of an ordeal for those who did not reside in the town. Even residents were subject to searches and detentions, in theory if not practice. Lea and Thomas had crossed dozens of times, and could no doubt do so again, but that would leave evidence of their passing, and that was something they were trying to avoid. The river patrol made it all but impossible to simply take a boat across the river, and the other land routes were days away on foot, and far more heavily guarded. Their best bet was to cross into Delmont from Gainsport; they would just have to do it as someone else.

The two avoided the main road into town and snuck in through an alley that ran between two shops. The morning was almost upon them, and venders, hawkers, and shopkeepers were just starting to begin their day, setting up their carts and stands, and unlocking their doors. Lea and Thomas kept away, walking fast and keeping their faces down, making as straight a path as they could to their destination.

The Dancing Wolf was not the fanciest tavern in town, but it had a reputation for a seedy sort of clientele that kept the local constabulary away under most circumstances. Of course, it was not really the law they were worried about, but they hoped that it would keep any others away, as well.

The Innkeeper was a gruff man, but his clothes were impeccable, if common. Finely made trousers and vest over a simple but well-crafted tunic contrasted with the scruff of several days, and the eye-patch that did not quite cover the whole scar on his left eye. They paid the man for two nights and two bowls of some kind of porridge.

They sat in a darkened corner of the common room, even though they were the only people in it. The porridge was not nearly as awful as it appeared, though they both ate it so fast they barely tasted it. The exertion of the evening had caught up with Lea, and she found her eyes starting to close of their own volition. They pushed the empty bowls away and made their way to their room, locked and barred the door, and collapsed on the bed, spent.

Nothing mattered to Exra, anymore. He knew the gods were truly gone, as he had prayed to them all, and yet he still lived. He had answered every question he was asked, and still Madu would not kill him. His only hope was that Ana was being spared this pain.

"Tell me, again," the High Cleric said, "from the beginning."

"Why?" Exra asked, defeated. "It will not change. I have told you so many times..."

"Perhaps you will remember something, yes? Some detail you have forgotten," the old man said it as though Exra was deliberately holding back, as if he had the will to do so. "Perhaps, in the retelling, something will occur to you that did not, before? Something that will help me to end this? From the beginning."

It was a hot spring day, the kind that signals that summer was almost here. They had just finished a dig outside the city of Trahmn, in the Golaan Desert. Trahmn was one of the ancient city-states that made up Zahir, and a hotbed of archeological activity. Since its rediscovery, every so-called 'legitimate' archeologist had staked a claim, there. And, while the discoveries being made gave great insight to the daily lives of the citizenry in the once great empire, it was not the sort of discovery the four companions sought.

Through Tomas' diligent research, they had determined that a royal necropolis once stood a handful of furloughs to the north of the city. Though there was little in the way of a local government since the collapse of Zahir before the Upheaval, any number of museums would pay handsomely for rights to the interred remains and funerary possessions of the old Trahmnasi.

Exra and Ana were hesitant about disturbing the dead, but as Zahirites observed a secular burial not in accordance with the gods, they were less uncomfortable than they normally would have been. After all, it was not as if they could have made it worse. And they were not going to disturb the dead, only uncover them. Perhaps, in doing so, they would finally get rest they deserved.

There was often no shortage of merchants and nobles who wanted to tie their names and fortune with uncovering the treasures of the past, but the four had no luck in securing funding this expedition. Fewer and fewer digs were proving fruitful, and many believed that glory days of the treasure hunter was behind them. Thomas claimed that nothing could be further from the truth, that the best finds were still out there, waiting. It was the easy digs that were exhausted, is all. Knowledge and fame were there for those who took the risk.

Of course, their last few delves did nothing to support this opinion. An old Aelfin colony outpost turned out to be nothing but ramparts and rubble, interesting only as a dot on a map. A supposed entrance to the fabled dwarven lands in the Frostmore Mountains was so obstructed that it would have taken a team of a hundred men ten years to completely excavate it. The last anyone had heard, the mining company who bought the claim had gone bankrupt. Before that, a pirate refuge turned out to be nothing more than a reef of sunken ships and a few tree-stands.

Because of this, Thomas had funded the Zahiran dig, entirely. His family's fortune was wholly invested in the mercantile business that had built it, but he had managed to direct enough away from it for one last attempt at securing their place in history.

The necropolis was right where Thomas had predicted. His talent for deciphering the puzzles of the past often amazed Exra. It was little trouble to enter the city of the dead. The city's defenses had long ago been tripped, triggered, and broken down. The necropolis may have been lost in the Upheaval, but it had been looted long before that. Tombs and crypts had been smashed open and plundered, and even anything decorative that could have been of use to a museum had been either taken or destroyed. At most, they would have a footnote crediting them for the rediscovery.

And with that, the funding was gone. It would take years for Thomas to save enough for real delving. If they could not find a patron, the most they could hope for was to lend expertise to other delvers. While it may provide the excitement, it left out all the fame and fortune. Not to mention that it was a humiliating step backward for any treasure-hunter.

The four delvers sat in a small open-air café in a town that was little more than a camp that explorers used as a stop before braving the scorching sands of the Golaan. They all sipped the bitter quawa tea that was served without milk, pouring over Thomas' notes, and trying to determine their next course of action.

"What about The Golden City?" Thomas asked, igniting the old argument.

"A myth," Lea said, not for the first time. "And a ridiculous one, at that."

"But it's the sort of ridiculous that might attract investors?"

"To what end? How many expeditions to the city have returned? And those that did had no proof the city even existed. We'd be digging for the sake of digging."

"Nothing else has proven fruitful," Thomas said, "why not try for something fantastical?"

"You're the one who's supposed to keep me grounded, Love; I don't like being on this side of the conversation. No, we have to find something big enough to bring in money, but realistic enough to reap the benefits of."

"What about...Killerman's Fleet?"

"I am not familiar," Ana said.

"Captain Gaius Killerman was a privateer," Thomas explained, "under commission from King Reginald XI to raid Aelfin ships who came too close to the Ingelean border. He had three ships in his fleet. Legend has it that, of his own volition, he took them to the Aelfin provinces on intelligence of a vast treasure. Most historians believe it was a trap set by the Imperial Navy, as neither he nor his fleet was never seen, again.

"However, some sources claim that Killerman sent a final missive just weeks after he set sail, addressed to the king. It supposedly said, 'I have found it, Your Majesty, and it is all we had dreamed.' But as to what he was referring, no one knows. The Crown denies any of it."

"Perhaps it is just that, then," Exra said, "a legend. People love a good mystery."

"Indeed. That's one I'd love to solve. Even if it were a trap, and there's no treasure, just to know his fate would be enough for me."

"But not for an investor, Love," Ana reminded him. "Besides, the Iron Sea is quite large, and we wouldn't even know where to begin. And we'd need to hire divers, since none of us have any experience."

"True. We could try for Icehold. There hasn't been a foray south in almost a century."

"There is a reason for that, my dear; it's suicide."

"That was before Eimurial vehicles and tools. A well-equipped expedition..."

"Would cost a fortune. Besides, you know how Ana is in the cold."

"It is true," Exra said, "she steals all the blankets."

"Silence is prudence, my heart," Ana said with a too-sweet smile.

Thomas sighed, a long and exasperated sigh. There had to be something they could do, but Exra did not have the facility for history that Thomas, or even Ana, had. He Loved the thrill of the hunt, but the details...he was content to leave that to the Porters.

"How about," came a booming voice from behind them, "a dig in Esisria?"

They all turned toward the source of new voice. A large, corpulent man stood at the edge of the café tent. He was dressed finely, in Delmonti or Ingelean fashion. He carried a cane, intricately carved and adorned with jewels, and wore a cape. His skin was dark, and his eyes were deep-set, indicating an eastland heritage. He was flanked by two servants, locals by the looks of them. He removed his somewhat ridiculous stovepipe hat.

"Forgive the intrusion," he continued. "I did not mean to be so rude. Allow me to introduce myself. I am Markus Blackmoore, Lord of Arlond." He bowed, deeply. The four companions made to stand.

"No, no," Lord Blackmoore said, waving, "please, please sit. May I join you?" He didn't wait for a reply but grabbed a chair from a nearby table and slid it over to theirs.

"Lord Blackmoore," Thomas said, "you are most welcome, of course. To what do we owe the honor? You mentioned Esisria?"

"Yes," said the rotund man. "I have been looking for you. I would like to finance a dig in Esisria."

Exra immediately recoiled. There were many reasons to not delve in Esisria.

"Not to seem ungrateful, My Lord," Lea said, "but why us? You've travelled a long way to find us when there are many other skilled archaeologists out there, and to be blunt, with better success rates than we."

"Very astute of you," Blackmoore agreed. "But I don't want them. I want you." He took a long drink of his quawa tea.

"Again, My Lord, I must ask: why? If you have a location in mind, surely any team of delvers would do? I don't mean to appear suspicious, but if we are to take the job, I must know everything."

The large man smiled, a crooked and toothy smile that reminded Exra of a river lizard. He set his tea down upon the table and shifted in his seat, the chair creaking under his weight. He sized the four companions up, as though he were best deciding how to cook them. It made Exra's skin crawl.

"But you are suspicious, my dear, and you are right to be. A strange man who is not what he appears to be has travelled far to hire you, you who believe yourselves to be failed treasure hunters, to hunt for treasure in a land that is hostile to delving, at best? Yes, I see that nothing escapes you, and that is exactly why I am here.

"You say you are unsuccessful? I say you judge success by the wrong merit. You think because you haven't found riches that you failed? I say that it is not what you have found, but what you have sought that makes you the best in your field."

"I'm afraid I don't understand," said Thomas.

"This necropolis, for example. No less than six expeditions have been made over the last three centuries to find it, yet none have. Until you. May I ask how?"

"Well," Thomas began, "In truth there were at least eight digs that I know of who have searched for the city. Each made extensive notes that I used to check against the writings we have about the Trahmnasi royal family. Once we eliminated the possible places that it could not be, it actually became quite obvious. Most of the work had been done, really."

"And yet no one had found it. You give yourself too little credit. You have found things others had searched a lifetime for. The Dwarven Pass, the Aelfin outpost? How many people died searching for those? And yet you four danced in like a harvest festival parade and planted your flag."

"'Danced' is somewhat understating things," Lea said, "but I'm beginning to see your point."

"What I have in mind isn't nearly so grandiose, I'm afraid, but I need a team that I can trust. It would certainly be cheaper for me to hire just any group of lummoxes with picks, but would they know what they were even looking for? No, I need the best, and I can pay for it."

"And what are we looking for?" Ana asked.

"I'm sure it hasn't escaped your notice that I don't look like a typical Delmontian. My grandmother was Esisrian, you see. And, while not unheard of in the lower classes, amongst the nobility it was quite the scandal. The Queen-Regent at the time threatened to strip my grandfather of his titles and lands if my grandmother did not renounce her Esisrian heritage. To what end I'm sure I'll never know; one look at her was evidence enough that she wasn't born in Arlond, or anywhere west of the Purple Marches. But politics are politics, and so she cut all ties with her homeland.

"The new king, Henri II, is a much more progressive monarch. I have petitioned him to reclaim my Esisrian heritage, and he has approved. Unfortunately, my grandparents were very thorough in purging all records and references to her parentage. The only clues I have are heraldic symbols I found on some of my grandmother's jewelry. They are incomplete, however, and my contacts in the Cultural Ministry have been unable to find a match."

"If the ECM can't identify them," Thomas interjected, "I'm not sure of what use we can be to you."

"I have found, though various sources, what I believe is the location of a pre-Upheaval municipal building, along the edge of the Great Silt River. I can show you the research, if you like, to scrutinize, but I believe it to be good."

"If your sources are certain, then why not have them lead the dig?" Exra asked.

"They are scholars, Basaa Khattab, not diggers. I need someone who is both."

"You believe that it may be dangerous?" Lea asked.

"I believe in being prepared."

"Assuming we accept, what are your terms?"

"I will pay for the entirety of the expedition, plus two hundred-pound, sterling, each, regardless of outcome. Any records or artifacts that directly relates to heraldry or lineage are mine, outright. Anything else of value is yours to do with as you please, minus the cost of the expedition plus one-fifth of the total value of the find."

"That is a remarkably reasonable offer," Lea noted.

"I hoped you would feel that way," Blackmoore replied. "My only real interest is in the records that may exist, there. Anything else I would consider a bonus."

"My Lord Blackmoore," Thomas said, "would you object to us looking over your research and discussing this among ourselves?"

"Not at all. I anticipated as much." The large man stood from the table and tossed down a rather large notebook, as well as enough coin to pay for the five cups of tea twice over. "I will await your answer in the morning."

Less than two weeks later they had begun the delve that had led Exra to this place, and to this pain. He cursed the name Blackmoore.

"But as we have discussed, Basaa," Madu said, "there is no Lord Markus Blackmoore in Arlond, or anywhere else in Delmont."

"That cannot be. Thomas wired funds to his bank on the morning we left. It was Blackmoore who sent us to this place."

"I have checked with the banking guild. They have no record of Thomas Porter making any transfer other than to his own Ingelean accounts. Is it possible, Basaa Khattab, that he lied to you? That this 'Lord Blackmoore' was a ruse of some kind that your partners put together? That their real goal was the phulassein, and knew that you would surely object, if you knew?"

"Impossible," Exra replied, but he was not sure, anymore. He wasn't sure of anything. He had not slept in what felt like days, but he had no real idea how much time he had spent in this hell. His mind had begun to play tricks on him, and the cleric's words had begun to take on a suggestive quality. He had known Thomas and Lea a long time, longer than anyone save Ana. Was it possible that Thomas knew about the prison? Was he that good an actor to fool Exra? No, it couldn't be. Could it?

"Impossible," he repeated. Madu simply shook his head, sadly.

The man named Amsu appeared out of the shadows. He passed a small piece of parchment to the High Cleric, whose face upon reading it betrayed a moment of panic. It was gone as quickly as it appeared, and he calmly asked Amsu, "Are you sure?"

A low and subjugated nod was the cold reply. Madu collected himself for a moment, then addressed Exra.

"When I return, we will end this." Then, to Amsu and Neb er Khalid, "Come with me."

The three men left Exra there, in the dark. His eyes began to close, try as he might to keep them open. He would not sleep, he told himself, but he would just rest his eyes for a few moments, taking advantage of this respite without his tormentors.

Just as unconsciousness threatened to overtake him, there was an explosion. He was rocked back to the waking world as dust and stone flew about his face, cutting him. What in the Underworld was that? It sounded like blasting gel, the Eimuria-infused substance the miners and diggers would sometimes use to open tunnels. But where was it coming from? Another explosion, this one definitely above him. He felt a support pillar collapse, and part of the room he was in came crashing down.

He heard then the screaming, the yelling. The sounds of men fighting and dying. What was happening? Was he under attack? By whom? He heard the familiar hum and thud of the strange weapon that had brought him down in the alley, along with the clanging of steel on steel. It sounded like a war.

Another explosion, and the world was ripped apart. Sunlight was thrust in from all sides, so suddenly that it blinded Exra. The blast had been so close that all he heard was a high-pitched ringing sound. He was both blind and deaf! He could hear voices, but not make them out. They were strange, distorted. The words ran together in his ears. He could also see shapes, like shadows against the sun, but could not make out who or what they were.

He felt a warm liquid run down his face and into his right eye. Blood? From where? His head hurt, but it hurt all over. He could not tell where the blood might be coming from. His vision started to dim, again. He was losing consciousness. He knew he was about to die, and his death bothered him far less than the mystery of what was happening. With luck, Uru would tell him what had happened before denying him entrance to the Golden Fields.

"Exra!"

His name! Someone had said his name. But, who? Where were they? He heard it, again. It was deep against the ringing in his ears, muffled.

A black blob blotted out the sun, but he could not tell if it was a figure or just death approaching. He was slipping fast, now, out of the waking realm. He heard his name, again, and this time it sounded familiar. The last thought he had before the darkness claimed him was one that made no sense, at all.

Ana had found him.

CHAPTER SIX

The storm ripped and tore at Thomas as he was led along the path. The wind was so fierce and course that it wore away his uncovered skin. The Thos guardians pulled on the chain around his neck, jerking him forward. The wolf-headed soldiers seemed unfazed by the torrential rain and lashing winds that beat Thomas, slowing him. They showed no concern or mercy, only pulling him forward, impatiently.

The walk seemed to take an eternity, as if it were part of whatever gruesome torment for which he was fated. He thought that he should feel scared, horrified, or at least apprehensive, but all he felt was...hate? Hate for whoever had done this to him. Hate for those who did not recognize his magnanimous altruism. Well, they had their chance. There would be no further warning.

Thomas looked to the sky. It was a swirl of dark purples and reds. There was no sun in the sky, but neither were the moons or stars visible. There was nothing on the horizon in any direction; only the path he walked stood out from the bleak and desolate vista. Wicked looking birds, with wingspans as long as a man was tall, circled above. Dreadful and awesome lightning flashed in the distance. Wherever he was, it was not of the natural world.

Eventually he was led past two giant pillars, each adorned with a colossus of staggering size. The carved figures were that of an ure bull that stood on two legs, its horns twisted and malevolent looking. They wore full plate armor, as if human, save for their bare hooves, and each wielded a double-bladed axe in its human-like hands. Thomas had never seen or heard anything like it.

Past the giant statues Thomas saw more pillars with even more hideous beast-men. Some he recognized, like the Thos guardians. Others were in the likeness of beasts that he had never seen depicted as such, including a vulture and a type of lizard that Thomas could not readily identify. Others were totally alien to Thomas, not resembling any sort of beast he had ever seen.

The pillars formed a circle, and in the circle stood posts with chains attached. The posts, themselves, were in a circle of runes, two posts to a circle. There were scores of runic circles that Thomas could see. Many of them of them were vacant, but some had figures in them, each of their hands chained to a post. The look in their open eyes was vacant and vacuous, as if dead.

As the Thos led him past many of the circles, Thomas looked at the prisoners. At the sight of some, he felt a pang of recognition, though he did not know why. At one of the captives, he stopped. It was a woman, dark skinned and black-maned. Despite her hawkish features and the scars that lined her face, she was the most beautiful woman he had ever seen. He knew her, but he could not recall how, or what her name was.

When Thomas looked into her eyes and saw the same dead look that the others had, he became enraged. He ran toward her, bound hands outstretched. He would free her. He would free her and all the others. A sharp jerk from the chain around his neck pulled him back. He strained against it to no avail. He let out a wail as he endeavored in defiance of his captors, pulling until he exhausted himself. When he had no more insolence left, his imprisoners continued to lead him deeper into the grove of shackles.

Finally, they reached his set of posts. The wolf-headed fiends that had directed him took each of his hands and secured them in the irons. Wordlessly and without ceremony they walked away, leaving him chained there. No sooner had they gone than a figure flew down from the swirling sky. Its wings swooped for a moment before it landed. It was a giant eagle that stood upright, as a man did. As it landed, he watched the beast's form change, until it was no longer a bird, but a man, tall and broad. He wore shining gold armor with a red cape that whipped behind him in the wind. His skin was alabaster white; not the pale of the eastern folk, but white as bone. His hair was yellow, long, and curly, and his eyes were a piercing green. Thomas was not sure how he knew who he was, but he did.

"Gol-Adam," he said. His voice was low, much lower than normal. "I am honored." The words dripped with sarcasm.

"You were honored, once," Gol-Adam said, his voice reverberating through Thomas' body and mind, "you, who were first among all others. You, who were trusted with the power of the Gods. You, who were given the secrets of the Ei'Mur'ai. You, who were loved above any-one, were most honored, once."

"Love?" Thomas' felt the vitriol in the voice that was not his. "What you called love, I call chains, as binding as these I wear, now. What you called trust, I call control, leaving no room for dissent or free thought. What you called honor, I call domination, the subjugation of my entire race."

"It did not have to end this way, my son. Whatever you may think, I am saddened. It brings me no joy to do this, child."

Behind Gol-Adam walked up another man, this one with skin as dark as the other was white. His hair was white, however, and straight as an arrow. He was shorter than Gold-Adam by a head and wore robes of such a dark blue that they looked almost black. Besides having eyes that were the same shade of green, the two men could not have been more different. In his hand he held a wooden staff, blackened, and twisted as if from fire.

"Arrak." Thomas said.

"You brought this on yourself, manling," the dark man said. "On yourself and those who followed you. Look around, child. Where once they called you and your brethren Exalted, they now call you The Wretched. Doomed to this oblivion, you will never see the Waking

Plane, again. Tell me," he gestured with his staff to the woman Thomas had tried to free, "was it worth it?"

Thomas did not answer but smiled despite the rage he felt. Arrak shook his head and leveled his staff at Thomas. Thomas began to feel himself slip away, not into the nothingness he was expecting, but into a prosaic confusion. He was losing himself, who he was, as the winds of the Wailing Prison whipped around him. He struggled as long as he could to hold on to himself, to not slip away into malaise of uncaring. As he felt himself disappear at last, he looked at Gold-Adam, one last time.

"This is far from over."

Thomas snapped awake, awash in sweat, and breathing heavily. He started upright, eyes darting around, as he tried to figure out where he was. He was in bed, in his room at The Dancing Wolf. He sighed a heavy sigh of relief as he felt Lea stir beside him.

"Love?" she asked, somewhere between sleep and waking, "Are you alright?"

"Yes," he said, still breathing heavily. "Just a nightmare, is all. Go back to sleep, Love."

"Would you like to talk about it?" Lea propped herself up on her elbow and ran her fingers through her husband's hair. "It sometimes helps. Jewel used to have the most awful nightmares when we were girls, and she could never go back to sleep until she told me about it. I have lots and lots of practice," she said, smiling.

"I was...somewhere else," Thomas started, but he could already feel the details fading away. The feelings of persecution and hate clung to him, but the particulars became elusive.

"I was being imprisoned, I think, in a particularly horrible fashion. I was...I can't remember where I was. Or who I was. I'm sorry, Love, but it's all slipping away from me. I just remember the hatred I felt for my imprisoners. And there was a woman...I think..."

"Oh, really?"

"Not like that," he rebuffed, pushing her, gently.

"I know, you great lummox. It's called levity." She stuck her tongue out at him, then kissed his forehead. "I'm sorry, dear. Considering all we've seen and all we've been through over the past week, I'm surprised we haven't all been having nightmares about it, especially that gruesome prison. Oh, Thomas, I wish I could help."

"You do, my love, you do." He kissed the top of her head. "Now, let's get back to sleep, if we can. It's going to be another exhausting day."

They kissed one more time and both settled back into comfortable sleeping positions. Thomas closed his eyes and tried to focus on anything except his dream. He felt sleep begin to take hold.

"Thomas," Lea said, a light annoyance in her voice, "you're doing it, again."

Thomas stopped rubbing his leg.

"Sorry," he said, "I didn't realize."

"I know," Lea said, yawning as she did, "I know. Good night."

Thomas tapped whatever object he had been rubbing in the pocket of his nightshirt.

Still safe.

The two treasure hunters-turned-spies slept for only a few hours the day of their arrival at the inn. They woke around midday to meet with the shady character who identified himself only as Hawk. He was, according to Lea's sources, a master forger. As strange as they come, she was told, but mostly harmless. Mostly.

The man wore as many pieces of clothing as he could, it seemed, none of them matching. When asked about it (as politely as possible, of course) he claimed it was to blend in as many places as possible, though Lea was certain the man would stand out wherever he went. After telling him what they needed and agreeing on a price, the man said:

"Ye have bearing a lady. Git ye a bouncy frock, ani topper. Ol' lad'll be thee man, so git him a dirtman wrapper and lid. Meet me here, come sunup. I'll polish my emerald, but if ye play the game a cropper, we'll all get clapped."

After he had gone, Lea asked the innkeeper what any of that meant. The man roared with laughter, gripping his sides, and doubling over.

"He says that that you have the bearing of a lady, and your husband your servant." He fell into another bought of laughter, and Lea felt her face flush. She would not apologize for her upbringing, but the fact that Thomas deferred to her in some things did not make him a servant, or her lesser. She swallowed the words that almost sprung from her lips.

"Says you need to get yourself a fancy dress and hat, and him a workman's outfit. He said his job will be flawless, but if you don't do your end well, you'll all get caught." He continued to laugh as they left the inn, Lea practically marching as she willed herself to remain silent.

They spent the rest of the day shopping. It was horribly short notice to have a dress made, but enough coin in the seamstresses' palm convinced her to tailor a showroom dress. The most time-consuming part would be removing the embellishments that identified it as a child's garment.

Thomas was far easier to shop for, naturally. Workman's clothes were sold at practically every corner and were expected to be ill fitting. He balked at the shoes, however, making an uncharacteristic fuss about the low-quality of the footwear.

"For someone who is supposed to be on his feet all day, this is unbearable. Imagine wearing these to dig into the necropolis! I'd have blisters the size my head by the end of the first day. Dear gods...is this what Lyle wears? How has he not strangled me, by now? That is the first thing I'm fixing when we get back. Are you absolutely sure this is necessary?"

"Thomas, you know that I love you with all of my heart. But, if I have to wear petticoats, a feathered hat, and thrice-damned heels, then the very – and I do mean very – least that you can do is wear slightly uncomfortable shoes until we are out of Gainsport." She patted his cheek for emphasis, perhaps a tad harder than she needed to.

"At least you seem to have your part down," Thomas said, sullenly.

"It sounds like someone wants to be cleaning the stables," Lea said casually as she walked away.

They ate dinner at a small bistro that was tucked into an alley. It served Delmonti cuisine, exclusively, for which Thomas also complained. It wasn't like him to be so contrary; usually Thomas was the optimistic one, his spirit never faltering, no matter what dire circumstances they found themselves in. Lea began to worry about him.

"It's the texture," he said. "Everything In Delmont is slimy and covered in sauce. I miss Esisrian food, already."

"Thomas. Love," Lea said between bites, "is everything all right? You seem not yourself, today."

Thomas stopped pushing the river mollusk around his plate with his fork and sighed.

"It's that damned dream," he finally said. "I keep getting flashes of it. Little moments that I see clearly, then are gone, again. I wish I could remember it...but, it's the feelings that I still feel, the emotions I felt in the dream. So angry, Lea. More angry than I think I've ever been, awake. It's...unnerving, to say the least."

Lea reached out and put her hand on his.

"You're not an angry person, Love. I don't think I've ever seen you angry, even when you were frustrated. You take it in stride, always. It's something I love and admire about you. And it's something that I strive to be. I get angry all the time. I get angry at the smallest and stupidest things, and you're always there to level me back out, to calm me down, even when I really don't want to be calm. And when you're not there, I just take a step back and ask myself, 'what would Thomas do?'"

"You do not," said Thomas, incredulously.

"I most certainly do! Why, if I hadn't asked myself that a few days ago, I surely would have punched that smug Cultural Minister right in his smug, smuggy face! But, I asked, 'what would Thomas do?' And I knew that you would try to see it from his perspective and try to be rational. Which only made me angrier, of course, because you're always so damned calm and I don't know how you do it! But...I didn't punch him, which for me I consider a smashing success. Thanks to you.

"You see, Thomas, I've learned to deal with my anger. But it's something you're unfamiliar with. I promise that it will fade with time, as will the dream, and you can go back to being the infuriatingly calm man I fell in love with."

"Perhaps," he replied. "It does feel better to talk to you about it, Love, thank you."

"You're welcome. Now, finish your sauce covered slime so we can get back to it. We still have a lot to do. And stop rubbing your trousers, it drives me batty."

Thomas stopped and put his hand back on the table.

"Didn't realize I was doing it, again."

"I know," Lea sighed.

They returned to their room late in the day with the spoils of their shopping. Most of it was to complete Lea's ruse. Ornate jewelry the likes of which Lea had never owned, even when she was considered nobility, she lay out on the nightstand for the morning. She knew she would be selling it, the first chance she got. Or perhaps she would give it away. It hardly mattered to her. Alongside the jewelry she placed an elaborately embossed and pearl-handled lorgnette. Her spectacles were deemed decidedly unladylike (as if ladies had no need to see), so she had purchased the ridiculously cumbersome and gawdy accessory to compete her disguise.

There were moments, over the years, that she had regretted relinquishing her title. Not for any specific reason, but on the general principal of the thing. It was a useless accoutrement to her, something that she had never desired or earned, and would never use, but it was hers, nonetheless. One look to her beloved Thomas and she knew it was more than a fair trade, but the moments still presented themselves. Now, as she looked over the trappings she was forced to wear just to pass as something she once was, she was glad she had given it up. What a silly and impractical lifestyle. She would take utility over being lady-like, any day.

Thomas, for his part, had lightened up for the rest of their outing. He even resumed the spouting of trivia, as he was wont to do. Lea simply smiled and acknowledged each fact as he stated it, as if he had not told her many times, already. He was happiest in knowledge and sharing knowledge. It was endless endearing, even when it was slightly annoying.

They prepared for sleep, changing into their nightclothes. Thomas had become silent, once again. Not somber and sulking, as before, but almost contemplative. He definitely had been out of sorts over the last few days, and Lea wished she knew what she could do to help. She supposed he would have to work through it on his own, but it was not an easy thing to watch unfold. Thomas was never an assertive man, but neither was he indecisive. As she watched him get ready for bed, he took off and put on the same tunic three times. Then, he looked confused for a moment, and went into a panic, frantically searching through his clothes that lay crumped on the bed. He did this several times, and once she could have sworn he whispered, "it's safe."

"Thomas, love," she broached, when he seemed to have finally settled down, "are you alright?"

"Of course," he said, getting under the blankets. His face betrayed no sign of distress.

She lay down beside him, wondering if now was the time to discuss this. It had been on her mind since it was brought up, dancing at the back of her consciousness. But obviously, there were greater – or, at least, more immediate and pressing – concerns, at the moment. They were searching for what could possibly be the greatest treasure of all time while being chased by parties unknown, and their best friends had been captured...or worse. But she felt like if she did not say anything, now, she may never.

"Did you mean what you said?" she blurted out, ungracefully.

Thomas turned his head to her, obviously unsure of what she meant.

"To Jewel. The other day. About...about me being pregnant."

"Well, no... I mean, yes, but not...you know..." he stumbled over his words, flustered. "It was a hypothetical, wasn't it?"

"Yes, and it was presented as the alternative to our current predicament, so I know your response was also hypothetical, but...well, we've never really talked about it, have we? Don't you think that's odd? Did we both just assume that it would happen? Or did we assume that it wouldn't?"

"I suppose," Thomas began, "that I assumed that you didn't want children, or that you wanted to wait. After all, the life we live is hardly conducive to child rearing. Can you image scaling the Great Cenotaph with an infant strapped to your back?

"I grew up with my parents mostly away on business. I don't resent them for it, but it's not the kind of father that I would like to be. I want to see my children grow and be part of their lives. It may sound strange, but I do harbor a small resentment for them dying on me."

Lea rolled over and buried her head into Thomas' chest. His heart was beating strong and fast. She placed her hand on top of it.

"I didn't mean to put you on the spot, Love, it's just been on my mind since Jewel said it. We don't have to finish the conversation, now."

"At the very least, my dear, I think we should wait until this ordeal is over." He kissed her forehead. "Then, we can decide if the time is right. And, who knows? Life sometimes has a way of deciding these sorts of things for you."

Lea reached her head up and kissed him. She appreciated his understanding but was annoyed at the non-answer. Sometimes she found his noncommittal attitude infuriating. This was not the sort of thing for one person to decide, like what to eat for dinner, or what show to see at theater. Sometimes she just wanted him to have a damned opinion about something. But he was right about it being the wrong time to finish the discussion.

She pulled back from the kiss, but he stopped her. He looked deep into her eyes and kissed her, again, and then again. He pulled her up to him level and held her tight against him. His hand went to her cheek, then to her hair, gripping it tightly in his fingers. He kissed her deeply and firmly.

She returned the grip, and the kiss, pulling herself fully on top of him. His hands moved from her face, down her shoulders and to her sides. With little effort, he hoisted her the rest of the way up. She grabbed the front of his nightshirt, tearing it open with no regard for the buttons. She heard one plink against the floor. She kissed his chest where it opened as his hands moved from her sides to her behind.

They made love, then, in that strange bed. It was intense and passionate, more so than it had been in some time. Thomas was normally very giving in bed, but tonight he was aggressive, almost rough. It was not unwanted, quite the opposite, but it was surprising. In fact, Lea found that she was more aroused than she had been since their first nights together. Not that their usual lovemaking was ever lacking, but the change brought a sense of newness to it that Lea found welcome and invigorating. It did not last as long as it normally did by a good measure, but the intensity was more than enough to make up for it.

It was not until they had finished, and Thomas lay asleep beside her, that it dawned on her just how different it had been. She had never been with another man; not out of any sense of prudence or modesty, but because until she had met Thomas, she had never had the desire to dally with a man. There were simply much more important things to occupy one's time. But as she ran her fingers through his hair, she realized that was exactly what it felt like. That she had made love to another man. The thought disturbed her for many reasons.

Thomas' eyes darted beneath his eyelids, and he scrunched up his face in disgust. Another nightmare, Lea thought. She almost woke him, but after a few moments, he calmed, and settled into a deep and restful slumber. She continued to stroke his hair, gently, until she faded off into sleep, herself.

"I feel like a peafowl," Lea said, twirling in her dress. "Absolutely ridiculous. How does anyone get anything done dressed like this?"

The bell-shaped gown was a bright yellow with white embroidering. She could barely walk in the gods-blasted thing, and she had not even put on the shoes, yet. The fitted bodice was far too tight, pushing her breasts to what felt like her neck, and making it all but impossible to breathe. Luckily, it was rigid as stone, because the necklace she wore was so heavy that it threatened to pull her head down. The hat was also substantial and was so tall that it stood at a height with Thomas. Some of the rings were nice, she thought. She might consider keeping them when this was over, impractical as they were.

"Women dressed like that aren't expected to do much of anything," Thomas replied. "That's why they have men dressed like me."

"And a good thing. I can't even scratch my own ass in this."

"Well, if it's any consolation, I think you look stunning."

"Oh, really?" she said. "Prefer me this way, do you? Well, I can start dressing like this all the time. We can bring Lyle on our delves to follow behind me and keep my skirts out of the dirt."

"I didn't say I preferred it, just that you look quite lovely. Personally, I prefer your trousers; the tighter the better. I like to see where all of you is at all times. For safety purposes, of course."

"You know I will probably have an exceedingly difficult time walking a straight line. I'm liable to step on your feet with those very sharp heels."

"It's a good thing these shoes are so thick, like wearing wooden blocks. And I'll just tell everyone you had too much wine at breakfast."

"Ass."

True to his word, The Hawk's documents were flawless. They listed Lea as Lady Miriam Castelberry, and Thomas as her servant, Jurgan Klugman. They had full diplomatic credentials, including the seal of the Office of Delmonti Trade. No matter how Lea looked at them, they looked totally authentic. And they must have fooled the border guards, as well, for they let them pass with hardly a second glance. Lea wondered if the whole subterfuge was even necessary. Well, better safe than sorry, she supposed.

Once on the other side of the Gains, the pair was able to let down their guard a little, but the ruse was far from over. They had chartered a carriage with the foremost service in the city. A lesser known and less reputable service would have asked fewer questions about the two, but no self-respecting lady would have been caught dead in one of their carriages, so they had to maintain the charade until they reached the next town of Orser.

They could have ditched the disguises once over the bridge, but there was still the possibility that they were being looked for, so they thought it prudent to keep up the act. As painful as it was to the both of them.

In Orser they could ditch the fancy trappings and go back to a less grandiose masquerade. There, they had arranged for a private carriage to be provided by a business associate of Thomas'. It would be filled with provisions, hopefully everything they needed for the rest of their journey, including supplies for camping, in case they were forced off the main roads. It also came with two armed men as protection, courtesy of Thomas' company, as well. They would not be told who they were guarding to prevent loose lips causing their downfall. This was standard caravan practice, anyway, to deter theft.

It was not long before Gainsport was beyond the horizon, and they both heaved a sigh of relief. The bulk of the journey was still ahead of them, but the hardest part – or so they both hoped – was now behind them. As the sun set on that first night, Lea said a silent prayer that Exra and Ana were safe and would meet them at the rendezvous. It was unlikely; she had come to terms with that, now. But, if the gods existed, and any were listening, she hoped they could hear her.

Please...please, hear me...

CHAPTER SEVEN

Exra's eyes shot open, and he regretted it immediately. Never before had his head hurt so much. He did not know his head could hurt so much. His hand went to his forehead. He noted with unreal delight that his hands were not bound and could be brought to his head. He would have laughed and danced if he were not afraid it would make his head worse. He seemed to be lying down, but the swishing nausea and vertigo made it hard to tell.

"Exra!" It was Ana's voice.

"Ana? Are you all right?"

"Am I all right?" she said it as a laugh, but Exra could hear the tears in her voice. "Of course I am all right! It is you I worry about, my heart."

Exra tried to sit up, and instantly thought better of it. Though he was no longer in restraints, it seemed he was still immobilized.

"Be still, husband," Ana said soothingly. "The effects of the foul sorcery may linger for some time. Do not try to sit. I am going to give you some water; you are very dehydrated."

A thousand questions swam in Exra's mind, but he held his tongue as his wife trickled water into his parchment-dry lips. She gave him only a little and he was about to ask for more when his stomach cramped, violently.

"You must take it easy, Exra. You were extremely near death."

"Where..." Exra attempted to stifle a cough and inadvertently turned it into a spasmic coughing fit. "Where are we?" he asked when it finally subsided.

"A safe place," Ana replied. "Everything else can wait until you are better."

As unsated as that left his curiosity, he trusted Ana's judgement. If she said he was in no condition to do anything but rest, he knew it was true. She would never coddle him or hold him back like some Westlanders did with their spouses.

"More," he said, as the cramps subsided. Ana obliged.

Hours later Exra sat on the edge of a cot in the same severe and un-adorned room in which he had awoken. The headache and nausea were better, if not gone. He had only been only able to stomach broth, so far, but it had helped to return much of his vigor. On a pair of utilitarian stools, he was joined by Ana and a middle-aged man with a beard. The newcomer had the dark skin-tones of the Esisrian people and dressed in a modest and unassuming manner.

"My name is Tirdad Jaleh," the stranger began. "I am the leader of the Tanrin Eli, here in Esisria."

"I am not familiar," Exra admitted.

"I would be quite surprised if you were. We are a very decentralized organization, if we can even be called that. We operate in cells; small groups that operate independently of each other. Only I know the names and locations of the other cells in Esisria, and only my superior knows the names of the other regional leaders. This way, no one can betray the information they do not have."

"I imagine this makes communication difficult," Exra interjected.

"Difficult, but not impossible. We have ways, if needed. We have been doing this for a very long time."

"And what," Exra said, adjusting himself on the cot, "is it that you do, exactly?"

"We seek to prevent the rise of The Wretched."

"And who, or what, are they?" Exra looked to Ana. Her stoic face implied that he must hear and judge this information for himself.

"Before the Flood," Tirdad began, "There were nine sorcerer-kings: The Exalted. The most powerful mortal magicians that the world had ever seen, they were entrusted by the gods to rule in their stead. And, so they did, for many generations. Until Chey-Luk came to power. He was said to be the most powerful man who had ever lived. He somehow convinced or corrupted the others to join him in open revolt against the gods, and a great war was fought. Our teachings say that it lasted for many, many years, and that hundreds of thousands lost their lives.

"In the end, The Exalted were all captured. The clerics devised a way to keep them imprisoned for all of time, to be forever known as The Wretched."

"The bodies we found in our delve," Exra extrapolated.

"Yes. All but Chey-Luk, himself. He was imprisoned far away from the others, in a place he could be guarded at all times, and that was extremely defensible."

"The Garden." It was not a question.

"Yes," Tirdad replied. "You and your wife are remarkably well-informed. Very few outside our order know this."

"Thomas...my friend Thomas is a scholar with no equal. It was he who deduced this."

"So Ana has said, as well. It speaks well of you that you give credit where it is due, and that you respect your friend as you do. Unfortu-nately, it is his knowledge that puts he and anyone with him in grave danger."

"It was you and your men at the station." Again, it was not a question.

"Yes, but not only us, as you are aware. Please believe that we were not there to kill you."

"Not before finding out how much we know," Exra accused. Tirdad smiled.

"Again, you and your wife's intuition do you credit. Yes, we were prepared to kill you and your companions, and would sleep soundly at night for it. I make no apologies when it comes to protecting the world from the evil that The Wretched represent."

"But this has changed?" Exra assumed defensive posture.

"After a fashion, yes. We need your help."

Exra's eyes narrowed as he studied this man. He did not trust his motives, yet, but he believed him when he said he would kill them without a thought.

"You know where the Garden is," Exra said.

"Of course. But we are not alone in this. You see, The Wretched did not act alone. They had foot-soldiers in their war against the gods, and not all of them were dealt with when the war was over. They have acted through the ages to release their masters, just as we have opposed them. In disgrace, they were called Blighted, but they have since taken this name as a badge of pride. To them, being forsaken of the gods is an honor they wish to share with all of humanity."

"They were also at the train station?"

"Yes. They are the ones that captured you and your wife."

"And the others?"

Tirdad paused before answering. He looked pensive.

"We do not know. Hired men, by the looks of them, but they had no clues as to who hired them."

"Then, they are all dead?"

"Not all. But many. This is perhaps the most troubling of recent events. The Tanrin Eli and the Blighted have been bloodying each other's noses for millennia; that someone else has entered the fray, and that we saw no sign of them before this, is beyond worrisome."

"They were there to kill us," Exra said.

"Yes. And they knew to expect us and The Blighted. Whoever is behind them is powerful."

"But that is not why you need us."

"No. We need your help because the phulassein of Chey-Luk was not among the artifacts recovered at the dig. If we are incredibly lucky, it was never there as recorded, and the worst that will happen is that your friends will perish in the Garden..."

Exra started to interrupt but Tirdad raised a hand to stop him.

"If it was there, and your friends have it, you two may be the only people in the world who can stop the new reign of The Wretched."

Exra and Ana sat together on Exra's cot. After Tirdad had left the two of them alone Exra's demeanor had completely changed. Ana saw just how much his ordeal had taken out of him, both physically and mentally; perhaps spiritually. He slumped, now, propping himself up with his arms. Ana had never seen him so drained, so tired.

"Tirdad told me what they did to you, in captivity," Ana said. "I did not understand all of it, but I may be able to answer questions, if you have any. I understand if you don't wish to speak of it."

"It is over," he replied, "and in the past."

"Let it be so," Ana replied, the traditional indication of finality in conversation.

"You were not harmed?" Exra asked.

"No. They kept me in a dark place, like a well. They told me they were torturing you and would release me if you told them what they wanted to know. If I told them, they would make your death merciful. I knew that was not what you wanted, or I think would have told them anything to get them to stop."

Exra looked away, then.

"They told me that you felt everything I did. The thought of you suffering like that..." he looked back into her eyes, tears welling in his own, "if I had known...I would have told them. I have done you a great dishonor."

"There is no dishonor in love. Do you understand?"

"I am a coward!" Exra spat, unexpectedly. Ana's reaction was just as unexpected to her: she slapped him, hard.

"Do not speak of my husband so! He is my pride." She took his face in her hands. "He would have died for me. To call him a coward insults me. Do you understand?" She repeated.

"Yes, but..."

"Then let it be so."

"Let it be so," Exra replied. He took a moment to compose himself, raising slightly on the cot. "The weapons they used in the market?"

"Eimurial. They have scholars who are harnessing Eimuria in many ways before unknown. Even the Tanrin Eli do not know all they are capable of."

"This Tirdad and the Tanrin Eli...do you trust them?"

"I believe them," Ana said, "but I do not trust them. They rescued me, yes, but it was only as a distraction to draw the cleric and sorcerer away. We are but a means to an end, and I believe they will do anything necessary to achieve that end, no matter the cost."

"So, they knew the High Cleric was a member of these Blighted?"

"Yes. Unfortunately, his political power is so great that they have been unable to route him."

"And the sorcerer? Can it be true?"

"I do not know," Ana sighed. "Tirdad claims he is Neb er Khalid, one of the nine Wretched, but without his kagh he is directionless. Essentially, a weapon to be pointed at their enemies."

Exra ran his hands across his face and through his hair. Ana thought about letting leaving him to rest, but she would not do that to him, coddle him like a child. Especially after slapping him. He would tell her when it was time.

"Do you think Lea and Thomas have this phulassein everyone wants so badly?"

"They have never kept anything from us. Besides, if they had it, do you think either of them could stop talking about it?"

"Fair point," Exra agreed, smiling. "If Thomas had it, then no doubt I would have heard its entire history three times. And Lea..." he trailed off, his smile fading. "Do you think they were protecting us, perhaps? Westlanders have odd notions of nobility."

"Perhaps. But I would think that they know us well enough to know what we would think of that."

"I hope so."

They sat in silence for a moment. Ana knew how much it was much to take in, especially after what he had been through. She had been given the luxury of time to absorb all of this, while he had been unconscious, recovering, hovering between life and death. They would have to take action, soon, whether he had regained his strength or not. She hated doing that to him but knew he would have it no other way.

"The hired killers," Exra said, at last, "do you think they are with Lord Blackmoore?"

"I do not know. You said the cleric told you that there was no lord by that name in Delmont; could he have been lying? That is not a mistake I would expect Lea or Thomas to make."

"It is possible, and something we must discover. He and they are unknowns, and unknowns are dangerous. But, first, we must find our friends."

Ana smiled. There was her husband.

Amsu stared with dispassion at the bodies that lay at his feet. Less than a minute ago they had been alive, initiates serving the High Cleric. One was named Jalil, and he was left in charge of guarding the woman. Amsu never learned the name of the other. To his knowledge, the man had done nothing wrong, but had the poor fortune of standing next to Jalil at the wrong time.

Jalil was bowed before Madu, explaining how the Tanrin Eli had slipped past their defenses and taken the woman. With a swift motion to the Sightless Sisters the throats of both men were slit. The other initiates gathered in the room fell to their knees in supplication. Amsu distractedly watched the blood run through the cracks of the floorboards.

"How!" the High Cleric yelled. "...did they know?" The initiates looked to each other, not knowing how to answer, nor wanting to be the next target of the Sisters' attentions. To Amsu, it was obvious that Madu was not expecting an answer from them.

"You may leave," he said to the terrified underlings. They practically fell over themselves running out of the room.

"Basaa and Bassara Khattab are of little consequence. It was clear that they knew nothing." Madu had taken to speaking to Amsu as a way of thinking aloud. Amsu wondered if he had done this before he entered the High Cleric's service, perhaps with the Sisters, or just to an empty room.

"What concerns me is how the sandal-lickers knew where they were being kept, and how they managed such a response so swiftly. They have never been highly organized; our spies rarely get worthy information. Of course, if we have spies, so do they...but I took the usual precautions. What has changed?"

Amsu knew what had changed, but he was unable to speak it to the High Cleric. He could, of course, write it for Madu, but His Grace did not ask it of him. A small tingling in the back of his mind wondered if he should volunteer this information, but something stopped him. If he did not know better, he would say it was because he did not want to. But that was impossible...wasn't it?

"The Ingeleans are clever, very clever. They are surely planning to search for the Garden, but our agents report that they have not left their estate. Are they waiting for their friends? Or have they given up the chase? That seems unlikely from what we know of them...if they really do not have the phulassein, however..."

"We will wait no longer." Madu placed his hand on Amsu's shoulder. "Bring me Cleric Ptol. We will have him send word to raid the Ingelean home. Find the phulassein, if possible. Capture the Westlanders, if not."

Amsu turned to leave, to fetch the cleric, but Madu held firm to his shoulder, and turned him back around. He looked deeply into the young man's eyes.

"You are the only one I can trust, now, Amsu," he said. "Even the Sisters could betray me, should they forsake their vows." The two veiled women gave each other a look that Amsu did not understand.

"But you...you can never betray me. Now, go."

As Amsu left, he felt something...relief, perhaps? Relief, that he could not speak. For, if he could, he would have been compelled to do so, to tell the High Cleric that he was wrong. Amsu could betray him. But he could not speak. And Madu did not ask.

Lyle chuckled to himself as he carried the bedding to the washroom. Poor Petyr was still sleeping on the floor, and Miss Jewel was still teasing the poor lad, who was too naive or dense to figure out she was only having fun with him.

She had been laying in the center of the bed, spread out as far as her tiny frame would allow, wearing her night shift.

"There's simply too much room on this bed, Petyr. So much larger than my own bed. I think I should sleep on the floor, tonight."

"I couldn't allow that, my lady!" he proclaimed, indignantly. "What would your sister think? And I promised Thomas that I would keep you safe! The floor is no place for a lady, my lady."

"Then you must sleep up here with me. I shan't sleep a wink, otherwise, and I think that's much worse than the floor. Besides, it's so cold, up here. No matter how many logs Lyle throws on the fire, I still get chills. If I had some body heat from a big, strong man, I just know I would sleep so much better."

"It's improper, my lady!"

"You are my cousin-by-law, how could it be improper. Unless...are you having improper thoughts? You scoundrel! Well, don't worry, dear Petyr. I shan't tell Thomas. If you come here and keep me warm, that is..."

So now Petyr lay on the bed, as far to the edge as he possibly could, while Jewel giggled to herself like a mischievous schoolgirl. They had left the chamber door open, so Lyle was unsure how much impropriety the poor boy thought could take place. But every time Lyle walked by or checked on the two, Jewel had somehow moved closer to Petyr while pretending to be asleep. The lad looked terrified.

Lyle dropped the bedding off and was making a last round of checks with the under-butlers. Thomas had increased the guards, but Lyle did not yet trust them, and so had assigned them to veteran household guards, many of whom had been with the house for decades.

All was quiet, just as it had been for the past three nights. Lyle began to wonder if Thomas' fears were less founded than he had thought. It was not likely, however. If anything, Thomas tended to downplay danger, both physical and financial. At first, Lyle thought him to be oblivious to it, but came to realize that Thomas was just immensely calm under duress. In fact, the only thing that seemed to faze the man was his wife.

Lyle did not know Lea nearly as well as he would like. She obviously tried to attain the casual demeanor that Thomas had cultivated with the staff, but there was still something that kept her distant. Her noble upbringing was the most obvious, but she had never struck Lyle as one to adhere to formalities. More likely, it was because she still felt like an outsider in her own home. The couple spent more time away than at home, and it seemed to Lyle that she had not quite found her place, yet. He had to admit that he had not done all he could have to make her feel like one of the family, but truth to tell, he found her immensely intimidating. He vowed to make more of an attempt to be welcoming in the future, especially after her greeting the other day.

No, the danger must be as real and pronounced as they had said it was. In the brief time he had known Lea, he had seen her excited, frustrated, exuberant, and so angry he thought she would catch fire, but he had never seen her afraid like he had that day. He hoped he never would, again.

He checked in on the fore guard, who took their charges very seriously, and having found them alert and vigilant, decided to turn in for the evening. He retired to his chambers, threw a few more logs on the fire, and slipped into bed. Within moments he was fast asleep.

Lyle shot awake at the sound of the alarm. The drone of the horn and the clash of the bells was unmistakable, though he had never heard it outside of practice. Quickly, he jumped into a pair of trousers and a tunic and grabbed the cudgel he kept by his bed. He burst into the hallway to see chaos.

The guards were fighting men in plainclothes, who seemed to outnumber them two-to-one. How had they gotten this far into the house? The alarm should have been raised long before this. The question would have to wait, however. Jewel and Petyr were Lyle's top priority.

He ran down the corridors of the manor, ducking blows when he had to and landing a few of his own along the way. He saw that not only had the under-butlers joined in the fray, but so had the maids and cooks. By rights they should have all been escaping out the back of the house, not trying to fight off intruders. He would be sure to have words with them, later. Bless them.

He reached the main bedchambers and found four attackers fighting a lone guard and Petyr. Jewel ducked behind Petyr, cringing, and shrieking with each blow. To Lyle's dismay, the two were not only holding their own, but were definitely dominating the fight. The boy might not be the smartest, but the steely-eyed look on his face as he fought off his attackers was nothing short of inspiring.

Petyr brandished a fire iron like a magical sword from legend. He deflected the long knife of one assailant and swung the iron with tremendous might directly into the side of his head. The man dropped in a heap, and Lyle had no illusions that the man was alive. The ferocity of the blow had a visible effect on the other attackers, making them take pause. They were clearly not expecting such resistance. Petyr took advantage of the pause they gave and shoved the fire iron into the midsection of another. The poker erupted from the back of the assailant. Petyr gave one tug to remove the iron, but when it did not give, he released it and kicked forward, sending the man flying backward.

Lyle ran up in the confusion and brought his cudgel down on the head of one of the men facing the guard. The man collapsed, giving the guard a chance to plunge his offhand dagger into the last attacker's side, just under his arm. The man cried out in pain, and bright crimson blood burst from his lips. A pained look on his face, he dropped to the floor and was still.

"Many thanks," Petyr said to Lyle. Dear gods, that man wasn't even winded!

"I hardly think you needed my help, sir," to Jewel, he said, "my lady, are you alright?"

"It's true!" she said, breathlessly, "it's true.... it's true..." she just kept repeating those words. She was in deep shock.

"Pippin!" Lyle said to the guard, "how did they make it so far into the house?"

"I don't know, sir," Pippin said. "One moment all was quiet, the next they were everywhere. What do we do, sir?"

"We get them to safety," Lyle said, indicating Petyr and Jewel.

"No!" Petyr said, fiercely, "I can fight!"

"No shit," said Pippin under his breath.

"It's these men's jobs to fight, Petyr; it's yours to keep her safe."

Just then, Jewel screamed. Lyle's hand shot out and covered her mouth, somewhat more forcefully than he had intended.

"My lady... We must get you to safety. Your sister expects you safe when she returns, and I fear her far more than these common ruffians. My lady, may Petyr carry you?"

Jewel's eyes shot to the big man who had gone from someone to tease to her savior in short order. She nodded her head.

"Good, my lady." He took his hand from her mouth. "We will take the hidden entrance to the wine cellar, as discussed, do you remember? I will lead the way, and Pippin will take the rear. Are you ready, my lady?" Again, she nodded.

"Good. Follow me."

Lyle led the group through the sliding panel in the wardrobe to the hidden hallway behind it. The narrow passage was created for just such an occasion, though it was always assumed it would be a business rival or an unhappy trading partner that would attack in the dead of night. At the end of the passage was a camouflaged trap door the led to the wine-cellar. The door at the end of the passage opened into the galley, an attempt to throw pursuers off their track.

Lyle brought them into the wine cellar and barred the trap door behind them. Wine cellar was something of a misnomer. There was wine, to be sure, but most was rare vintages of sentimental value to Thomas. The rest he gave away to the staff or in trade; he and Lea were not much for drink. Now the cellar was filled with tokens of the pair's adventures that were not on display in the main house. Thomas was not one to hoard things, but he did attach emotional value to objects, a practice Lea put up with, but quite obviously did not share. And so, to placate her, many of Thomas' 'treasures' ended up here.

The small group navigated the maze of sheet-covered statuary, furniture, and artifacts to yet another hidden door. The cellar exited out the side of the house, but it would almost certainly be watched. This passage led to one of the many outbuildings on the estate, this one dedicated to groundskeeping. They emerged into the small building and, as before, barred and re-hid the trap door.

Lyle looked out the small, barred windows toward the manor. He could see hired men wandering around the perimeter of the house, obviously looking for something, most likely them. He wondered about the poor staff who should not have stayed to fight; what would happen to them? He knew the answer but tried to think of ways for it not to be true.

Petyr set the tiny Jewel down, who had regained at least part of her composure. He looked at the gardening tools hung on the walls. First, he grabbed a large spade. He put in back in favor of a scythe. His eyes lit up when he saw a sickle, putting the scythe back and grabbing it off the hook. He took a few test swings in a small arc and seemed quite satisfied with it.

"Now what?" Jewel asked.

"Now...we wait." Lyle was surprised at how calm he felt during the entire ordeal. It felt as if the entire world had melted away, and all that had mattered was what was right in front of him and getting the two fake lovers to safety. Now that he had a moment to pause and think, a flood of panic caught up with him. He felt light-headed and struggled to not vomit. He was almost unsuccessful.

"Wait for what?" Pippin asked.

"An opportunity. We need to get away from the estate. Our best chance is the stables if they are unguarded. If nothing else, we can slip off the back of the property."

"Can't we stay here? Surely the duke will send his men when he gets word?"

"And who will send that word, my lady? We must assume they will allow no one to escape, and that they will find us, eventually. We will stay as long as we can, but as our needs grow, so will the danger. Right now, they are focused on the main house. Once they realize that neither you nor your sister are there...? I don't know what they will do."

The four spent several hours in the outbuilding. Lyle and Pippin took turns keeping an eye on the intruders. Jewel was jumpy and alert for roughly the first hour or so, then suddenly fell asleep. Petyr held her close, protectively. He looked ready for anything.

As the sun rose over the horizon, Lyle saw that the men became more active. One who looked like he might be in charge started barking orders at the others. Lyle could not make out what was being said. Over the course of the next hour or so, the men began to dissipate, until none could be seen around the manor. Lyle knew that there were many inside the house, still, however.

"After the sun crests, we head for the stables," he told the others. "We will ride west, toward Eddleston on The Green. The sun will be in our eyes, but it will be in theirs, as well, if they pursue. We just need to reach the roadguard."

The others could offer no better plan, so they waited. It seemed a painfully long time until noon. When it looked clear, they opened the door and started toward the stables. Lyle was amazed that they looked unguarded. They all crouched at the side of the building next to the door. Jewel cowered behind Petyr as a small child hid behind her mother's skirts. Pippin had a comforting hand on her shoulder.

Lyle pushed the door open and crept inside. He had expected to have to soothe the horses as he entered, but he did not seem to disturb them, at all. As he sidled along the inner wall, he realized that the horses were not only not reacting to him, but they were making no sound, at all. He froze. Something was wrong; they had to get out, immediately. As he turned to exit the stable and warn the others, a metal-clad fist rocked his head back.

The world went insane.

He was on his back but did not remember how he got there. His vision came and went, and everything sounded like his head was under-water. He thought he lost consciousness a few times, but time seemed to jump around in flashes. There was a man standing over him, then was gone. Then there were two men. Petyr and Jewel were suddenly next to him, on their knees, then Pippin lay next to him. Pippin's eyes were wide as if in shock, and Lyle saw that his throat was slit; his eyes would never close again.

There was a third man standing over them, now. He wore rust-colored robes and carried an air of authority. The other two men flanked him on either side. Lyle's vision started to clear, and he could start to make out what the new man was saying to them.

"...understand why I find that difficult to believe," he was saying.

"It is the truth, sir," Petyr was answering. "We have no idea what you're talking about."

"'Your Grace,'" the man said in a condescending tone. "Clerics are referred to as 'Your Grace.' An understandable mistake in this heathen country. Not that being devout has done much for anyone, but the formalities should still be observed, my son. After all, man's strength is his discipline, his spirit. Without it we are no better than beasts. Well...some of us, anyway. Now...the vial: where is it?"

"What vial, your grace?" Petyr spat the title as an insult, causing the robed man to smile.

"It seems you do have spirit, after all. Good. But it won't serve you long if you don't answer my questions. Whether or not you have it remains to be seen, but a scholar of your experience and renown is not ignorant of these things. You know. And the sooner you start being honest with me, the sooner this unpleasantness will end."

Lyle tried to speak, but his mouth would not work. His head was killing him, and he was still quite disoriented. He wanted to save the poor lad any further duress; he knew Petyr would keep the ruse up as long as he could out of loyalty to his cousin. He managed a moan, and one of the men next to the cleric looked down at him and smiled.

"It may please you to know that many in your service remain alive. It's true. I even paid these men extra to avoid killing as many as they could. You can imagine their disappointment, but I need your cooperation, my son. Violence may be the shortest solution, but not always the best. Now...where is the phulassein?"

"I don't know!" the boy practically yelled. His desperation was becoming apparent.

Just then, laughter sprang forth from Jewel. From the looks the cleric and his men gave her, Lyle could tell he was not alone in thinking her crazy. It started small, but quickly turned into an almost hysterical fit. She clutched at her sides, and tears ran down her face.

"What?" the cleric demanded, angrily, "What is so funny?"

She continued to laugh, however. She paused once, and Lyle thought she was finished, but she cast one look at the cleric and started again. The three men stood over them in uncomfortable impatience. When she finally stopped, she hung her head, and wiped away the tears from her cheeks.

"You...absolute...fucking...idiot..." The words stung the cleric like a slap to the face.

"What? You dare..."

Jewel sprung to her feet. The men flanking the cleric both reached for their sheathed swords, resting their hands there. The one closest to her looked embarrassed at being startled by the small woman, but his hand did not move from the hilt.

"My sister is the smartest person I have ever met, matched only by her husband, and you think you can match wits with her?" She took several steps toward the cleric, who towered over her. "You think they would wait for you to plan and execute this foolish, juvenile little raid?" She looked up fearlessly into his eyes, her neck craning at his height. "I don't have the slightest idea what you're after, and you can believe that or not, but whatever it is, I can promise you this: she is three steps ahead of you. Always. You will only see what she wants you to see, when she wants you to see it."

The cleric's eyes widened in surprise.

"Decoys! We've been tricked!"

"Intelligence, your grace. Intelligence is what separates us from beasts. Well," she paused, "some of us."

The cleric's face writhed in anger, and his hand reeled back to slap Jewel, who did not so much as flinch or duck at the sight. With no hesitation, Petyr leapt to his feet and pushed her to the side and out of the way of the cleric's wrath. The mercenary closest to them drew his sword, and in one seamless motion drove it into Petyr's stomach. In response, Petyr's forgotten sickle was suddenly in his hand, and then into the hired man's neck, the force of the swing so great that it all but decapitated him. Blood sprayed from the wound and the man's mouth, covering Petyr in gore. The two men toppled to the side together.

Jewel turned back to the scene, recovering from Petyr's push, and saw him fall.

"No!" She threw herself on top of him, fingering the sword and then his face, unsure of what to do.

The cleric, for his part, looked nonplussed about the loss of his man, but was furious at being deceived.

"Gather the men! Send word to Madu. The Ingeleans are gone, as far as three days ahead of us! Don't worry about loose ends, just pull out, now!" The cleric turned with a flourish and all but ran out of the stables.

The mercenary standing over Lyle looked down and smiled. He pulled back his steel-gauntleted fist once more and brought it down against Lyle's head. His skull smacked into the hard-packed dirt, and his vision blurred, once more. Lyle struggled to stay conscious, but the darkness overtook him, anyway. The last sound he heard as he slipped into the black abyss was the sound of Jewels racked sobs over Petyr's body getting farther and farther away from him.

CHAPTER EIGHT

Thomas winced as Lea removed the old bandage from his arm. The blood had clotted to the cloth and pulled part of the fresh scabbing off with it.

"Sorry!" said Lea, abashedly. "You think I'd be better at this by now."

"It's my own stupid fault," Thomas replied.

"Nonsense. You handled yourself quite admirably, Love."

"Hrmm," he grunted in grudging agreement.

The pair had left the carriage at the border entering Baryo, and bought two Delmonti draught horses, well known for being among the heartiest of breeds. Anonymity and going unnoticed would be essential throughout Baryo. While the cities were as civilized as any Ingelean city, the dense woodlands and hinterlands were next to lawless. Banditry was commonplace, and much worse.

They dressed down from their noble ruse and put on rather tattered clothing they purchased from two Delmonti crofters who had clearly never seen so much money at once. Jewel had given them most of her jewelry, as well. The ring she kept, however, "just in case." Her disheveled clothing practically fell off of her, completing the look. They rubbed some dirt on their faces and joked that they spent most of their time like that, anyway.

Several main roads were patrolled by militia, so they felt relatively safe, though they still kept their guard up. Taking the Emperor's Highway would take a good deal longer than the straight route, but they both agreed it was worth the time to avoid any trouble. Trouble, however, found them.

Baryo City was just cresting the horizon as the sun dipped behind the tree line. Ahead of them on the road they saw a woman, as disheveled as they, if slightly less dirty, pulling a board with a rope that she had strung under her arms like a yoke. On the board was a man, sitting. He was at least twice the size of the woman, save for the fact that he had no legs.

"Werter Frau!" Thomas called, "Do you go to Baryostadt?"

Lea almost gasped. Thomas spoke to the woman with the perfect clipped accent and inflection of a Baryon. She had never heard him speak with any accent. Quite a surprise, indeed. The woman stooped pulling the man and looked to Thomas. She appeared cautious and wary.

"Who asks?" the woman replied, her voice dry and cracked.

"Mine wife and I travel to Baryostadt and have ridden long. I admit I am a poor horseman, and mine legs need stretching. Would you care to ride in my stead? Mine horse is strong and could carry you both."

"What do ask in return?" she said, her eyes squinting in distrust.

"Nothing," Thomas answered, laughing. "As I say, we have travelled long, and would be glad for the company. Mine wife is surely tired of my voice, by now."

"I accept. But I ride with the woman. And your horse can pull mine husband; he is in no form to ride."

"Aye."

Lea shot Thomas a questioning look. He just nodded a knowing nod and dismounted. He approached Lea and whispered, "They're looking for two, not four, and definitely not a cripple." He smiled up at her. She nodded back. It made sense, she thought, but it still made her nervous. Not to mention that she could not imitate a Baryon accent if her life depended on it.

He took the woman's hand and hoisted her up onto Lea's horse.

"I am Mads, and this is mine wife, Greta," Thomas said. "Please excuse her; she has a beautiful voice, but I am afraid she has not spoken since our child..." he looked away, tears in his eyes.

Lea was astounded! If nothing else, Thomas had a wonderful future as a play actor. She had no idea he was such a gifted performer.

"Inga," the woman said, then pointed to the man, "Gord." Gord just grunted.

"A pleasure to meet you." Thomas said.

He attached the rope on the board to his horse's haunch straps and remounted. The going was much slower than before with the extra weight, and soon the sun had disappeared, completely. The plan was to reach Baryo City before dark to secure a room at an Inn, but Lea supposed the delay would be of little significance.

As the sight of the city came into full view, they spotted a group of four riders riding in their direction. At first, Lea thought it would be the militia, patrolling the Emperor's Highway, but as they got closer, she could see that they were most definitely not. They were garbed in leather armor, helmeted, and armed with short swords. The militia wore mail and flew the colors of the Baryon Empire.

Bandits, she thought.

"Hallo!" the lead rider called, a smile on his face.

"Hallo!" Thomas called back. "May we be of assistance?" The rider's smile widened.

"Indeed. If you could kindly open your saddle bags for us to peruse, it would most appreciated."

"Werter Herr, look at us," said Thomas, "we have nothing you'd be interested in. If you would just let us on our way, I assure you..."

Lea suddenly felt a knife press up against her throat.

"We'd like to take a peek, anyway," the woman called Inga said.

"Is it them?" the man who had been call Gord asked the lead rider.

Lea was surprised to see that he was standing next to Thomas, long knife pressed against his side. She glanced back at the man's board and saw that there was a cutout for him to fold his legs under to make it appear he had none. It was an effective deception, to make travelers feel pity for the legless man and the woman who had to pull him. Downright insidious, Lea thought.

"They fit the description, don't they?" Inga answered.

"Search them. Find the vial."

"Down," Gord said to Thomas, who climbed down off his horse.

Two of the riders began to go through the pair's saddle bags, looking for what Lea could not say. They had mentioned a vial, but they had nothing like that on them. When the marauders did not find what they were after, they turned to their leader.

"Not here," one said.

"Check their persons," replied the lead man. "We only get half without it."

Inga, if that was actually her name, swung down from Lea's horse.

"Come on, now, princess. Down with ya."

As Lea prepared to dismount, Thomas sprang into action. With no warning, he slapped his horse's rear. The poor animal was spooked, causing it to kick violently with its rear legs. Gord caught the end of one of those directly in the head. His neck jerked to an unnatural angle as he was thrown through the air. Lea knew he was dead before he landed.

Before the bandits had time to register what was happening, Thomas had his sap in hand and thwacked it square against Inga's head. The woman crumpled like a sack of grain. Thomas reached down and scooped up the dagger that had been held to Lea's throat and flung it side-handed at the lead rider. The hilt hit the man in the forehead, and he cried out in surprise and pain.

"Damn," Thomas said, "That always looked easier."

One of the mounted men rounded Thomas' horse in an attempt to flush him toward the others. As he circled around, Thomas grabbed the board that Gord had ridden upon and brought it down on the head of the mounted man's horse. Dazed, the horse toppled sideways, pinning the man beneath.

"Go!" Thomas yelled to Lea, "I'll catch up!"

Lea was about to do no such thing, of course. She steered her own horse toward the remaining bandits and, pulling back on the reins, caused him to rear. He struck one of the bandits in the chest, and he fell out of his saddle. One foot remained caught in a stirrup, and the horse frightfully pranced in a circle, taking the man with it.

Meanwhile, Thomas had remounted his own horse, and had somehow found the time to grab the short sword of the man he had knocked over. He pulled up next to Lea and made a motion with his head to run. They spurred their horses on toward the city.

With both horses running at full speed, Lea spared a moment to look back. Rather than take a moment to tend to his men, as well as the lump on his forehead, the bandit leader was putting up a chase, along with his last mounted man. It looked as though Thomas and Lea were outpacing them, however, and she sighed in presumptive relief.

Just then, an arrow whirled past her head. She looked back to see that the lead bandit was firing from horseback, and still maintaining speed.

"Shit!" she yelled.

Thomas looked back as well, then looked to Lea.

"Yes. Shit."

"Now what?" she asked.

"I didn't really have a plan to begin with," he replied.

Another arrow whizzed past, barely missing Thomas. He looked back to the bandits. They would outrun them soon, but could they do so before an arrow finally found its mark? As close as that last one was, Lea doubted that. Thomas looked back to her with an excited look on his face.

"The ring!" he shouted, "throw it to me?"

"What? Why?"

"No time! Throw me the ring and ride hard toward the city."

"But that doesn't..."

"Just do it!" Lea was taken aback. Thomas had never so much as raised his voice to be heard, and Lea was the first to admit that she sometimes made it difficult for him to be heard. His yelling at her was almost as bad as if he had struck her. Perhaps worse. She felt like she was going cry, which was the silliest thing she could imagine, considering the circumstances. Cry and shout at him. She would throw the ring at him, all right, and a few other things besides. But the look on his face was earnest, and she had no better idea...or any ideas, at all.

She fished the ring out of her inner pocket. It was in a small, tufted fabric bag she had purchased in Esisria, years ago. Esisrian weavers made the best crushed and tufted fabric. She made sure the drawstring was tight, checked the heft a few times, and tossed it, underhand, to Thomas.

At first, she was certain he would miss the catch. She was not the best toss on the few occasions she had taken an interest in sport, and Thomas, well...Sacred Mother help him, he did try. But, to her delight, he reached out and nabbed it. Then, stuffing it into his own pocket, he spared a backward glance to their pursuers.

"Go!" he yelled to her. "I'll find you."

Thomas steered hard to the right and peeled away. What in Anthumbra was he doing? Then, she saw. The two riders looked torn. Finally, the leader motioned for the other bandit to chase Lea, and he veered after Thomas. The bloody fool was going to get himself killed! But at least now there would be no arrows flying in her direction.

Lea thought extremely hard about chasing after him, saving him from himself, but she had no idea what she would do when she got there. The best she could do for the moment was to make it to Baryo City and mount a rescue with the city militia.

Lea began to notice that her horse's gait was changing. The poor dear was exhausted, frothing at the mouth. She knew that she could push it to keep running, and that it would most certainly die from the exertion. Could she do that to it? She honestly did not know. As frightened as she was, the thought of killing the horse made her stomach clench in pain. It began to slow to a light gallop, and she decided she would let it, if for no other reason than if it died before she reached the city then it would have died for nothing, and she simply could not allow that.

The bandit behind her was gaining, now, and would be on her in moments. She had no weapons or means of defense, which seemed like a severe oversight, at the moment. As her horse came to a stop, she dismounted and began running. She knew she could never outrun the man, even were he on foot, but she could think of no other course of action.

She had barely begun to make her escape when she heard a distinctive whooshing noise behind her. A bola made of two weighted wooden balls and a braided leather cord wrapped itself around her knees, and she tumbled to the ground. She searched frantically for something to cut the cord with as the rider approached. He had a smug smile on his face, and spit from the side of his mouth.

"That was exciting, wasn't it? Been a long time since I had a chase like that." He reined his horse in and trotted toward her. "You are a lucky one, you are. Lovely girl like you, I'd normally have a little fun with, first. But someone wants you untouched and is willing to pay handsomely for it."

Lea struggled against the straps around her legs. They were so tight that she was beginning to lose feeling. From the corner of her eye she saw another horseman approaching, riding fast. She wanted to believe that it was Thomas, but deep inside she knew the awful truth: that Thomas was likely dead or captured. Several sobs escaped her lips.

"Oh, come, come, My Lady," the bandit said, turning the title into an insult, "as long as you be a good girl this will go easy as silk. I promise. But if you try anything like your fool husband," he drew a long dagger from a sheath on his saddle, "and I will have some fun, yeah? I like money, but...money isn't everything, is it? Or would you even know, having never been without?"

He hopped down next to her and crouched low. Running his dagger along the outside of her leg, he tapped the flat of the blade against her calves, then her thighs. He moved the blade to the inside of her legs, sliding it slowly down to where the leather cord was. With a tug, he cut through. Almost immediately Lea could feel blood return to her lower legs. She groaned loudly with the pain that the initial rush brought, followed by the sharp tingling as feeling returned.

"Now, dove...will you tell me where the vial is? Or do I get to search you for it?" His eyes told her which option he would prefer.

She was about to tell him yet again that she had no idea what he was talking about when the sound of hooves against the ground drew her attention. They were not slowing down. The bandit must have noticed the same thing, for he turned his head, as well. But he was too late. From seemingly nowhere, Thomas came flying off his horse, crashing directly into the bandit. The man's head smacked against a rock, his leather helm doing little to absorb the shock. His eyes rolled back, and the color drained from his face. Thomas, who had landed right on top of him, gave him no respite, however landing blow after blow with his bare fists until it was certain the man was unconscious.

"Are you...okay?" he asked, breathlessly.

"Oh, Thomas!" she said, sobbing. "I thought for sure that he got you! Where is he?"

"Oh...he's still coming. I managed to put a great deal of distance between us, but he's still after me. At least he's out of arrows. I think..." Thomas stood and put his fists on his hips. He stretched backward with a groan and took a deep breath. "Stay low and safe, Love. I'll be right back. I hope." He pointed to the leather straps still clinging to Lea's legs. "Bolas, eh? Incredible."

He bent over and drew the fallen bandit's short sword. He gave it a good looking over and grunted. He then walked past his horse and bent over, propping himself up with the sword. Lea could clearly see just how exhausted he was. In the distance, the lead bandit came in to view, and was closing fast.

Thomas picked up the sword and readied himself. He held it with two hands, not the stance of a swordsman, but rather how a rounders player held a bat. To the best of her knowledge, Thomas had never played rounders. In any case, even she knew that if he intended to face down a mounted swordsman, untrained, with that stance, he would lose.

The rider was almost upon him and raised his own sword to attack. Lea wanted to scream at Thomas to move, to run; anything but to just stand there with that stupid sword. But only moments before the mounted bandit was ready to strike, Thomas drew back and threw the sword! It was ridiculous, Lea thought. What in all the god's names...?

But then she saw. The rider was just as surprised as she was, and though he easily ducked out of the way, he was forced to abandon his own attack, and he drew his arms in as he ducked. And that's when Thomas acted.

As the bandit's horse passed, Thomas reached up and pulled the man right of his horse! The bandit landed hard on the dirt and Lea heard the loud exhalation as the wind was forced from his lungs. Thomas was on top of him, knee to his throat, dagger in his right hand.

"Who hired you?" he demanded. Lea had to admit that he did not sound the least bit intimidating.

"Don't know!" the man coughed.

"Oh, come now," Thomas said, digging his knee in deeper, "who told you about us, then?"

The man sputtered and gagged, unable to answer. Thomas eased up, bit.

"Terribly sorry, is that better? Now...how did you know about us?"

"Job is posted at guild hall. Anyone can take it."

"How many others?"

"What?"

"How many others took this job? Who else knows?" Thomas dug in, again, causing the bandit to choke. He left his knee there for a moment before easing up, again. The man coughed in a fit before he was able to answer.

"Whole city, at least. Who...who are you?"

Thomas seemed to think for a moment before answering.

"A historian." He cracked the hilt of his dagger into the man's temple, rendering him unconscious. He stood and groaned again. He did not seem to notice the blood that was pouring in a small, steady stream from his right hand. He walked back toward Lea and knelt next to where she still lay.

"Thomas!" Lea pointed to his arm.

"Oh, great Gilafred!" he exclaimed, "he really got me good, didn't he?"

Lea tried to stand, but her legs buckled beneath her. Thomas caught her before she fell. He smeared blood all over the side of her overcoat. It would hardly be noticeable against all the grime once it dried, but

Lea could not help but worry at the amount he seemed to be losing. She steadied herself and drew bandages from her saddlebags. She used almost the whole roll, as the gash was deep and kept bleeding through the cloth.

"We'll have to get more, soon, Love. This is bad. It needs cleaning and suturing. I'm no healer; we'll have to see someone in the city."

"Out of the question. Not after what our friend over there said."

"Thomas we must! If it's not taken care of you could lose the arm. Or worse."

"Let's find a place to camp, first. We can make plans, from there, but the horses need water and rest, badly."

They walked the horses deep into the forest until they found a cave near a small stream. The water was fast moving and clean, and the horses took to it, immediately. Thomas and Lea made camp at the back of the cave, which was luckily occupied only by bats. Once they were settled, Thomas proposed to head into the city by himself for supplies. Lea resisted the idea, even knowing he was right. Thomas was far more likely to go unnoticed, alone, and they did need supplies.

He was not gone long, but to Lea, every moment was filled with anxious paranoia. They had done as much as they could to cover their tracks and hide their presence in the cave, but she was sure that bandits or worse would come rushing in for her at any moment. When Thomas finally did return, she almost broke down into tears. She did not like this habit of crying that she was developing.

He had brought several rolls of bandaging material, as well as needle and thread. He also had purchased some fresh fruit and cheese, a loaf of bread, honey, and some wine.

"I don't know that I'm in the mood for wine, Love," Lea said.

"It's for my arm."

"I know. Attempting levity." She began to undress Thomas' wound. "Sorry! You'd think I'd be better at this, by now!"

"It's my own stupid fault."

"Nonsense. You handled yourself quite admirably, Love."

"Hrmm."

Lea scrubbed the gash and dabbed it clean, all the while Thomas kept telling her to ignore his winces and moans. Unable to find the cleansing acid that would have been available at any chemist's shop in Ingeland, she was forced to rub honey in the wound. When it came time to suture, she balked.

"You know I can't sew with any skill," she lamented. "I'm sure I will do more harm than good."

"Just take your time, my dear. And don't worry about how it looks. Besides, I hear women find large, disfiguring scars to be handsome."

"Jewel does, perhaps. Of course, Jewel could sew you into a dress without breaking a sweat."

"I've never been under the illusion that you married me for my looks."

"Oh, shush! You're the handsomest man I've ever seen."

"That's the nicest lie I've ever heard," Thomas retorted. "There, see? Who could do better than that?"

While it was true that the stitching was much better than she had thought she could do, it was still quite an ugly job of it. The banter had helped her focus.

"Don't ask," she replied, tying the thread off.

She soaked the bandages in the wine and wrapped his arm back up.

"We'll have to clean it tomorrow, and again the next day."

"We're already slowed, considerably," Thomas said.

"There's nothing for it, Love. If we don't..." She did not need to finish the thought.

"Ah!" Thomas exclaimed, reaching into his pocket. "Here is your ring back."

"What did you need it for?" she asked, taking it from him.

"I had hoped that they would assume it was this vial, or whatever it was they are after, and follow me, rather than you. It sort of worked."

"Do you have any idea what they were talking about?"

"Not a clue," Thomas answered. "I didn't think to ask that ruffian, back there. I'm sorry. Also...I'm sorry I yelled at you."

"It's alright," Lea lied. "It was the heat of the moment, and we were in a predicament. I think it can be forgiven."

"No," Thomas said, genuinely upset, "It can't. I don't know what came over me. I wasn't angry, Love, I promise. There was just...a voice, in my head, that told me to yell, that I didn't have time to explain. And before I knew what I was doing..."

"This voice," Lea said, choosing her words carefully, "You've heard it before? The other things you did, today?"

"Yes," Thomas replied. "I know it sounds crazy, but I'm not mad. It's not a different voice, it's my voice, just stronger, more confident, somehow. It's like...an instinct, perhaps. When I think about what it says, it makes perfect sense, but it comes to me without having to think about it. I just know what to do, and I do it. Except for yelling at you. I shouldn't have done that."

"No. You were right to. I won't lie, Thomas; it hurt. But it was the right thing to do."

"Well, I wish I hadn't. And I'm sorry."

"I forgive you, Love," she sighed, and this time she meant it. But she found it worrisome, perhaps more so than his arm. Thomas had never been an indecisive man, but neither was he a flippant one. The man didn't so much as pick out a shirt without thinking about it. For him to take action spontaneously, at the behest of a mysterious voice...it was worrisome, indeed.

Petyr's chest rose and fell in deep, erratic breaths. Jewel sat in a chair to the side of the bed, staring at the floor. She had cried for hours, until there were no more tears to shed. The only time she had stopped was when the doctor was tending to Petyr's wound, Lyle thought she would pester the man as he worked, but instead she watched everything he did, studying it with astute reverence, and offering help when needed. She demanded to know how to treat the wound, change the dressing, and anything else she could do to help.

When he had finished, the doctor pulled Lyle aside and told him that even though they had done everything they could do, his chances of surviving were not good. Several major organs had taken damage, and he had lost too much blood. If he could make it through the night, his chances improved greatly.

For his part, Lyle had a giant bandage around his head covering a massive lump beneath. The doctor had told him to try to stay off his feet and to not sleep for several hours. Two of the maids insisted on following him around, everywhere, and he was much more grateful than annoyed. Mostly.

The damage to the house had been surprisingly minimal. It seemed that the cleric had been true to his word about keeping casualties to a minimum. Including Pippin, they had only lost three guards, the other two being new. Among the staff, they lost two. Mother Lizbeth, the head seamstress, was known to have a weak heart and died of fright. Her grandson, Simon, who served as an under butler, also perished when he fell down the stairs and broke his neck. Lyle would have to draft a missive to his father, a respected farrier in Rhoslyn, telling him that his last remaining family had died under his service. He did not look forward to that.

When the cleanup was complete, save for the repairs that would have to be made, Lyle called all the house together in the great room. The servants stayed to one side of the room, the guards to the other. They all stared at him expectantly, waiting for the soothing words that he still had not managed to find. Finally, he could make them wait no more.

"Last night," he began, "we suffered a great loss. And we should never forget those who are not with us, now, who died to protect us, as well as those who became casualties of that effort.

"Mother Lizbeth, who has been with us since before most of us were born, serving the Porters three generations back. Her grandson, Simon, ever eager to please, to do right by us and our employers. Rickard Hunter and Kristofer Potterson, who I knew for only days, but seemed good men, and proved their loyalty with their lives. Pippin Waddle," he choked on the words. "My friend."

Lyle paused a moment as the lump in his throat worked itself out.

"Too often this house is empty," he continued, "but when Mister and Mistress Porter were lost at sea, Thomas kept us all on. I've oft heard him say that we are all his family, as much so as Lady Lea. And I believe that we have done them proud. To the guards, who courageously kept the invaders at bay, so our charges could escape," a cheer rose among the servants, "to the staff, who bravely stood their ground with pots and pans," a cheer rose among the guards. Both groups looked proud.

"I know that they will mourn our losses as much as we do. Perhaps more. But now we carry on and make their home – our home – ready for their return. Thank you all." He turned to walk away.

"That's all?" a gruff voice called after him. It belonged to Blake Quilter, the head guard.

"Is what all" Lyle replied.

"We're just going to pretend everything is normal?"

"Certainty not, Mister Quilter. We are going to do our jobs, as we have always done."

"Gods' piss, man!" the guard replied, "they attacked us! Attacked Thomas and Lea! In their own home! Are we just going to ignore that?" Cries of agreement rose from the gathered mob.

"And what would you have us do, Mister Quilter? We have alerted the Sheriff, who has pledged to increase the patrols, but the assailants are surely gone, knowing Thomas and Lea are not here."

"We take the fight to them!" Willem, a young under butler, cried, "make sure they don't catch up with Thomas!" There were more murmurs of approval.

"I don't doubt the courage of anyone here. Nor the ability to fight. I saw both in great measure, last night. But we are not a militia! The most help we can be is keeping their house until they return."

"And if they don't?" Lyle could not tell who spoke that time.

"This is hardly their first adventure! They don't need us to come to their rescue."

"Suppose we put it to a vote," Blake Quilter suggested.

"We are not a parliament, Mister Quilter. There will be no vote. Now, until we get word otherwise, we will do as we have been instructed. We will care for Thomas' cousin Petyr, and the Countess Barracourt. Or have you forgotten about them? To work, all of you!" With that, he stormed out of the great room.

Lyle entered the bedchamber as silently as he could. Jewel had pulled her chair close to the bed and was talking to Petyr in low, hushed tones. When she noticed Lyle enter, she kissed Petyr on the cheek and sat back in her chair. She closed her eyes and took several deep breaths, letting the silence linger.

"Do you know why Lea dyes her hair the way she does?" she asked without opening her eyes.

"My Lady?" Kyle replied.

"I doubt even Thomas knows." She opened her eyes. "When we were younger, people confused us, all the time. As much as we deny it, we know that it is true. We look alike. Do you know what that's like?"

"No, My Lady," Lyle said. He grabbed a chair from the end of the room, pulled it closer to the bed, and sat facing the countess. "I'm afraid I was an only child."

"We're not even twins," Jewel continued, "She's two years older than I am, and even our own parents would confuse us, at times. It was maddening." She dried her eyes with a handkerchief.

"I can't imagine what it would be like to be compared..."

"I longed to be compared to Lea!" Jewel cut him off, "Because then, at least, we would be different people in their eyes. We were dressed the same, had the same tutors...I know my life hasn't exactly been difficult, Lyle, but as a young girl it hurt. To be seen as not only something meant only to be married off, and not even unique, at that..."

Lyle felt immensely uncomfortable. He desperately wanted to console the woman, but there were about ten layers of etiquette that stood in his way.

"When Lea was fourteen, and I was twelve, we had just finished a dance lesson and had decided to play a game of seek-and-find. Lea had hidden in a wardrobe in the foyer, and as I was looking for her, we both overheard out parents speaking to our dance tutor about courtship. It turned out that he also tutored the son of Count Berryman, who had begun looking for suitable matches for marriage for his boy. We were all still too young to marry, but a betrothal could be arranged. And when asked which of us would be more suitable, our father answered that it didn't matter. Who would notice one way or the other? Our own father!

"Lea leapt from the wardrobe. I was too shocked and hurt to call 'found.' I followed her as she marched into the washroom, and taking a pair of sewing shears, cut her hair short. I know it would surprise you to know, but she had the most beautiful long blonde hair, as did I. She cut it and grabbed some purple fabric dye – rather expensive, I might add – and dyed her hair right there. Our father was furious, and for some reason nothing could have made me happier. No one ever mistook us, again, though." She paused, sniffling, and wiping her face. She took several deep breaths.

"Do you know what the irony is in all of this, Lyle?"

"No, My Lady?"

"Lea is everything I could ever hope to be as a woman. Oh, I don't care about all the treasure hunting and such, but...she is so confident, and strong, and determined. If you mistook me for her, today, I'd call it a compliment." She giggled at the thought.

"My Lady," Lyle began.

"Oh, Gilafred's ass, Lyle! Stop with the 'My Lady' nonsense. I have a name, damn all. Start using it, or...I'll elbow you in the stomach!"

"Jewel," Lyle said, still very uncomfortable with the name in his mouth, "I think you are much more like your sister than you realize."

She put her head on his shoulder and wept.

Jewel still sat next to Petyr, singing a soft and wordless tune that Lyle recognized as a popular lullaby. He hypnotically watched Petyr's chest rise and fall, each breath coming shallower and farther apart. It would not be long now, Lyle knew.

Petyr had regained consciousness a few times but was not coherent.

"Wait by the shore," he said, looking at no one. "Wait by the shore. To keep Uru away. Wait by the shore."

Up and down, his chest went. Rise and fall. Jewel held his hand and brushed his hair away from his eyes. Up and down. Rise and fall.

Suddenly his eyes opened. He looked about, disoriented, until he saw Jewel next to him. He smiled up at her.

"My Lady," he said.

Lyle felt a rush of hope. He rose to his feet and was about to join Jewel at his side when he noticed that she was crying. Staggard and ragged sobs shook her shoulders, and it took Lyle a moment to see why. Petyr's chest no longer moved. It had stopped forever, his eyes on Jewel, a smile on his face. He was gone.

An anger rose up inside of Lyle where he thought sadness should be. A red-hot fury unlike anything he had felt before. He wanted to break something, to take the chair he had been sitting in and smash it against the wall. There was a pit in his stomach and from it rose a growl, an inhuman sound of agony and hate. It was not until Jewel put her hand on his shoulder that he realized that he had been making that sound. He slumped back into his chair.

"What now?" Jewel asked after a moment of silence.

"Now? I will contact his family on Thomas' behalf."

"And then what?"

"And then? We wait for Thomas and Lea." Lyle had no other answer for her.

"No," Jewel replied. "I won't do nothing."

"My Lady..." Lyle said, soothingly.

"No!" she shouted. "Don't 'My Lady' me! I can't – I won't – just sit here and wait for them, knowing what is after them. Knowing that Petyr died, for what? A distraction? Absolutely not!"

"But where would we even start? And how can we help? We are none of us delvers, scholars, or mercenaries. Do we just charge off after them and hope we find them? And once we do, then what?"

"I don't know!" she stomped her foot for emphasis. "Something! We know their plan, more or less. We know their contacts. You can stay here if you like but that is my sister out there. And my cousin-by-law, who lays in this bed, gave his life for me and Thomas and Lea. And what of Pippin? Would you let his death count for nothing? I will not!"

Lyle laughed unexpectedly, then. A guffaw that escaped his lips before he even knew what was happening. Jewel's face turned bright red, and she put her hands on her hips.

"What is so gods-blighted funny about any of that?"

"For a moment," Lyle said, "I actually thought you were her. Come with me."

Lyle led her in the great room and sent word to gather everyone once again. It was just past dark, but no one wasted any time in answering the summons, many showing in their night clothes. When everyone had assembled, he turned to Jewel, and looked her in the eyes. For some reason he felt the need to take her hand in his. She looked puzzled, but not alarmed or offended. She squeezed his hand, gently, and he knew he was doing the right thing. He turned to the assembled crowd.

"Alright," he said. "Let's have a vote."

CHAPTER NINE

Duck, the voice in his head said, and Thomas did. Just moments later an arrow flew past his head. It would have surely struck him if he had not moved.

The road to the docks wound around a mountain. It twisted and turned as it descended, and sudden cliffs, forks, and obstacles were all too abundant. It was hardly the best place for a chase on horseback for even a skilled rider, let alone Ingelean archeologists. More than once, now, Thomas was sure he was about to plummet to his doom or have his horse trip over an ill-placed log. Each time he had been saved by the voice in his head. The voice that was his, and yet...somehow not.

Lea was doing much better, at least outwardly. She was a much more experienced rider than Thomas, but the path was still incredibly treacherous. She could have easily outpaced him – and he told her to do so several times – but she stubbornly kept pace with Thomas.

Two more arrows whizzed past, one grazing Thomas' arm. It was a light scratch, at most. He would have called it lucky, but he seemed to be getting lucky an awful lot, lately. He refused to count the dowry before the wedding, as they say, at least until men were not trying to kill him.

The path straightened out as it made its way to the Southern Sea. To the left, the mountain loomed tall, and Thomas could see the pursuers further back along the trail. *Swerve right,* said the voice. Without hesitation, Thomas did. A man landed directly to his left, where Thomas would have been, had he not dodged. The man had thrown himself from the cliff above and would have landed squarely on Thomas.

Instead, he writhed on the ground, howling in pain, as both his legs were certainly broken.

The straight road allowed several riders to catch up with Thomas and Lea. They wore uniform robes and head-coverings, desert brown, but had nothing on them that could be used to identify them. Thomas found it infuriating. So many people had been trying to kill them, and he still did not know who in the Hundred Hells they were!

One of the men rode close to Thomas. He brandished a long, curved blade, more akin to something seen in the Aelfin provinces than something an Eastlander would wield. He made a couple of quick swiped at Thomas to test him. Thomas dodged them, handily. The next attack was more aggressive, plunging the rider close, so their horses were mere hands length apart. Thomas was unable to dodge, fully, and took a gash to left side. He could not tell how bad it was, but it felt quite deep.

Swing, now! the voice said. Thomas made a backhanded strike with his fist, landing it soundly in the man's face. The attacker was still off balance from his last swing at Thomas, and the blow finished the job, causing him to tumble off his horse.

Lea was busy dodging attackers of her own. Her diminutive size, coupled with her riding skills, were making it much harder on her assailants. One was on either side of her, and they were pressing in. Thomas aimed his horse toward her. He pulled up along the rider on her left and grabbed the sap from its place on his saddle. He made an awkward swing that failed to connect. The attacker, who had up until that moment not even noticed Thomas, turned his attention to him.

"Oh, piss..." Thomas said.

The man swung his straight short sword at him, missing only because of the distance and the spontaneity of the attack. Thomas knew that advantage was over.

Stop! said the voice. Thomas pulled back on the reins, significantly slowing his horse, if not stopping it outright. Thomas' attacker smiled in victory, thinking that he had successfully chased him off, but his victory was short-lived. A volley of arrows rained down from the cliffs, above, and would have made a pincushion of Thomas. Instead, two of the arrows meant for him struck the other man. One lodged in his side, the other in his neck. The man gurgled sickeningly as blood sprayed out onto his horse. Thomas sped back up and passed the man as he fell to the ground.

Lea was still evading strikes from the other attacker, but her skill and luck were bound to run out, soon. Thomas made straight for him.

Go left, the voice decreed. But Thomas balked. He needed to help Lea, and that was to the right. Before he could make up his mind, the leather cords of a bolas wrapped around his midsection. He still held the reins in his hands, but he could no longer raise his arms. *Damn all!* he thought. *I should have listened.*

He turned his body to see who had ensnared him just as a man was leaping from his horse. He landed on Thomas' horse skillfully and grabbed Thomas by the sides. Thomas yelled in pain. The man was wearing gloves with spikes on the insides, similar to what some Muruk tribesman used to climb ice cliffs. Tied and secured with spikes, Thomas could do nothing to fight back.

"Stop the fucking horse!" the man yelled into Thomas' ear.

Throw your head back, the voice commanded, and Thomas obeyed. The back of his skull connected with the man's face. As his hands were attached to Thomas' sides, he could neither deflect nor dodge. Thomas felt the warm gush of blood that must have emanated from the man's nose run down the back of his shirt. Instinctively, the assailant removed his hands from Thomas and brought them to his face, yelling obscenities the likes of which Thomas had never heard.

Rear, came the voice. Thomas pulled back on the reins. His horse skidded to a stop, and reared up on its hind legs, sending the distracted attacker flying off the back of the horse. Thomas kicked, starting the horse toward Lea, once more. He was still bound from the bolas, but there had to be something he could do to help. He just hoped he thought of it by the time he reached her.

Ram him!

Thomas coaxed full speed from the horse. The animal clearly felt his intentions and was not in favor of the maneuver. Thomas kicked it ahead, anyway. *Gods' blood!* he thought just moments before the horse crashed into Lea's foe. Neither enemy horse nor rider were prepared for the onslaught, and the horse toppled sideways as the man's sword flew wildly from his hand. He became pinned beneath his horse and cried out in pain as multiple bone broke under the weight of the beast.

"Should we stop?" asked Lea, seeing they had evaded their pursuers for the moment. "The horses can't take much more of this."

"Slow," Thomas replied, "but don't stop. We're almost there, but there is at least one more group behind us. They were firing from the cliffs."

They slowed to a lighter gallop, checking behind them every few moments. Oddly enough, Thomas had yet to see any further followers. He did not let his guard down, however. It seemed most unlikely that their shadows would give up, now.

The great blue waters of the Southern Sea appeared over the horizon, its magnificent water shimmering in the waning sun. The docks would be close, soon. Though he could not see them, he had memorized the map that the smuggler had given him. He could find the slip that the Randy Brute was docked in blindfolded.

Soon, the waterfront came into view. It was truly a sight to behold. The docks gave way to the boardwalks, the endless shops, restaurants, and peddlers. The throng of life always amazed Thomas. He knew that water had been the essential component for civilization, but to experience its importance, even today, was breathtaking. Whoever controlled the waterways of Anthumbra, controlled the world. At least, to its post-diluvian, pre-Upheaval citizenry.

"Isn't that our dock, there?" Lea asked.

Thomas immediately saw why she had asked. The whole of the surrounding area was filled with people, many mounted, and all wearing the garb of desert warriors.

"Uru's Peace, can't we catch an even die, for once!" Thomas exclaimed.

They both slowed their horses to a trot, and then stopped.

"We do seem to have the Gambler's own luck, lately. How in the world did they know? You don't think Ana or Ex...?"

"Never," Thomas replied, "at least not willingly."

"So, what do we do? We can't wait them out. The ship will leave whether we are on it or not. If it hasn't already. You heard what that mealy-mouthed smuggler said..." the sentence went unfinished as she was interrupted by low rumble coming from the south, along the same road they had been travelling.

Squinting to see what new annoyance the day had thrown at them, Thomas could see plumes of smoke in the distance, growing larger as the rumble grew louder. Soon, several distinct columns of smoke could be seen, and a cloud of sand a dust could be seen behind them. Lea gasped, coming to the conclusion a few moments before Thomas did.

"Eimurial carriages!" she exclaimed.

Surely enough, Thomas could make out the forms of several Eimurial-powered carriages heading their way. Though they were still far off, they looked like no carriages Thomas had ever seen, before. They were twice as big, at least, and looked to have some sort of armored covering. Mounted to each appeared to have the long tube-like weapons that were used in the Esisrian train station.

"Gilafred's rotting teeth!" Lea swore. "Do you recognize those?"

"All too well. We can't go back, that way...forward?"

"Forward."

They resumed their trek to the waterfront, setting a fast pace with the tired horses. It was not long before they realized that the carriages were closing in on them, and fast. Thomas tried to push his horse to go faster, but it was no use. The animal was already giving all it could.

A low, dull 'thwoom' rang out from one of the carriages. The sound travelled in a straight line toward Thomas, passing him on his left. He felt an enormous wave of heat with the sound, and a pressure shoved against his side. It felt like a large invisible projectile had flown passed, narrowly missing him. Perhaps that is what it was. All Thomas knew was that he did not want to find out by being struck by one.

"If we reach those men below," Thomas started, "they'll either stop firing into their own men, or we'll give them quite a few more targets."

They raced toward the docks, still some distance away. The low drone of the unseen weapon came constant and steady. So far, the two had not been hit, but Thomas had felt several that were far closer than he would have liked, and one almost blew Lea off her horse. The carriages had almost closed the gap, now, and it would all be moot when they were just run over by the colossal machines.

Thomas' attention was drawn below, where they warriors surrounding the docks had seen the chase taking place and had become riled. Many started hooting and waving swords, and several kicked their horses into action, heading straight for the pair. It seemed their luck would hold, Thomas thought.

A voice cried out in the throng of advancing warriors, somehow familiar. He could not quite make out if it were words the voice was yelling, but it was definitely familiar. Thomas, the voice inside of him said. But that didn't make any sense. Why would his newfound inner voice just be saying his name? Thomas, it repeated. *What?* he thought back to himself in frustration.

"Thomas!" He heard the word clearly, now, coming from the warriors ahead. It was his name...someone was calling his name! He recognized the voice, now.

"Exra!" Thomas yelled.

"What?" Lea exclaimed.

"Lea!" came a female voice from below.

"Ana!" Lea cried, tears streaming down her face.

The Esisrian couple were leading the charge toward them. Thomas laughed a relieved peel of laughter, almost crying, himself. He did not realize just how much the loss of his friends had been weighing on him until now. All of the doubt and guilt and worry seemed to melt away as they approached. They were dressed as the others, in the sand-tan colored Kheptha and Uhlan as they others, and wielded traditional kaltesh swords.

"I don't think swords will be enough," Thomas yelled to Exra as they drew nearer.

"Don't worry," Exra called back, "neither did we."

As the Eimurial vehicles crested the rise, several of the mounted men and women drew shepard's slings and began twirling them. Thomas could not imagine what sort of projectile they could sling that would even make a dent to the armored carriages. Certainly not rocks.

As the mystery warriors let fly their slings, the vehicles' weapons fired. One horseman was thrown at least twoscore hands backward from his horse. Another seemed to be hit directly in the head, which twisted at an unnatural angle as he slowly slid from his saddle. The third appeared to narrowly miss a horse, who neighed and bucked against its rider.

The slung projectiles struck the armored carriages with a sound like broken pottery. In fact, shards of what appeared to be fired clay flew from where they hit. In their place, a black tarry substance clung to the outer shell of the vehicles. The goopy material held its shape, but began to change color, from black to blue, blue to green, and then from green to red, all in a matter of moments. When it became red, Thomas was sure it was also glowing. There was a hissing, sizzling sound that grew louder, and then an explosion. One after another, the clinging jelly exploded against the armor of the vehicles.

The left-most carriage was thrown into the air, flipping end over end until it finally landed upside-down, its Eimurial-powered wheels still spinning, fruitlessly. The blasts against the center carriage rocked it up onto its two right wheels while the fore section of the roof was blown completely off. The vehicle's driver and co-pilot were only exposed for moments before they were peppered with arrows. The remaining carriage was hit from below, having run over a missed projectile. The front end flew upwards, and the vehicle came to rest on its rear. Its wheels spun and twisted, the driver trying in vain to right the carriage. There was a hum and 'thoom,' as the vehicles strange weapon fired. It must have been damaged in the blast, however, as the tube exploded, violently, and the whole giant machine was thrown to the side, crashing into the carriage next to it. Sparks and flames flew against the grind and crash of steel. The mounted warriors cheered.

"Blasting gel?" Lea asked Exra. Exra just laughed a hearty laugh as a reply, a giant grin on his face. "Where in the afterlife have you been? We've been so worried about you? Are you all right? Who are these people? What in The Hell of Boiling Lead are those weapons? How did you get here? Who are these people?"

"Slow down!" Thomas said to her. "I'm sure they have just as many questions for us."

"Indeed," said Ana, putting her hand on Lea's shoulder, "but right now, you must get to the ship. We will stay here. There are many more after you, and they must not be allowed to reach you or the Garden before you."

"No!" exclaimed Lea, "We need you! We can't do this without you!"

"Of course you can," Exra interjected, "you have made it this far by your own skill."

"Not to be contrary," Thomas began, "but this was the easy part. And I would be lying if I said I was sure we'd get this far. We need you, my friends. Can your new acquaintances not hold these ruffians at bay?"

"He is right, Basaa," came a deep voice. Thomas turned to see a dark, bearded man approaching. "We are not sure of the dangers they will face on the island. The Garden is older than we can fathom, and it was not left unguarded. They will need you."

"Forgive me, Basaa...," said Thomas.

"Tirdad Jaleh. Mister and Mistress Porter. Your friends speak very highly of you."

"They are extraordinary people, Basaa Jaleh. We are fortunate to know them."

"Indeed. And they speak the truth. There will be many more after you, if not ahead of you, and you must reach the Temple of The Garden first. Especially if you have the phulassein."

"What is this phulassein?" Lea asked. "And why does everyone think we have it?"

"A phulassein is..."

"Thomas, I know what a phulassein is, Love," Lea said, somewhat harshly, "but what is so special about this particular vial that has the whole of Anthumbra in a fit? And why should we have it?"

The man who called himself Tirdad Jaleh squinted slightly at the two, almost as if he did not quite believe that they did not, in fact, have the vial. If that was what he thought, however, he kept it to himself.

"I will allow Analeytuua and Exra to fill you in on the ship. But you must go, now. More attack vehicles are on their way, our scouts report. We will hold them at bay as long as we can, and follow when they are dealt with, Gol-Adam willing. Now, go!"

Thomas did not question the man, though he was hesitant to determine if it was out of the man's good sense, or fear of the coming attack. He supposed either was a good enough reason. The four friends, reunited, made for the docks.

They easily found the slip where the Randy Brute was moored. A large man, the very stereotype of a sailor, down to the peg-leg, was there to greet them, waving impatiently for them to board. From the outskirts of the waterfront, the sounds of explosions and screaming could be heard.

"Hurry, hurry!" the captain said, ushering them aboard.

The four dismounted and gave their reigns to waiting longshoremen, who would take the horses to the stables to be boarded. They grabbed what they needed from the saddlebags and watched the animals being led away. Thomas had grown most fond of his horse. They were in such a hurry when they purchased them that he had neglected to ask the ostler their names. He vowed he would find a name for him by the time they returned. If they returned.

"'Aveya anymore carga?" the captain asked.

"No," replied Lea. "Do you have the supplies we requested?"

"Aye, aye, I've yer things. Come, come, come..."

The four hurried up the slipway and onto the ship. It was a rather large ship, though Thomas was the first to admit he knew relatively little about ships, or seafaring in general. He had a tendency to become ill when they travelled on water, and this was the largest body of water he had ever been on. He had always wanted to voyage across the Iron Sea to see the Aelfin lands but had not summoned the fortitude to try. Maybe this experience would strengthen his stomach.

The captain was yelling orders at his crew, who barked them back with an "aye!" each time.

"All able-bodies, clear the moorings! Mister Paris, weigh anchor! Boatswain, get yer men on them rigs or I'll have ya on double watch! Mister Bustos, tack the Fair Lady; I want to be out of sight of the shore by two bells! Mister Baca, this ain't no Delmonti virgin to be gentle with! Put your back into it, man! Work her hard, or she'll work you!"

Soon the ship was gliding out of the dock and was under way. Thomas could not help but look back to the shore. In the distance, he could see the plumes of smoke and dust from more attack carriages. How many, he could not say, but the clouds were huge and many. He hoped Ana and Exra's new friends had enough blasting gel. It was not long before the shore, and the dangers they had left there, slipped behind the horizon.

Lea rubbed Thomas' back gently. She thought for a moment that he may be finished, but she had thought that, before. Even though he had nothing left to give, it was like he kept trying, anyway. In a way it was just like everything else about her husband, though somewhat less pleasant for everyone involved. His shoulders jerked, suddenly, and he doubled over. He made a dry retching sound, the contents of his stomach having long since been emptied. Somehow it was worse when there was nothing left.

"There, there," she said, reassuringly. "I'm sure this will pass."

"Not likely," the captain's voice said, approaching from behind them. "This here's the calm part. Much, much rougher waters ahead. Given time, aye, he could stomach the sea, but ye won't be aboard long enough, this time.

"I apologize for the lack of a formal introduction, earlier," he said, extending his hand, "but we were in somewhat of a hurry. Captain Neto Pedraza, at yer service."

Lea shook his hand. His grip was gentle, but his hand was rough, more calloused than even the most experienced diggers she had met.

"Lea Porter," she replied. "You'll forgive my husband, Thomas, I hope?"

"Aye. Sea life is a hard one, I hold it against no man – or woman – who ain't yet earned their stomach. Why, in my youth I was known as 'Black Bile.' On account of all the retching, ya see. It was a good year before I could keep a meal down. Musta weighed less than you, little lady. Of course the name followed me 'til I was a captain, and I told my crew I'd take the liver of any man who so much as thought the name. Now they only call me that when I cancel the dog watch."

"Do you have a very large collection of livers, then?"

"Nay. The gods gave every man the right to hate his captain, from time to time. Truth to tell, I oft deserve it." He leaned in close as if he were about to tell a great secret. "Let 'em think they got away with something now and then. You'd be surprised what it does for morale. Now, let's take this discussion back to my cabin, and then you can get settled in. Come on now, lad; I've a bucket for just such an occasion."

Thomas sat with the bucket between his knees, and he stared down at it as if it may actually save his life. Lea sat next to him, with Exra beside her. Ana, who looked almost as pale as Thomas, sat next to him. The cabin, itself, was sparsely, but finely, decorated, and everything was secured to the floor or walls. Across a large, meticulously crafted wooden table sat the captain. He had spread a large map of the Southern Sea out upon the table.

"This is the area yer lookin' to go," he said, pointing to the map. "It's an archipelago smack in the middle of The Storm."

"What's The Storm?" Lea asked.

"The Storm is just that," he said, "a storm that never dies. At its best, it'll batter you about like a child's toy. At its worst, the winds will rip the staysails from the bow and break a ship in half. No one with half a brain in his pan goes there, anymore."

"But they once did?" asked Exra.

"Aye. Many captains braved The Storm looking for whatever treasure it may hide. Most never returned, and those who did say they found only a string of deserted islands with nothing on them. I've not heard of any ship trying since before my father's grandfather's day."

"It makes sense," Thomas said, almost a croak. "The natural Eimuria there would be astounding. Who knows what sort of effects it would have on the area?"

"Thomas?" Ana said.

Thomas passed the bucket down to Ana, who looked on the verge of using it, but managed to hold off for the moment.

"But you will do this for us?" Exra asked, not taking his eye off Ana.

"If The Storm is tame enough, aye. I'll not risk the lives of my crew for any sum, and I've been at sea long enough to know what my ship can and can't take. If that's not acceptable to ya, I'll drop ye in port, and ya can keep yer money."

"That's more than acceptable, captain," Lea said. "How long can we expect you to wait for us, once we reach our destination?"

"Assuming you find what you're looking for, and assuming the weather holds steady, two days. Any longer than that, and my cargo will spoil. I can try to make a go at it on my way back to Altera, but there are no guarantees. I recommend ya be back afore I leave."

"If we are not back in two days, captain," Exra said, "it is unlikely that we will return, at all."

The four friends were to share a cabin. It was close quarters, but they had endured much worse for much longer. The women objected to taking the two cots, at first, but they could not argue with Thomas' assertation that the men's height would make them uncomfortable, anyway. When they had finished setting out the bedrolls and making themselves at home, they sat on the cots and began the task of filling each other in on what they had all been through and learned.

"That's horrible, Ex!" Lea said, in response to his being tortured, "and by a High Cleric, no less! This is unimaginable. That this secret order has infiltrated the highest levels of the Temple..."

"I'm much more worried about these Wretched," said Thomas, "especially if one is already up and walking about. If mankind has truly lost the ability to manipulate Eimuria on a primal level, then these individuals would be all but unstoppable. Our journey has stopped being about being proven right and has become an actual quest to save the world. I must say that I have reservations."

"Assuming we do, in fact, reach the Garden," Lea began, "and we do so before these Blighted, manage to defeat or circumvent any and all defenses, and reach the phulassein...what do we do then? Do we dare give them to the Tanrin Eli? Can we be sure they'd act with any less malice than the Blighted?"

"No," Exra said, "nor can we destroy them. It would take long, perhaps many years, but the Bagh would eventually make their way back to the Pagagh. We must hide them where no one else will dream of looking, and then take the secret to our graves."

"Is that all?" Lea said. "And here I thought it would be something difficult."

"I'm just thinking out loud," Thomas said, passing the bucket back to Ana, who sat across from him on the other cot, "but from an academic standpoint, do we not have a responsibility to study all of this? Not to mention the theological implications. Real, tangible proof of the existence of the gods? Men who can bend Eimuria to their will...what could they teach us, do you think? The ramifications could be world-changing."

"Thomas," Lea said slightly taken aback, "you know I value knowledge and truth above all things. But you said it, yourself. These Wretched would be all but unstoppable. I can't allow us to be the cause of the chaos and misery they could cause. Knowledge at any cost? The price is too high."

"We are assuming these stories are true. We have heard only one side of this tale. After a few thousand years, is it not possible that it has become distorted in the telling? After all, didn't you say, Exra, that they were once called the Exalted? Perhaps it was jealousy that tuned them from heroes to monsters."

They all stared at Thomas, almost in disbelief. Lea knew that Thomas could be single-minded when it came to the pursuit of knowledge, but even she had never thought he could be so reckless.

"Are you willing to take that risk?" asked Ana.

Lea saw what she thought was a flash of anger in Thomas' eyes. No, not anger; hatred. A deep and powerful hatred that terrified her. She had never been afraid of Thomas, but that briefest of glints made her blood run cold. And then it was gone, and Thomas smiled that goofy smile of his.

"Of course," he said. "As I said, just thinking aloud. Can't ignore any possibilities, at least."

"Of course," Lea replied. She wanted to feel relived, but her heart was still pounding loudly in her chest.

Amsu walked among the bodies. Where once he would have found the sight revolting, now he only noted the severity of the damage to the remains. The Eimurial cannons could either be used to incapacitate or obliterate human tissue. Amsu was no doctor, but these were not the relatively clean wounds left by bladed weapons. This was rending, tearing, exploding...violence the like Amsu had never seen. It seemed...effective, if excessive.

Madu was busy combing through the dead. He was searching for Tirdad Jaleh, Amsu knew, the effective leader of the Tanrin Eli in the Eastlands. With each corpse he turned over, the more frustrated he became. Amsu supposed he had good reason; they had suffered a rather heavy loss, here, today. Fifteen Juggernauts, not to mention the men inside them. A cursory glance told Amsu that the Tanrin Eli had lost a comparable number of warriors, but significantly less equipment.

"We will need to fortify the Juggernauts against blasting gel. The greatest weapon in the world, laid waste by men on horseback. Disgraceful! And where are the Khattabs? The Ingeleans?"

Amsu thought the answer obvious but was glad he could not speak it. Madu was in no mood for it.

"We must catch up to them," he said to Amsu, "if they are lost in The Storm, the phulassein may be out of reach, forever! And no one knows what awaits them in the Garden."

But Amsu knew. Amsu knew wait waited for them, there, patiently. Dormant until needed. Unsleeping, unyielding, undying. To be lost at sea by The Storm was a much better fate.

Neb er Khalid grunted next to him. Amsu was...surprised? Could he even be surprised? Since his awakening Khalid had not made a sound. Only his initial scream that had ushered him back into this world, then silence. Madu did not seem to notice. Amsu looked into his eyes and saw a glimmer of recognition.

Yes. You know what awaits them in that cursed place, don't you, old friend?

"Come," Madu commanded them, "We must set sail, immediately. If luck is with us, we can overtake them before they reach the islands."

But Amsu knew there was no such thing as luck. Only will. The will of gods and men to shape the world as they saw fit. Those who relied on luck merely rode the will of others, hoping to not be pulled under by it. Madu would reach his precious Garden, but he would have no luck.

CHAPTER TEN

Lea flew across the deck as if tossed by a giant. She landed squarely on her backside and bounced, twice. The Storm had increased in intensity as they pushed forward. The captain had insisted that she go below decks, but she was just as battered about, down there. This was the first she had been thrown about with such force, however.

"I told ya to stay below!" Captain Pedraza yelled at her.

Lea climbed back to her feet and pushed her wet hair from her eyes.

"Tossed up here, tossed down there...what's the difference? At least up here I can see what's happening."

"Aye, and get ye tossed over the side, too. Is that what ya want, lass? Is it worth that to know what ya can't change?"

"Then let me help!" she said, fiercely.

"Ahahaha!" Pedraza bellowed. "Do ya know yer way around the rigs? Which is the jib, and which is the main? Do ya know yer tack from yer jibe? I thought not, and I've not the time to teach ya."

She marched up the man and stared him down.

"You can point, can't you?" she asked. "Tell me which rope to pull, and I'll pull it!"

The captain looked deep into her eyes for a long moment.

"Mister Baca!" he called, not taking his eyes from hers, "The lass wants to help. Use her as ya see fit. Teach her the difference between ropes and lines. And if she can't keep pace, use her for ballast. Is that suitable, Mistress Porter?"

"Aye," she replied.

Lea fell to her knees. She watched the water run off her head in small, steady streams. She pressed her hands flat against the deck and felt the ache of the stretch. Her back and shoulders were one giant knot. She breathed slowly and deliberately, taking pleasure in exhaling, and watching the rivulets of water fall from her lips.

The Storm had died to a light wind and rain. Ahead of them could be seen light, breaking through the black clouds. Lea had lost all track of time, but it felt like days she had been on her feet. They had come close to several small islands while navigating the rough waters, more than once almost running the ship aground. Now, they passed another island, the largest Lea had seen, so far. She imagined that it could be inhabited, perhaps, but what sort of people could live in this persistent gloom and rain?

"That's the worst of it, fer now," said the captain. "Mister Bustos, rotate the men out, I want no man on more than four bells. We'll need all hands on for the trip back. Mister Baca, damage report!"

"Several sails need repairs, but no damage to the masts. We don't appear to be taking on water."

"Casualties?"

"We lost Barda," Baca sighed, mournfully. "Went over and under. I looked for him, but..."

"Barda was a good lad," Pedraza said, "like his father and brother. Born o' the sea, and to the sea returned. May Andrella guide him to port. Any others?"

"Justin has a broken arm, but it looks clean. Coulda been a lot worse."

"Aye. Carry on."

The captain walked over to Lea and extended his hand. It took an enormous amount of willpower to take it. She had to deliberately think about each motion she made. As he pulled her to her feet it felt as though she were being torn from the deck, a sort of violent rebirth. She could not have stopped the loud groan she made if she had wanted to.

"Come on, lass," he said, "let's get ya inside."

Lea was not surprised to hear that Ana and Exra had slept though the worst of it. She supposed it was their time in the Esisrian military that had taught them the ability to sleep anywhere and anytime. Thomas had spent the entire time with his head in the bucket, much like a horse in a feedbag. She had hoped he would be feeling better, by this time, but he only looked the worse.

Lea was huddled under a thick blanket as she sat in the captain's cabin with the others. She felt like the water was sucking all of the warmth from her body, but the blanket was helping, immensely. The captain pulled a large jug down from one of the shelves behind his great chair and pulled the stopper. The smell was strong and pungent, yet somehow savory. Thomas' head went back into the bucket, and Ana's face became quite pale.

"Here," Pedraza said to Lea, "this will help with the fatigue and the soreness."

"What is it?" she asked hesitantly.

"While the other gods may be gone, the beautiful Andrella still provides for those who work the sea and keep the faith."

He poured a white, viscous liquid into a large tin cup. Lea was sure she saw chunks in the sludge. He handed her the cup.

"You don't want to know. Plug yer nose."

Lea did so and gulped the liquid down. It was the most vile concoction she could have ever imagined. It assaulted her senses and stomach. With each swallow she was sure it would come back up, but she managed to finish it all, and slammed the cup on the desk.

"Blech!" she cried.

"Aye," said the captain, laughing. He handed her a second cup, this one with a hot steam rising from it.

"Tea?" she asked.

"Aye. It'll wash the taste away, and warm ya up." He poured a cup for everyone else as well. Thomas merely held up a hand in refusal, but Pedraza insisted, saying, "it'll calm yer stomach, Mister Porter. Asides, yer liable to die of dehydration if you don't keep something down, lad."

"Thank you," Thomas replied. "And, please, it's Thomas."

"How close are we to the island, captain?" Lea asked.

"Close, but this'll be the slowest going part. We're approaching the eye of The Storm. We'll have little wind to tack and may find ourselves in irons."

"In irons?" Ana asked.

"Aye. Stalled out, as they say, sailing directly into the headwind."

"You know much about this Storm, captain," Exra said.

"Aye, all who work this part of the sea know it well. Some call it Andrella's wrath. Some still tell tales of a vast treasure The Lady put there to test us. But all know to avoid it." He put the tea kettle down and drew out an ages-old ledger from one of the desk's many drawers.

"But yer right," he continued, tossing the book on the desk, "I do mayhaps know more than most."

Lea picked up the book and began thumbing through the pages.

"A journal?"

"My great-grandfather's, aye. I may have been a touch less than truthful with ya."

"Incredible!" Lea said, "He was an explorer!"

"Aye, and a bloody good one. Sailed the nine seas for lost relics of the old world, he did. And found many. But his greatest quest was for Andrella's treasure at the heart of The Storm. For years, he studied everything about The Storm, before and after the Upheaval. He mapped out every expedition he knew of, and claimed he found the path through. He took his ship and crew into great winds and was never seen again."

"Did he leave his journal behind?" Lea asked.

"Nay, though he did leave notes and a crude map. When I first made boatswain, my father passed them on to me. And, like the young fool I was, I followed."

"You've been here, before!" Lea exclaimed.

"I took a small sloop and a crew of three and headed into The Storm by the route my great-grandfather laid out. We all but lost the ship on the way in. We put in on a small island and made repairs. When we camped, that night, we heard noises like no man has ever heard. Beastly noises. Not a one of us slept a wink that night.

"We had to row most of the way from there and arrived at the island near sunset. We chose to sleep on the ship, that night. My first mate, Kirk, took first watch. He never woke me to relieve him, and when we roused at daybreak he was gone, never to be seen, again."

"What did you find on the island?" Thomas asked.

"We hardly got a score of paces inland when we found a pile of loot. Weapons and armor, clothes and coins. Some so old they were falling apart. Many we did not recognized. Atop the pile was the journal you have there. Read the last page."

Lea flipped through the book until she found the last entry and read it aloud.

"'There is naught but death, here. We should not have come. All have been lost to the wrath of Gol-Adam. Turn back, now, Neto. Turn back.' Captain," Lea said, "is this addressed to you?"

"That wasn't the most unnerving part, lass."

"The handwriting," Lea said, realizing what he meant, "it's different."

"Aye, and afore I could think as to what that meant, a rumble came, like I would imagine a stampede to sound. Thundering footfalls that sounded like giants coming our way. We turned and ran. I saw Monty lifted into the air and disappear into the think jungle, his screams I can still hear to this day. We last two made it back to the ship and rowed for our lives. The jungle rumbled and shook along the shore we had left.

"Aldric became sick almost as soon as we pushed off. He wasted away so fast, there was nothing to be done. He didn't survive the trip back through The Storm." He became silent, then, and looked down at the desk.

"If this is true," Exra said, "why would you willingly take us here?"

"On the contrary," Pedraza replied, "I was the only one crazy enough to take this job. If you were just some too-rich for yer britches thrill seekers, I woulda turned right around and taken you back to Atera. But if ya were the golden fish, as they say, I could finally find the answers I sought, and put my crew and kin to rest."

"Ex," Lea said, "did the Tanrin Eli say what they thought protected the Garden?"

"They had only scant writings on which to base suppositions, but besides the physical and Eimurial traps they believe are there, they mentioned only The Deathless. Men and women so devoted to the gods that they willingly forsake the afterlife to remain bound to the physical world. They cannot be killed, no matter how much damage they take, and will always regenerate, given enough time."

"And how are we to deal with them?"

"They do not know."

"The Gambler's luck," Thomas said from inside his bucket.

Lea stepped from the dinghy onto the shore. The captain's foul concoction did, as he said, help with the soreness, but her muscles stilled ached, fiercely. Thomas practically dropped to his knees in the white beach sand. She would not have been surprised if he tried to kiss it.

"Whatever is in that jungle," he said, "can't possibly be worse than that blighted ship." Ana patted his back, comfortingly.

"I'll wait here, just offshore," the captain was saying. "We'll rotate out once a shift, but someone will be waiting for you. Two days," he reminded them, "that's all I can wait."

"Thank you, captain," said Lea.

"Andrella's grace upon ya," he replied.

They took their first steps into the dense foliage of the jungle. They each carried a long, curved blade similar to a cutlass that the captain called a matchet. It was used both to clear a path through the roughage as well as a weapon. Lea hoped her lessons came back to her, and that the blade was similar enough to a falchion to be relevant.

Thomas and Exra took the lead, hacking away at the myriad vines and shrubbery. As Pedraza had said, it was not long at all before they reached the pile of loot he had described.

"Dear gods," Thomas said, "he said it was a pile, not a mountain..."

It was indeed massive, three times the height of a man. Lea could not see the entire width of it. It was made up of anything and everything a person would carry in the jungle, and then some. Weapons and armor from countless cultures and eras stacked so high that one could not so

much as see over it. Coins and jewels were tossed casually about like so much refuse. Thomas looked equal parts excited and terrified.

"This is a warning," Exra said.

"Yes," said Thomas, opening the captain's journal. "We landed at what Captain Pedraza the Elder had noted as the only feasible place to come ashore. The rest of the island is surrounded by reefs, sand bars and cliffs. These were placed right here as a deterrent. We are being told to turn back."

"What worries me more," said Lea, trying to get a feel for climbing the giant heap, "is where are the bodies?"

"I assume they are dead?" Ana posited, climbing behind Lea.

"Quite certainly. But why not leave the bodies as a deterrent? Surely, a huge pile of bones and corpses would be more effective? It would certainly smell much worse."

"I do not know. Perhaps they were given proper burials. Perhaps the goods are left to be returned, the way the journal was. Perhaps the mystery of the missing bodies is more terrifying."

"Perhaps they were eaten," Thomas said.

"By wildlife?" Exra asked.

"No."

Ana gasped and looked at him in horror.

"I haven't seen so much as an insect since we stepped foot, here. Which is odd, because bloodbugs love me."

"They really do," Lea confirmed. "Welts the size of an apple."

"Assuming that whoever, or whatever, lives here needs food..."

"How terribly macabre," Lea said.

"Just a theory," Thomas said, shrugging as he climbed. "Until we know more, it will remain a morbid mystery."

They reached the top of the mound of discarded goods. Lea counted it as nothing short of a miracle that no one was cut by a hidden blade in all the debris, but it seemed that the years had settled the huge pile sufficiently enough to eliminate such surprises. As tall as it was, they were still unable to see over the tops of the giant trees. Deeper parts of the dense jungle almost seemed black as the sun was blocked from the jungle floor.

"And here I hoped it got easier," Thomas said.

The four started down the other side of the pile of discarded items. Lea thought Thomas was going to fall end over end more than once, but he managed to reach the bottom without incident. He looked back as he stepped foot onto solid ground, once more.

"I could spend years just going through all of this this. So many relics that could be studied. Such a find."

"Perhaps when all of this is over, we can come back and you can play in the trash until you're blue in the face," Lea said, playfully.

"Perhaps," Thomas replied, but he sounded very unconvinced.

Despite the denseness of the foliage, and the years of uninhibited-ness, there was still a sort of path leading from the pile into the heart of the island. They were nonetheless forced to chop and hack away at the many vined and low-hanging branches every few steps, however. The work was far more tiresome than Lea would have guessed. In fact, she almost thought of it as a break from manning the lines aboard the Beast. But less than half an hour into their trek she was already exhausted.

They decided to take a rest after an hour.

"We're not even close," Thomas said. "At this pace, we have another 8 hours or so to the temple."

"At least the path will be clear on our way back?" Ana said.

"I love your optimism."

They switched to a quarter-hour rotation, with two people at a time taking turns hacking. The pace was noticeably slower, but they had to stop and rest far less frequently. They seemed to be making much better progress this way. At least to Lea, the constant moving felt more like progress.

"We're more than halfway there, according to this map. We have still yet to encounter any of Captain Pedraza's giants. Where do you suppose they are?"

"Personally," Lea answered between cutlass swipes, "I've been count-ing ourselves fortunate."

Night began to fall, and the four found themselves hacking directly into the fading sunlight. Rather than make camp, they decided to press on after a short rest. The unknown jungle at night was not a place any of them had wanted to stay.

As the last rays of sunlight slipped away, they felt the wind pick up. It had been very calm until the point, though Lea had assumed that the thickness of the plant life had keeping any breeze out. But now, it blew, picking up speed. It was enough that Lea had to catch her hat from blowing away.

With the wind came another surprise; sounds of life. Not all at once, but the darker it got, the more wildlife they heard. Birds began cawing and singing, and the hum of insect life could be heard. The companions all looked at each other, askance.

"I think we had better pick up our pace," Exra said.

"I concur," said Lea.

They all four began to hack and slash at the foliage. Soon, this had to be abandoned, as it became so dark that none of them could see. Lea lit a torch and held it up while the other three continued the clearing away.

Suddenly, Lea's heart leapt into her throat. She heard the sound that she had been praying they would not hear; the thundering of large, heavy footfalls.

"Oh, no..." she whimpered.

Directly in front of them, the thudding grew louder and closer. Suddenly, the jungle parted, and gave way to the most horrific thing Lea had ever seen. Its shape was that of a man, but it was half again as tall as Exra, and it had the muscular bulk of a heavy laborer or circus strongman. But its size was not what made it monstrous.

Parts of the man-creature's flesh were rotten, almost dripping off of its form. In other areas, particularly its face, it seemed to be melting, like wax down a candle. It was clothed – if one could even call it that – in strips of mismatched sack cloth, torn and aged, falling off its giant body. The stench of it as it appeared was shocking and sent Lea reeling back. It smelled of death and fermentation. Lea had had long ago learned to deal with the smell of decay and corpses, but this was on a scale heretofore unknown. It only intensified when it roared an ear-shattering scream at the companions.

The gust of wind caused by the creature's roar blew out the torch, and they were left in blackness. Lea backed away as fast as she dared in the dark. She scrambled for her flint and striker, rummaging furiously through her satchel. She felt the various tools and implements as her hands passed over them, many falling out and to the ground in her haste. Ahead of her she heard her friends yelling, grunting, thudding...as well as the deep, guttural noises of the creature. She found it!

Lea raised the flint to the torch and struck. The spark did not catch, as a first strike often didn't, but in that brief flash of light she saw a terrifying scene. There were now two of the giant monsters! One was poised over Ex, a giant fist reeled back for a crushing blow. The other had its arms spread wide, crouched over Thomas and Ana, who were both on the ground, apparently backing away.

Lea tried several more times for a spark, but her hands were shaking and sweating. The striker kept slipping in her hand, and when she did manage to hit flint, the strike was not powerful enough or was off angle. Finally, another spark. In the flash of light that accompanied it she saw a giant, mere hands away from her. She could have extended her arm and touched it. It was mid-stride, coming for her! Whether it was attracted by the spark or could see in this pitch blackness, she did not know. If they could see in this dark, then they were surely all doomed.

She shrieked, a high-pitched scream of pure terror. She was not even sure where it came from, it sounded so far away. Instinctively, she dropped the torch and flint and dove to the side. She felt the air pressure of the behemoth behind her as she dove. It had barely missed her.

Lea landed onto damp loam; a blanket of leaves covered in the freshly forming dew. She crawled, then, not knowing what direction she faced. The sounds of thudding and crashing were behind her, and that was all that mattered. Fear gripped her heart like ice. She had never been so afraid. Vines grabbed at her, tangling her arms, catching her head. Low branches raked at her, and razor-sharp leaves sliced her. Where there had been no insects, before, suddenly they were everywhere. They crawled on her arms and legs and flew into her mouth as she gasped for air. They crunched beneath her, a sickening sound, their sharp appendages poking through her clothes. Through it all she kept crawling. She had to get away, to get away from that horrible thing.

When the sounds of the conflict had faded away, finally, she stopped. She stayed on her hands and knees, listening, still shaking with fear. Her breaths were deep. Even in this ultimate darkness she could see the colored stars and shapes of exertion. She forced herself to keep breathing. In and out. In and out...

Dear gods, what had she done? She left them. She left them, again! She swore she never would, not after the train, and here she had done it again. But she had been so afraid, so very afraid. Now she had nothing. Now she had no idea where she was. And she had left Ana, Exra, and her beloved Thomas to those things. But what could she have done? They who were giant, and she, who was so very small.

That was it. The question she had been asked her whole life. What could she do? The tiny Ingelean girl, Little Lady Barracourt. But she had shown them what she could do, hadn't she? At every venture, she had proven herself, she had fought and won. And she would be thrice-dammed if she stopped now. To the Hell of Clowns with prudence, she would not run away, now.

Lea stood up and brushed the grime and dirt and insect bits off as best she could. She spun in a circle, looking around, but everywhere was blackness. She had no idea where she was or what direction to start off in. In which case, any direction was as good as another. She started walking, keeping a brisk pace, and listening as closely as she could for the sounds of her friends...or those giant monsters. After roughly ten paces, she walked face-first into the trunk of a tree.

"Fuck!" she yelled, eternally grateful Thomas was not around to hear that.

She felt around the tree for a branch she would be capable of breaking off and found one. Using it as a sort of feeler for trees, roots, and other obstacles, she continued. Cautiously.

For once, her small stature served as a boon. She was much better suited to squeezing and slipping through the super-dense undergrowth she encountered. Of course, the brute strength of a dead-but-not-dead giant would come in handy, as well. Several times she paused, thinking she heard the heavy footfalls of the behemoths. Each time, the sound seemed to vanish just as she stopped. When it did, she adjusted her course to the direction she thought it came from. If her friends were alive, they were likely fighting or running from them. If not...well, it was a direction to walk in.

The trek was rough, and the soreness and fatigue of the last week were taking their toll. Muscles Lea were sure were not there before began to ache and sting. More than once she tripped, falling to her knees. Each time, she contemplated not getting back up. Just lay there and let the insects devour her, or one of the giants could squish her beneath its rotting feet, probably not even noticing her. But that was fool's thinking, she decided. If she were to die, here - and with each passing moment she became more certain that she would – she at least wanted the satisfaction to die while trying. Uru couldn't fault her that, could he?

After what seemed like ages, she thought she saw light. At first, she thought it was a trick of her eyes, which had begun to manifest odd colored shapes in the absolute dark. But the closer she got, the more she was sure it was light. She pressed her way through the jungle to the source of the light: A clearing.

The light she saw came from the moons. Both were out, tonight, and they shined so bright over the clearing that it almost seemed like day. And they cast their light upon the most glorious sight Lea had ever seen.

In the center of the large clearing was a temple, huge and ancient. It looked like the pyramids of the ancient Esisrian temples, except it had a flat top, rather than pointed, and it had some sort of ramparts lining the walls. It was unlike any architecture she had seen before. Thomas would be ecstatic.

Thomas! She saw them just moments after she spotted the temple. It was all three of them, hobbling toward what looked like the main gate of the temple. Exra was favoring his left leg, and he and Ana were carrying Thomas, who appeared to be unconscious, or...

"Thomas!" Lea yelled, caution be dammed. She ran toward them.

Captain Neto Pedraza stood aboard the deck of the Randy Beast, hands clenched behind his back. He had not moved in hours, staring at the island of his great-grandfather's death. For a short while after his dinghy returned, he paced the decks, sometimes muttering, until he finally stopped and stood as he was. His crew seemed most uncomfortable around him. Some stopped and stared as they passed, but none were foolish enough to disturb him. He was in a rare mood, and they knew it. Woe to the first man to break that stony silence.

The sails and railings had been repaired, only minor cosmetic damage remained, and that could be taken care of in port. His crew had done an excellent job getting the Beast ready for sail. Now, scrubbed and checked. Scrubbed and checked until the deck shone, and each man knew the riggings were secured. They sang work shanties as they did, the good lads. Now, it was Ol' Janey Longlegs, a song about an elderly Delmonti prostitute who...

"SHIP!" came the call from above.

The cries of, "ship! Ahoy, ship!" were taken up from all around. Pedraza marched to the port railing and held out his hand. Mister Bustos slapped a spyglass into it. The captain raised it to his eye and looked.

Not just one, but two ships, were breaking through the edge of The Storm. They were smaller ships of an odd design. They had no sails, much like a coal tug, but were sleek like a sloop, and coming in fast. They flew no flag and had no markings. There was nothing about this that Pedraza liked.

"Recall the dinghy," he said, almost breathlessly.

"But sir..." Bustos objected.

"Recall it!"

"Aye, sir." Bustos turned to relay the order.

"The Porters, sir?" Mister Baca inquired.

"We're no good to them at the bottom of the sea."

"They've no sails, sir; coal?"

"Too fast. Eimuria, more like."

"Impossible!" Baca cried, incredulously. "There's no such ship!"

"Then prepare to be shivered by my imagination, Mister Baca. Unfurl and weigh anchor!" he cried. "Tack whatever ya can! Get this ship moving!"

"We can't outrun them, sir," Baca said.

"Nay, but we can draw 'em away. We know these waters better than they, if only by a little. Mayhaps we can run 'em aground. Get all hands ready for battle, Mister Baca. Prepare to be boarded."

"Aye, sir!"

As Pedraza stared at the new coming ships, his crew danced around him. They were well practiced and able-bodied. Good lads, all. He prayed to Andrella that they not all perish on his fool's errand.

Suddenly, a third ship broke through the dark waters of The Storm. It was large, half again the size of the Beast. Unlike its two predecessors, it had sails, but through the spyglass, Pedraza could see that it was furling them as it came through. This ship, too, had its own power. Andrella's grace, they were doomed.

"Buckets!" the captain yelled.

In teams of two, one man starboard, one port, they hurled large buckets off the bow. The handles of the buckets had lines tied to them that the men then used to pull the buckets down the sides of the ship. When they were a quarter of the way to stern, another team threw their buckets. As the men pulled, the ship began to move, albeit at a painfully slow pace. One man's line snapped midway to the stern, and he flew forward on his feet, striking his head on a mast. A crewman checked him, determined that he was unconscious but otherwise unharmed, and took his place in the bucketing line.

The Beast caught a bit of the wind and began to move on its own. It was still a slow pace, but it was something.

"Away buckets!" Pedraza yelled.

The men pulled the lines in and threw the buckets on the deck, then crouched low to catch their breath, all sweating heavily. They paused only moments though, then joined their comrades.

The two smaller ships had broken away from the island and were pursuing the Beast. It would still be several minutes before they caught up, giving the captain and his men time to prepare. The larger ship, however, maintained its course to the island.

"Aye," he said aloud, "you know what's there don't ya?"

The captain said a small prayer for the four he had left on that accused island, then another for his men. He closed his eyes, and took a deep, cleansing breath.

"Longbows and catapults!" he yelled.

The battle had begun.

CHAPTER ELEVEN

The grotesque creature roared, its breath smelling of rot and decay. The torch that Lea was carrying was snuffed out in the gust of rank wind, and Thomas was plunged into blackness.

Duck, his inner voice said. Thomas dropped to his hands and knees. He heard the woosh of the air move over his head in what would have surely been a killing blow from the creature.

Backwards. Thomas quickly began to back away, still crouched. Another whoosh told him he had barely been fast enough. A sudden flash of light came from behind. Lea was trying to relight the torch. In that briefest of illuminations, Thomas saw Ana next to him, also backing away. Could she see in the dark? Or did she have her own inner voice guiding her?

Get up. Thomas did.

Thrust. He had almost forgotten he was even holding the cutlass. He stabbed forward as hard as he could. He felt the blade strike something giving and tried to imagine that it was anything but flesh. The hilt of the sword stopped his hand. There was another flash of light, followed by a shriek. Lea!

Carve right.

But Lea!

Not now! Slice right!

The blade slid easily though the old carcass of the giant. There was a sickening sound, like stepping in tar, followed by two thuds.

Jump backwards.

The commands started coming fast, and Thomas began to anticipate them. They almost felt like an instinct, now. The voice was still there, still instructing him, but it almost sounded...excited? Thomas did not have time to worry about that, now, or to entertain the thought that he might be going mad.

Forward. Duck. Swipe up. Thrust. Step right. Stop! Back. Tree to the right. Duck. Slice left...

Suddenly the voice was silent, and Thomas could hear nothing except his own breathing and his heart pounding in his ears. He tried to call to Lea, but his throat and mouth were dry, and all that came out were raspy groans.

Cut your hand.

"What?" he said aloud in surprise.

Do it! Or you and your friends die here!

Tentatively, Thomas ran his hand along the blade of the cutlass.

Deeper, we need more blood.

He winced and grunted as the edge cut deeper. He could feel the warmth of his blood running out of his hand.

Coat the blade with your blood.

Confused, but not ready to argue, Thomas complied.

Xi'um taa ku, pa'ees taa ku, duatta ba'a ju'i!

The blade of Thomas' cutlass began to glow, dimly at first, but the light grew to equal that of any traditional or Eimurial torch. He could see the trampled battlefield. Parts of those giant creatures were littered, everywhere, enough to make at least a dozen of them. Ana and Exra were on the ground, both alive and conscious. Ana was holding her left shoulder, and Exra's left leg looked twisted and wrong. And Lea...

"Lea!" Thomas called. There was no reply, but he did hear the resounding treading of the giants in the distance. "Lea!" he called, again.

"Thomas," Ana said, getting to her feet, "Thomas! She is not here. We will find her, but you must stop yelling. There are more guardians, still, and we will bring them down on us. Thomas! We will find her."

"Yes," Thomas replied, shaking off the panic that had engulfed him. "Yes, of course we will, won't we? Are you all right? Your shoulder..."

"I do not believe it is broken, but it is severely dislocated. Exra's leg, however..." she trailed off.

"Ex? Your leg? Is it...?"

"Yes," Exra said, "in at least two places. The bones have not shifted. I should be able to walk carefully with a splint, for now."

"Are you sure?" Thomas asked. "Perhaps we could carry you? Construct a gurney of some kind?"

"No. We cannot afford the time, and I do not want to be prone, should there be trouble. I will walk. I am more concerned about your sword."

"Yes, well, uh..." Thomas fumbled for an explanation. "I really don't know. And I'm not sure I could explain it if I did."

"Can you dim it?" asked Exra. "I'd rather not attract any unwanted attention."

"I don't know."

Will it so.

Thomas thought about making the sword dim, and it did.

"I guess I can," he said with an awkward and nervous smile.

Both Ana and Ex looked warily at him. He knew what it must look like, to them. Actually, he had no idea what it must look like, but he knew how suspiciously Esisrians viewed any type of magic, if that was indeed what this was. Oh, who was he kidding, of course it was magic! This was not some Eimuria-fueled technology that a small-minded priest thought was evil because he could not understand it. He rubbed his blood on a sword and now it was glowing!

He looked at his hand. The wound from the cutlass had somehow completely healed. There was not so much as a scar to show where it had been. It had all happened in the dark; had he even cut it? He certainly remembered the pain. At any rate, he was not about to tell them about the blood. Magic was bad enough, but blood magic? That was enough to end their friendship, or worse.

"Before we can make a splint for Exra, I need your assistance," Ana said, approaching Thomas. "You must pull my arm back into place."

She extended her shoulder to him and placed a small length of wood in her mouth.

"Oh, I don't know if I can."

"You just need to take my hand and arm and extend it straight. Do it in one swift jerk. There will be resistance, but you must pull through it."

"I know what to do, but this will hurt. A lot."

"Of course it will hurt," Ana said, looking confused.

"I don't like hurting people. My friends even less so."

"I know," she said, kissing him on the cheek and smiling sweetly. "It is terribly misguided. But also quite endearing. Now, I need you to do this, Thomas."

Thomas took several deep breaths and grabbed Ana's arm by the wrist and forearm. He braced himself for what he had to do.

"The sooner you do this, Thomas, the sooner we can find Lea."

"That is not fair, at all."

"I know. Now, do it. Do it!"

Do it!

Thomas yanked with all his might. He felt the resistance she spoke of and then the loud pop as he broke through. Ana bit into the wood she had put back into her mouth just in time. Thomas could see just how far her teeth sank into it as she grunted, fiercely. He let go of her arm and backed away.

"There," she said, removing the wood and rotating her shoulder. "That wasn't so bad, was it?"

"I may throw up," Thomas replied.

By the glow of the blood-coated cutlass, Ana and Thomas made a makeshift splint out of branches and vines. It was crude and rudimentary at best, and Exra would need an actual doctor, soon, or risk permanent loss of mobility. But it would have to do. They also made a simple crutch to take as much weight off his broken leg as possible.

"Now, we must find Lea," declared Thomas.

"Of course," Ana said. The best place to start is the temple.

"But if she's hurt..."

"If she is, we can't just go trampling all over the jungle, not with Exra injured. If she is able, she will reach the temple. If she's not there, we can leave Exra to wait for her and you and I can go look."

"Yes...yes, of course, you're right," Thomas said after a short pause.

"I am worried, too, Thomas. She is my closest friend. But she is capable, and strong."

"I know she is, Ana. Far more capable than I. I just..."

"You have a need to help her. I understand this, my friend. But sometimes helping is best done indirectly. Come. The sooner we get to the temple, the sooner we can search."

The three resumed their trek to the temple. The pace was slow, both due to the denseness of the jungle growth as well as Exra's leg. Knowing how close they were to the temple made the slow going all the more agonizing.

Exra suddenly halted and held up his hand. They all stopped and listened. Soon, Thomas heard what had given Exra pause. It was the booming of giant footsteps approaching. Exra made a motion to dim the light from the sword, and Thomas willed the light out, completely. Once it was out, Thomas wondered if he could even relight the blade. The roaring footfalls passed, and Thomas found that he could, in fact, reignite the cutlass. He wondered how long this ability would last.

Exra gave the all-clear, and they began, again. Ahead, Thomas could see the leaves of the gigantic trees part, and there was a clearing. And in the clearing, he could see the vague outlines of what he knew must be the temple. It took all his willpower not to just run on ahead, throwing all sense of caution to the wind. It was, after all, the greatest theological and archeological find of all time. More important still, Lea might be there.

As they neared the clearing a sudden rustle cause them all to stop. Before Thomas could once again douse his cutlass, the rotting form of one of the giant guardians burst through from the clearing, ahead. It plodded toward them, menacingly, and was joined by a second, and then a third behemoth. The three companions backed away as fast as they could, but a low rumble from behind made Thomas look back. There stood three more unliving giants behind them. They were completely surrounded.

"I believe this is where we part ways," Exra said.

"We will at least die fighting," said Ana. "Uru will surely grant us the Golden Fields. I will see you there, my love. And you, Thomas."

Wait, Thomas' inner voice said. *Tell them to wait.*

"Wait!" said Thomas, obediently. "Wait, why?"

"Thomas?" Exra asked, puzzled.

Give me your voice.

"What? How?" Thomas replied.

"Who are you talking to, Thomas?" inquired Ana, still ready to dive into battle.

Give me your voice! the voice demanded, again. *Let me speak or perish!*

"I don't know how!" Thomas said, desperately.

Let go...

"Thomas, what is happening? Are you all right?" Exra seemed both concerned for his friend's life as well as his sanity.

"Alright," said Thomas. "Do what you must."

Thomas felt himself pushed back, almost like a passenger in a carriage. He could still see and feel everything around him, but his actions were not his own. He watched as his left hand went once again to the blade of the enchanted machet, cutting a large gash down his palm. He then tossed blood around the three of them, as if he were tossing bird feed in a circle. His sword was raised high, and the words came from his lips, unbidden.

"Xi'um pel da na pourii...Maa'et mo ram da na pourii! Xi'um taa ku, an am rah taa ku! Duatta maa'et mo ram!"

From the raised blade, a crackle like that of lightning came forth. It jumped from the sword to the nearest giant, then to the one closest to it. If leapt from body to body, until it looked like one, solid bolt of lightning connected all of the guardians together. The deathless corpses began to smoke, then caught fire. It spread slowly at first, but soon grew into a raging fire, bright and blue. Howls of pain arose from the guardians as the flames became so bright that Ana and Exra looked away. Thomas wanted to avert his eyes as they stung and watered but was unable to move of his own accord.

The forms of the giants crumbled as they became nothing more than ash, blackened piles now where the huge figures once stood. The lightning retreated back into the sword with a sharp crack, and Thomas' arm fell to his side. He dropped to his knees, no energy to stand. He felt as if a dam had broken inside him, and his life flowed out of him like water over a levee.

He tried to keep his eyes open, to stay conscious, but he felt as if he were falling down a deep well. The last thing he heard before he hit the bottom was Exra calling his name, begging him to stay. Everything was fine, though, Thomas knew. He would see his friend in the afterlife.

Another blast hit the side of the Randy Beast and rocked it in the calm waters. The bow had buckled, cracking the dense wood. Captain Pedraza could see that they were taking on water, now. It would not be long until the damage was too much, and the Beast would have to be abandoned.

"Get below, man!" he yelled to Baca. "She's cracked above the turn of the bilge. Get the men to bucket it out and patch it if ya can. One more hit like that, and we're done for."

The problem was that the captain had no idea what he was being bombarded with. Invisible projectiles hammered the sides of his ship, shot from some strange catapult or ballista by the two smaller ships circling him.

So far, the only thing keeping the Randy Beast afloat was Pedraza's skill and Andrella's grace. The smaller ships were too fast to be hit with the catapult, and the longbowman did too little damage to be counted. What few lucky shots they had gotten in with the ballistae were effective, but far too few. He had to think of something, fast, or they would all soon be at the bottom of the sea.

"Mister Bustos," he summoned, his mouth already dry with what he was about to say.

"Aye!" came his first mate's reply.

"Fetch the oil, Mister Bustos." It came out barely above a whisper.

"Sir?" asked Bustos, clearly hoping he had heard wrong.

"Fetch the oil, Mister Bustos," this time with far more command.

"But sir...the law..."

"To the swirling depths with the law!" Pedraza cried. "The law'll do us no good when we're fish food. Do you think these'n are following the law, lad? Attacking undeclared, and with what? The gods only know. I'll not lose all hands to hold to a code that weren't writ for this. If we survive this, you can string me up at the first port of call, Mister. Now, get the damned oil afore I throw ya over, myself."

Pedraza felt his hands shaking and hoped Bustos had not taken notice. The Law of The Sea was immutable, having lasted more than three hundred years as it stood. While not legally binding by the laws of any nation, the men of the sea clung to the Law more than any religion. He would face no criminal charges for what he was about to do, he knew, but if his men did not kill him outright to show they had no part of it, then he would never get another commission so long as he lived. He would not even be allowed to scrub decks aboard a garbage barge. He would be a drylander, an outcast. Shunned by his peers and forbidden from the one thing that gave his life meaning. Death was preferable. But he had meant what he said; he had no intention of losing his men to these cowardly knaves.

An explosion of water off the port bow showed where one of the invisible projectiles had missed, then another followed. The Beast continued to maneuver deftly despite the lack of wind. Her crew was well trained, and the attackers' obvious ineptitude at sea had managed to keep them just ahead of the attackers. Pedraza knew that could only last for so long.

Bustos appeared with two others, rolling large casks of the oil used for lanterns and cooking. The captain ordered the lids removed. He wrapped strips of cloth around the heads of several arrows and dipped them in the oil. Then, he ordered two of the barrels into the catapults.

His crew looked at him in open disbelief. Using fire in battle was forbidden by the Law. Since most confrontations between ships happened in close quarters and most often ended in one or both ships being boarded, fire could easily be spread from one ship to another, causing both ships to go down, losing all souls and cargo to the depths. For more than three hundred years, the use of fire had been anathema, and now Neto Pedraza would be, as well.

He grabbed a longbow from the hands of a young rating, who's mouth was agape. Pedraza clasped a hand on the boy's shoulder.

"Yer hands are clean, lad," he said.

The captain made for the catapult closest to him, but Bustos beat him to it.

"You know what this means," the captain said. It was not a question.

"On your mark," was all Bustos said in return.

Pedraza nodded, hoping the lad knew what he was doing was irreversible. He waited until one of the two ships were in range, calculating. Unlike a lead ball, the shot would only have to be close enough to spill a good deal of the oil on the ship, not a direct hit. Closer...closer...

"Fire!"

The barrel flew through the air. It reached its apogee and began to descend, now turning end over end, oil spraying in a wide, chaotic area. Pedraza waited to see just how much splashed across the deck of the encroaching ship. It was not much, but it would be enough to start. He lit his arrow and drew back.

"Andrella forgive me."

He loosed the arrow, which flew true, striking the bow of the ship and igniting the oil. The flames spread fast, engulfing the aft third of the ship. Behind the captain, gasps and prayers could be heard. This was a dark day, indeed.

Aboard the blazing ship, men could be seen trying to douse the fire, scrambling to avert their doom. Pedraza would give them no chance to. He signaled Bustos to the next catapult.

"Fire!"

The barrel flew much the same as the first, this time spilling far more oil on the ship. The blaze flared as the oil hit. The crew were now on fire, running around in vain, leaping from the deck to the waters below. But the oil on the water was aflame now, as well, and there was no quarter to be had there. The second enemy ship paused and made for the first, keeping its distance. It looked as though they meant to help but were unable. That moment of compassion would be their undoing.

"Fire!"

The third barrel landed soundly in the center of the second ship's deck, the metal rims giving way as the barrel exploded. Oil spilled everywhere on the deck, almost no plank was left dry. Pedraza grabbed another arrow, but before he could light it, the first ship detonated.

The force of the blast knocked the captain back on his feet. Several men near him were thrown to the deck. The flames of the explosion had ignited the second ship, which had capsized in the blast. Screams could be heard from the those who had not been killed outright. The captain was not a man without mercy, but he knew nothing could be done for them.

"Back us away...back us away!"

The Beast turned away, moving slowly in the calm sea. Moments later, the deafening explosion Pedraza knew was coming rocked the ship, spraying flaming debris on them from above. The men quickly put them out before they spread to the deck, or worse, the oil. Bustos called for hands to take the remaining oil to the hold.

Captain Pedraza turned to the men. They all stared at him with mixed emotions on their faces. He saw relief and fear, anger and shame. All of them justified. But they were not out of danger, yet.

"Aye, lads, I know. I've done the unforgivable, and I make no excuses for it. By Andrella's mercy, I wish I hadn't had to, but I'd do so again, under the same circumstances. You'll get yer justice, my boys, have no doubt. But until we retrieve thems on the island and put back into port, this ship still be mine. You have my word that once we do, I'll step down and face the Guild's judgment."

"And what is your word worth, Lawbreaker?"

The voice came from somewhere in the back, but Pedraza recognized it as Demos, a lad who had been at sea several years, but had only been aboard the Beast a season or two. Several men angrily made to confront him, but the captain stopped them.

"Nay, nay! He's a fair point. What credibility have I left? But know this: until my task is done, I'll not go from my post quiet, and I'll treat any attempt to force it from as insurrection. I'd not wish to fight you; I've done enough evil, this day. But I'll not leave those men and women behind, if they are still alive. I have that much honor left to me, at least."

He looked around at his men. The conflict within them all was evident. He did not blame any of them. But he would not let them rob him of the last of his dignity, either.

"Are we agreed, then, lads? Say 'aye,' and let's be on our way. There's fine folk a'countin' on us."

The cries of "Aye!" went up across the deck.

"Opposed?"

There was silence.

"Good lads. Now, make sail for that shore, there. We need repairs and restitutions before we can rescue anyone."

The ship made for the small island, limping on torn sails, and taking on water. The crew did not dally in their work, but the mood was dark and gloomy. It was the end, Pedraza knew. One way or another, this was his last voyage. Not even the Grand Lady Andrella could save him, now.

Amsu stood on the bow of the Carrion Crow next beside Madu. The High Cleric had found the name of the ship humorous for reasons that Amsu did not quite comprehend. Not that it mattered what its name was; there was only one ship like it in the world. The smaller speedcraft did not have names, though since they lost two of them coming through that storm, perhaps it was for the best. The two remaining ships had taken off after the ship that had ferried the Porters and their companions to this wretched place. Wretched? Amsu did not think that feeling was his own. He did not think many thoughts and feelings were his own, anymore. He idly wondered how much of him would be left, soon. Would he even notice? It did not really matter.

"Full ahead, captain!" Madu yelled.

The Crow's captain, a squat man with a severely receding hairline, had probably spent more days at sea than Amsu had spent alive. The man loathed Madu, or at least taking orders from the man, but was very careful to hide it when the cleric was looking. Amsu saw, however, and made note of it.

"Aye, Your Grace," the man replied. His voice conveyed nothing but obedience.

When they drew near the shore of the island, the captain called halt. Madu turned furiously to the man.

"Why are we stopping?" he demanded to know.

"We can risk getting no closer without running aground, Your Grace," the captain said, terrified. He sounded like a man trying to explain the simplest thing to a child, but a child that could kill with a word.

"From here, we must use the ship's boats."

"Of course, captain. My apologies," Madu said, that sickly false smile returning to his face. "Forgive my impatience, please. Please ready the captain's gig."

"Your Grace, I believe one of the longboats would be better suited..."

"Did I not speak clearly enough?" Madu asked, that facsimile of a grin never leaving his face.

"No, Your Grace...I mean yes, I understand, Your Grace. Bosun! Ready the captain's gig!"

For a man called 'grace' Madu certainly had none. Amsu found his contempt for the man growing with each passing hour. The man was a buffoon, but one that Amsu needed, for the moment. No, not a buffoon, a child. A child playing at a god. He could be taught, be brought to heel. Or he would be destroyed.

Amsu followed Madu onto the ship's boat, followed by the ever-silent Neb er Khalid and the Sightless Sisters. Twelve deck hands and under-clerics boarded as well, to row and assist in the excursion.

It was a short jaunt to the island from the ship. Madu complained about the comfortability of the boat the entire time. As soon as Amsu set foot on the island he felt it: Eimuria. The raw power of it filled him with elation. Could he feel elation? He must be able to. Yes, he could feel many things, now. One glace to Neb er Khalid and he saw the that the desiccated sorcerer felt it, too. He was stronger, here. So very much stronger.

The laborers hacked to widen the path left by the Porters and Khattabs. It would be an easy task to catch up to them, given that most of the work had already been done. They had barely begun their trek when the workers stopped, abruptly. In front of them was what could only be described as a mountain of discarded possessions. Hundreds, perhaps thousands, of years of clothing, armor and weapons lay before them, as well as various other accoutrements.

One of the under-clerics reached for a small pile of gemstones. Much more fascinating – and far more valuable to the right person – were the ancient Ateran coins next to the gems, but the young fool only saw the shiny and obvious prize. Madu slapped his hand away from the pile.

"Respect the dead," he said, looking about warily. "Especially in this place."

Worry not about the dead, Madu, Amsu thought. They will reclaim their own.

Amsu, Madu, and Neb er Khalid reached the other side of the mound. Several of the laborers were still clamoring down, cautiously grabbing at handholds. As Madu was brushing himself off, with very little warning, a giant figure burst through the side of the cleared path.

The beast's stench hit Amsu's nostrils as soundly as any fist. His eyes involuntarily blinked, sending tears down his cheeks. The scraps of clothing the creature wore for what passed as clothing were all but tatters. Its flesh was decayed like a worm-eaten corpse, bits of it falling off the bone. These were the Deathless, the undying servants of Gol-Adam. Fools who had given even their reward in death to that pompous fraud, and in return been granted this single-minded and grotesque form. Likely, they had added to their ranks over the years with the miscreants who had found their way to this place.

The giant grabbed the closest man it could, a poor young boy who tried backing away, but was not swift enough. In a casual toss, the young man was thrown aside, violently, as though he weighed nothing. He slammed hard into a tree and his back bent a severe and unnatural angle. He fell to the jungle floor, motionless.

A second worker turned to run and was greeted by the form of another monstrous guardian. The Deathless snatched him up from the ground with one hand and, grabbing him firmly with the other, tore the man in two as easily as a man breaks a crust of bread. Gore and viscera sprayed everywhere as the beast tossed the two halves of the man aside in fury.

Madu took cover behind Neb er Khalid. If not for his misguided sense of self-importance, the man would be cowering.

"Dispatch them!" he ordered the sorcerer, "Quickly!"

Neb er Khalid looked at the High Cleric as a man looks at an insect. The confused look on Madu's face was priceless. He has almost got it figured out, Amsu thought. If he were not so prideful, he would have, already.

The silent man-husk turned from Madu to the guardians. He raised a hand, palm out toward the Deathless.

"So Daa'a ku!" he said in a low, monotone register. The words startled everyone save Amsu. The guardian at whom Neb er Khalid had pointed flew

backward, pressed flat as if struck with a large sledgehammer. The giant crashed through trees, breaking them in two or tearing them from their roots. The sound of the monster flying lasted until it was well out of sight. Amsu wondered just how far it had gone.

"So Daa'a ku!" The second Deathless was propelled back in the same manner.

"Ha! Aha!" Madu cried, please with himself. "Well done! Well done!"

The thundering of giant footsteps brough yet another guardian into view, then another.

"Tu ra'e ma Daa'a ber'a!"

The words had barely escaped the desiccated magician's lips before the first of the new guardians raised into the air. Then, as if drawn and quartered by invisible horses, the giant's limbs and head were pulled from its torso, each landing with a sickening thud. Bits of the Deathless' decaying flesh rained down among the expeditionary group. One of the workers vomited.

"So ber'a, so Daa'a ka, so pet'esh!"

The remaining guardian burst into flames, a fire that reached impossibly high, burning so hot that many, including Madu, had to step back. It burned blue, then red, then orange. A loud and high-pitched whistling erupted from the pyre. When it finally burned out, the giant white bones of the Deathless stood on its knees, blackened loam all around it. It sat there, unmoving, and they radiated so much heat that none could approach.

"Yes...yes!" Madu said laughing. "Come, come now. We will reach the temple by sundown.

Amsu shared a look with Neb er Khalid. This was almost over.

CHAPTER TWELVE

"Thomas! Oh, gods...Thomas!"

Lea ran to her husband and friends. As soon as they heard her voice, the three stopped. Ana and Exra lay Thomas down close to the side of the temple. Exra fell backwards, awkwardly. His leg was set in a rudimentary splint. Ana, though appearing relatively uninjured, still looked as though she had been on the wrong side of an ure stampede.

"Oh, great Gilafred, Thomas! Is he...?"

"He is alive," Ana said, clasping her friend by the shoulder, "but he is unconscious. We have not been able to wake him."

"What happened? Was it those things? Those...dead giant things?"

"Yes, and no."

Ana and Exra took turns describing what had happened. Lea could hardly believe any of it. If she had heard from the mouths of anyone else, she would not have believed it. Her Thomas was neither warrior nor wizard. He had proven that he could hold his own in a fight, but this was insanity. Magic swords and lightning? It felt like a fever dream.

"I don't understand any of this," she confessed.

"Neither do we," Exra said. "Had I not seen these things for myself, I would not even believe them possible. Only the gods can do as such."

"Or perhaps an ancient sorcerer king," Lea mused.

"What do you mean?" asked Ana.

"I'm not sure yet, but I think we have been played from the start. Ex, your leg..."

"Is not as bad as it looks," Exra said. "Let's get to the entrance of the temple and away from the prying eyes of the jungle."

The entryway to the temple was as grand as the temple, itself. Bas reliefs and frescos lined the large outer double doors. They were scenes depicting the gods, many Lea did not recognize. Some she recognized but were out of context. Despite the supposed age of the structure and the time it had sat abandoned, the carvings and paintings on the walls looked to have been polished that day. Perhaps the guardians of the island spent their time not killing outsiders as janitors. The thought was so absurd it almost made Lea giggle.

They lay Thomas down, again, and trickled a small amount of water into his mouth. Lea sat next to him on the ground and gently stroked his hair. Exra took up a position of observation at the end of the entryway. He leaned heavily on his makeshift crutch. Lea felt a lump in her throat and tried with all her might to push it down. She bit her lip to distract herself. She would not cry, dammit! Not now, when they were so close.

"I wish you could see this, Love," she said to him. "I'd never be able to pull you away, but it would be better than the Golden Fields of Avar to you. I'll try to take some notes for you, but you were always the better scholar. I'm afraid you'll have a thousand questions that I won't be able to answer. So, if you could just wake up, please, it would save us all the trouble, later."

Her voice broke on the last few words, and she found herself crying despite her best efforts. She hated crying. She hated the way it made feel, the way it made her look like a circus clown...and worst of all, it made her feel weak. As a girl, she would cry whenever she got angry, and her father had said once that it made her seem frail. Men wanted vulnerable; they did not want frail. Like she gave a good god's piss what men wanted...

Would Thomas think her frail if he could see her? Would he see the ridiculous schoolgirl that she felt like? Or course he wouldn't. He idolized her, the silly sod. For the life of her, she did not know why, but she was grateful. Right now, she felt like she had not been grateful enough.

"I love you, you giant horse's ass," she whispered. "Please, please, wake up..."

Ana crouched and clasped her friend's hand in her own. She squeezed it, and Ana squeezed back. Lea burst into sobs, then. She tried to hold back at first, but it broke free, violently, like trying to hold back a sneeze. She sounded like a donkey braying, but she didn't care. Ana pulled her head into her shoulder and held her there until she stopped. Lea pulled back and, in the absence of a handkerchief, wiped her face with her dirty blouse.

"I'm sorry, Ana," she said.

"For what? For crying? There is no shame in crying, anymore than there is in laughing. Sadness must escape just as much as joy, or anger. And there are worse ways to let it out."

"Thank you."

"Let it be so," Ana replied. She glanced to Exra, who still held vigil at the end of the entryway. Lea was somewhat embarrassed knowing that Ex had heard her sobbing like that but knew he would never so much as mention it, not even to Ana, unless she brought it up first.

"He is lying," Ana said, her voice low.

"Lying? About what?"

"About his leg. He hides it well, but I saw it when Thomas and I set the splint. There are loose shards of bone at each break. If it is not addressed soon, it will turn to blood poisoning. If he were a horse, I would have put it down. As it is, amputation may be the safest course, if a healer cannot be found, soon. He will surely not survive the return trip across the sea."

"Why would he lie about that?"

"Because if we knew, we would force him to stay off of it. He does not wish to abandon us for his own safety."

"And why tell me?" Lea chose those words carefully. She knew that under normal circumstances, Ana would never act on this knowledge, respecting her husband's wisdom and skill. For her to be telling Lea this could be seen as a grave betrayal, and one Lea did not expect.

"Because you Westlanders may have strange ideas, but sometimes you are right. I cannot let him kill himself to satisfy his pride."

Now Lea understood. Ana wanted her to back her up should a dispute arise. Lea hoped that it would not come to that but gave her friend an understand nod. Nothing more needed to be said about the matter. A groan from Thomas drew her attention.

"Thomas? Thomas, can you hear me?"

Thomas opened his eyes, which did not seem to focus on anything. They darted about as if searching for something before finally coming to rest on Lea.

"Lea," he said, "are you dead, too?"

"No, my love. We are not dead."

"Oh." He almost sounded disappointed. "That's good. I was hoping the afterlife didn't hurt this badly. Are you all right?"

"That's what I'm supposed to say, you ridiculous fopdoodle."

She buried her head in his chest. Her body did not seem to know if it wanted to laugh or cry, and so a little bit of both slipped out.

"I was so worried about you," she said, raising her head to look him in the eyes. "What happened, Love? Do you remember?"

"He's...inside me, Lea," Thomas said, his face going stark. "I can feel him. Just Behind my eyes."

"Who, Love?"

"I don't know. One of the Wretched. He grows more powerful in this place. He's filled with anger. He wants free. Promise me, Lea... promise that no matter what happens you won't let him be free. I don't know if the world could survive it. Promise me!"

"What do you mean, Thomas? How..."

"If you must choose, if the time comes...you must not let him escape. You must do whatever it takes to stop him. No matter the cost."

"I don't know that I can, Thomas. Please don't ask that of me."

"It will be done, my friend," came a voice from behind. Lea nearly jumped. She had not heard Exra approach.

"Glad to see you still walk the land of the living," he said, extending his arm. Thomas took it, and he was hoisted to his feet.

"It has its benefits," Thomas said. "Speaking of walking, how is your leg?"

"It is to be as expected, painful and annoying. But, all things considered, it is fine, thank you."

Thomas' eyes narrowed, and a look of concern came over his face.

"No, Ex... it's not." He crouched to look at the leg and splint. "It's much worse than we thought. I'm surprised you didn't notice. If this isn't treated immediately you could lose the leg, or worse."

Exra look as though he were about to argue with Thomas, but Thomas did not give him the opportunity. He put both hands on Exra's leg and made a pensive face.

"I don't know if this will hurt or not, Ex. So... don't move."

Everyone waited for something to happen, but nothing did. After a few moments of holding Exra's leg, Thomas let it go and stood up. He looked at Ex, expectantly. Exra just stared back, seemingly unsure what to make of his friend's strange behavior.

"Well? Try it," Thomas said.

Exra look skeptical, but took a tentative step, putting weight on his injured leg. He then took another...and another. He tossed the crude crutch aside and began to walk faster in a circle. He even jogged a few paces before coming back to rest in front of Thomas.

"By all the gods," Lea exclaimed. "How?"

"If he's going to use me," Thomas said, determinedly, "then I'm going to use him."

Exra stood before Thomas with a conflicted look on his face. Lea knew that the Esisrian prejudice against magic was strong. Would Ex be upset that his life was saved by it? Did it matter that it was Thomas, or would he be wary because there was obviously some outside influence upon his friend? After a long moment, Exra extended his hand.

"Thank you, my friend." Thomas took his hand.

"Think nothing of it. Or consider it a partial repayment for all the times you've saved my hide from the fire."

"Promise me that you'll use this...power responsibly."

"You have my word, endiha," Thomas replied. They embraced.

"Now," Thomas continued, looking around at the temple for the first time, "I suggest we cease with the 'shill I, shall I' and get inside this cursed place. Just look at these frescos! Incredible..."

"I don't recognize many of the figures or poses," Lea said. "They don't seem to match any of the commonly depicted scenes from any mythology or history I know."

"These are older," said Thomas, "much, much older. The styling is definitely Prediluvian. This could be a history that's been forgotten or replaced. The pictograms are related to ancient Esisrian, but without any sort of reference we have no hope for translation. Only supposition."

"I believe that is meant to be Gol-Adam," Ana said pointing to bas relief depicting a man with golden, curly hair on his knees.

"I think you're correct," said Thomas, "but why is he on his knees? He isn't depicted thus in any representation I've heard of. Here he is, again, in this mural, but in chains."

"That cannot be," Ana said.

"As I said, Ana, we have no context for these. It could be purely metaphorical. It may not be Gol-Adam, at all."

"We could spend a lifetime trying to decipher these," Lea chimed in. "I know that would please my husband to no end – don't smile at me like that, you rapscallion – but time is not on our side, at the moment. Shall we?" She gestured toward the large double doors.

"Of course, Love," Thomas said, kissing Lea on the top of the head.

They all moved to stand in front of the doors. With a shrug, Thomas pulled the golden handles. The doors opened, easily, to everyone's surprise. Warily, they stepped inside.

Though the large room had no windows, there was a source of light emanating from somewhere. Lea could not see its source, but it illuminated the entirety of the room. It was round, with one giant mural painted the whole of the wall. It looked like one landscape, all around them, bleak and desolate. Lightning flashed in the oddly colored and swirling sky. There were four figures painted in the scene, in odd positions.

"Like the dreams," Thomas said, almost under his breath.

In the center of the room was a small pool of crystal-clear water and lined along the giant mural were stands on which stood jars. They looked like internment jars, to Lea, meant to hold the organs of the deceased. They were larger, however, and had no lids. On each was engraved an ancient Esisrian hieroglyph. Three small daises were spaced evenly apart in front of the pool, consisting of a small pedestal on a slight step, with a fourth behind the others. There were no other exits from the chamber.

"It looked much bigger from the outside," quipped Lea.

Suddenly, the outer doors slammed shut. Exra ran to them, pushing as hard as they could, but they would not budge.

"I think we are committed," Thomas stated.

"What now?" Exra asked, finally giving up on the doors.

"I believe we are to put the jars on the pedestals," Ana replied, "but which jars on which pedestals?"

"Awfully cliché," said Lea.

"I'm sure it was much more original four thousand years ago," Thomas answered. He walked back and forth along the wall, studying the giant painting.

"What is written on the jars?" Lea asked.

"Would it not be the various organs they should contain?" posited Exra.

"That would make sense," Lea said. "You don't suppose we'll have to fill them, do you?"

Ana and Exra gave each other a dark look.

"No," Thomas interjected, "I don't think it's organs, at all. I believe it's parts of the soul. After all, isn't that what all of this has been about?"

"So, we're to fill the jars with souls? That's not possible."

"The ancient clerics could do it. Perhaps they were the only ones meant to pass."

"And we're meant to starve to death, here?"

"I'm not suggesting we give up. I'm merely pointing out possibilities. Look," he said, pointing at the mural, "this woman is somewhat translucent, and see that her feet don't touch the ground? And this woman on the right in on one knee, clutching at her chest. This man in the center is lying prone. His eyes are opened, so he's not asleep. And behind him is another man, and see how he is glowing, slightly?"

"Thomas," started Lea, "what does is all mean?"

"I don't know," he replied after a slight pause.

"Oh, ure's bollocks..." Lea swore.

"Patience, Love, Patience."

"This jar, here," Ana said, "the symbol is Bagh, the body." Thomas turned to her.

"Quite right!"

"And here," she continued, "is Kagh."

"This one I recognize from your rubbing as Pagagh," Lea stated, pointing at a jar.

"That only leaves eight jars," said Thomas, somewhat dejectedly. "I wish I had my rubbings with me. I have my notes, but the reference would be invaluable."

He opened his satchel and retrieved his notes. He began thumbing through them, mumbling to himself as he did so.

"This one," Exra said. "I believe it means, 'answer.' It hangs above the archway to the cleric's vestibule in temple services."

"I think you're right, Ex," Lea said, smiling, "well done!"

"No," Thomas said, thoughtfully. "Not 'answer.' More like, 'sum.' Yes...yes! That's it! Look...the three parts – the bagh, kagh, and pagagh – make up the 'sum' of man. That's it!"

Thomas ran to the closest identified jar, ja'gagh, 'The Sum,' and lifted it from its stand.

"Place them on the pedestals as they are in the painting," he said.

They each took one and placed it on the dais. Nothing happened.

"Perhaps we need to stand on the dais, as well?"

He stepped up onto the small step. Lea stepped up behind her jar, kagh. Exra put on foot on his dais before Thomas turned to him and yelled, "no!" so forcefully that Ex took a step back. A small bolt flew past Exra and clanged into the wall, shattering. Exra stood there with wide eyes.

"How..."

"The painting," Thomas answered, pointing. Pagagh is female, Bagh is male. Switch with Ana."

Lea wanted to tell him how nonsensical that was but could not find a justification for it. After all she had seen in the past few days, it made about as much since as anything else. She looked to see where the bolt had come from but could not identify any holes or alcoves that could have hidden a small crossbow. In any case, that had to be a one-time trap. She hoped.

Ana and Exra stepped tentatively onto their new daises, but again, nothing happened. Thomas looked disappointed but determined.

"Should we fill them?" Ana suggested.

"With...parts of the soul?" asked Lea.

"With water. Perhaps it is a pressure plate."

"What if we overfill them?" asked Ex.

"The alternative is waiting until we die of thirst," Ana said. "I say we try."

"Since the bagh, kagh, and pagagh each make up a third of the soul, perhaps we should fill each a third full?"

"That makes sense," said Thomas. "And ja'gagh...should it be full?"

"Worth a try," Lea said.

They all took their jars to the pool and filled them. Thomas struggled with his, as it must have weighed several stone when completely full. Lea, herself, was almost unable to get hers back onto the pedestal with it only a third full.

Once they all had their jars in position, they stepped up onto the steps. Still, nothing. Thomas stepped down and began pacing.

"Maybe," Lea postulated, "the ja'gagh should be empty? To receive the parts of the soul?"

"Yes!" Thomas said. He grabbed his jar and hauled it over the pool, pouring the water back out. He placed it back on the pedestal and tried again. The silence was deafening.

"Dammit!" Thomas yelled. For a moment, Lea was afraid he might smash his jar. He put his hands to his head and grunted in frustration. She was not quite sure what to do in this situation.

"Love?" she quested.

He put a hand up to stop her and she almost yelled at him, but the look on his face made her take pause. His head was tilted slightly, as if listening to something.

"Yes, of course," he said, "of course! Everyone...pour your water into my jar."

"But, yours was just..."

"I know," he cut her off. "Just trust me."

They all did as he asked, then put their jars back in place. On his signal, they all stepped onto the daises. A loud, dull thud shook the room, making Lea jump. It sounded like it came from deep within the temple. The sound of running water could be heard, and when she looked, Lea saw that the pool was draining.

"What does that mean?" Ana asked.

They all stepped off their daises and approached the pool. The water had drained from it, completely, leaving an empty round indentation in the floor, only a few hands deep.

"Do you suppose...?" Lea asked.

Thomas just shrugged and stepped into the empty pool. Nothing malicious seemed apparent, so the others followed suit. Almost immediately as the last of them had stepped in, the floor beneath them began to drop. The four gasped in unison, as the pool slowly lowered them into the floor. Lea looked up at the long shaft that was left behind them until the opening was little more than a pinprick of light in the deep black of the ceiling.

There really was no turning back, now

The lift lowered the four companions into what appeared to be a cavern, at first glance. The same mysterious light source illuminated the area as the room above, though much dimmer. Lea supposed it made transition easier on the eyes. They stepped out into the large area, cautiously.

Thomas ran his hand along the wall.

"This was carved, not a natural formation."

The four made their way down the passageway which, natural or not, twisted and turned like a serpent. It was not long before Lea was not sure what direction the were heading, anymore. There was a definite downward slope the cavern, leading them deeper and deeper into the depths of the island.

"I was thinking," Thomas said, suddenly, "that it was serendipitous that we had exactly what the gate needed. To unlock it, I mean. Two men and two women. Seems an awfully specific coincidence, yes?"

"A little too specific, if you ask me," Lea replied.

"My thoughts, exactly."

The winding grotto finally opened into a much larger cave. The floor sloped downward and ended at an underground lake, complete with a dock. A small rowboat was moored there. The water in the lake was strange, shiny and metallic, silver in color. Lea could not see the other side of the lake.

"Not more boats," Thomas moaned.

"Be careful," Exra said as they approached the dock, "this is quicksilver."

"A whole lake of quicksilver?" Lea said, incredulously.

"I'm not a student of the physical sciences, Ex," Thomas said, "but wouldn't the quicksilver be absorbed into the ground?"

"Not if the basin were lined with lead. Look, the boat and dock are so protected."

Exra was right, Lea saw. The wood of the dock, steelwood, no doubt, had been painted with a coating of lead. The brush strokes were still viable on the planks. The bottom of the boat looked to be a solid plate of lead.

"How do you know so much about quicksilver, Ex?" Lea asked.

"I have studied poisons. And their antidotes," he amended, quickly.

"And what is the antidote for quicksilver?"

"There is none. Be sure to cover your mouths. The fumes can be deadly, as well."

"Fantastic," Thomas said smiling. "Rowing across sea of poison on a boat made of poison to unknown dangers on the other side. Remind me again why I didn't take that teaching position you talked me out of? 'You'd be bored,' isn't that what you said?"

"Get in," Lea said, shoving him.

The lake was not as large as Lea initially believed, the other shore being just out of sight and around a bend. The oars felt strange in the quicksilver, more buoyant than water. It was at once thicker than she would have guessed, and yet it was somehow smoother. It was definitely an odd sensation. Thomas, for his part, did not seem as ill either, thankfully. Lea felt a tingle run over her arms and body as she rowed, like pure Eimuria dancing on her skin. Whether that was a property of quicksilver or just the raw energy of the place, she did not know.

The other side of the lake had no dock, forcing them to step out into quicksilver. They made sure to get as much off their boots as they could. The passage continued for some distance until it ended at a door. It was a very plain door, like one might see on any building in Anthumbra, the frame carved into the rock of the cavern, itself.

"Surprisingly modern design," noted Thomas.

"What are these runes around the door, Love?"

"Some sort of protection glyphs, I believe. Wards of some kind."

"To keep something out?" Ana asked, "Or, in?"

Thomas reached for the handle and opened the door. It opened into a very plain, square, white room. Directly opposite the door they entered was a stone archway. It, too, had the same warding runes lining the frame. In the center of the arc was stained glass, its colorful surface permanently displaying the curvy symbols of a long dead language.

"Another coincidence?" Lea mused.

"What do you mean?" asked Ana.

"The language in the arch. It's called Vasik Lex."

"But why is that a coincidence?"

"Because Thomas is quite possibly the only person alive who can read it."

All eyes turned to Thomas, who looked somewhat abashed.

"Well, I... I don't really know if I can or not, to be honest."

"I don't understand," Exra said, "I've never heard of this language. What is it, and why is it here?"

"Well," Thomas began, "it's fiercely debated in academic circles. The language itself is nearly impossible to date, or to connect to any particular culture. It's been found in digs dating back to prediluvian times, but only ever in fragments, and all over Anthumbra.

"You see, it's a featural language, meaning that the symbols that make up the language go one step beyond phonemes."

Ana raised her hand.

"Right. For example, we are speaking Anthumbran Common, a language with a written phonemic script. Each sound of a word is its own letter. The letters are written and when read aloud, form the words, yes? Esisrian is syllabic. Each symbol represents a combination of sounds that make up a word, usually a vowel and a consonant sound, not necessarily.

"A featural system of writing, like Vasik Lex, is much more complex, with each symbol only forming part of a sound, and other symbols that can indicate inflection, tone, articulation. In fact, it is the most complex featural language ever discovered."

"But why is this of interest?" Exra said, problematically.

"Because!" Thomas said, astounded, "Because the oldest find of Vasik puts it at least five thousand years old, when every other written language was still logographic, meaning each symbol represented an entire word. The most advanced written language of all time supposedly existed while men were still painting a bird to mean 'bird!'"

"Perhaps it is not a human language," Ana suggested.

"That's actually the most prevalent theory. Some have suggested a form of Dwarven, despite it not matching known dwarven languages in style, or even being found in dwarven ruins. The Aelfin have outright denied it, but some still maintain they are lying to hide something. Some have suggested it belonged to another race, forgotten in Anthumbra, while other have suggested it's..."

"The language of the gods," Exra finished.

"Just so. Unfortunately, there's never been enough of the language found to perform accurate translation. Those who don't support the idea of it being a non-human language have perpetuated the idea that it's all an elaborate hoax."

"To what end?" Ana inquired.

"Who knows?" Thomas shrugged, "Some people don't need logical reasoning. I find that there are three types of people when presented with information they don't understand: attribute it to magic or the gods, call it a hoax, or keep looking for answers, knowing that they don't have to understand something for it to exist."

"This still doesn't explain why you might be able to translate this," Exra said. "If no one has enough of the language to decipher, how can you read it?"

"My linguistics professor, Doctor Bolivar, claimed he had found the key to translating Vasik Lex, an ancient stone tablet he called the Lex Apantisi. He spent years trying to translate every scrap of Vasik anyone had ever recorded. Before he died, he was practically obsessed with it. He lost his position at the university and fell into poverty. When he died, everything he owned was sold to pay his debts. The Lex Apantisi disappeared.

"I tried to track down who may have purchased it, but there was no record of it being sold with his belongings. I managed to get my hands on his notes, however, and studied them, extensively."

"Obsessively," Lea said, rolling her eyes.

"Yes, well...had it not been for Lea, I may have suffered the same fate as the good doctor."

"Do you think you can translate this, Love? I'm not opposed to simply smashing the glass, at this point, but something tells me that won't work, unfortunately."

"Let me see..."

Thomas studied the archway intently. He ran his fingers in the air in the lines and shapes of the lettering. He took out his notebook and started writing, glancing up on occasion. He crossed a few lines out and rewrote them. When it finally seemed like he had finished, he turned back to the others, a slightly bemused look on his face.

"It's a poem," he said.

"A what?" Lea said, skeptically.

"A poem. And not a particularly pleasant one."

"None of the roses and sunsets you Westlanders call romance?" Ana asked, smirking.

"I'm afraid not. Listen:

Woe, but built we in this place

The pillars of Eternal Grace

"Look upon these works," said we

"From shore to shore and sea to sea"

Thought we perfect in execution

Forgone the ire of ablution

Saw the world built for all years

Tumble 'round like falling tears

For in the haste to birth creation

Built upon a cracked foundation

And worshipped like the distant star

Said, "gaze upon how great we are"

Not knowing how we made, once more

The mistakes of those who came before

"Then this last part is separate: 'Abandon thy faith, oh faithful; Discard thy hope, oh hopeful; Cast off thy courage, oh courageous. Enter, and weep.'"

"I think I preferred the roses and sunsets," said Ana. "How is it that it rhymed?"

"Oh, I took some liberty. It's far more depressing in the original."

"So, how do we..." Lea said, making a gesture indicating entering the archway.

"Well, uh...I don't know."

"Oh, for the sake of the sacred!" Lea exclaimed. "Is there nothing on there that tells us how to open that damned thing? Just a bloody poem?"

"Perhaps the answer is in the poem, itself?" Ana posited. "Or maybe the final statement is telling us that we must abandon our faith to enter?"

Lea had enough maybes. She marched up to the archway, determinedly.

"Maybe I'll just push on the bloody thing and see if it opens."

Ignoring the protests from Thomas behind her, she extended her arm to cautiously push on the glass. As her hand touched it, the colored crystal rippled, like water. It was cold, colder than ice. The chill ran up her arm like Eimuria dancing along her skin. It was not painful, but it was startling, shocking...it took her breath away as it washed over her body

She tried to pull her hand back but found that she could not move. Her fingers broke the surface of the glass, as if it were a pond, but it felt oily and permeating as the ripples lapped her fingertips like small, prismed waves. She felt pulled into the glass, as if she were looking down at it from above. Something moved beneath the surface, or behind it; she could not tell which, anymore. Panic struck her and she redoubled her efforts to pull away. She tried to yell, to cry out to Thomas, but her voice was lost. She turned to him, and saw that he was frozen mid-stride, hand outreached to stop her. Ana and Exra stood motionless, as well, concern upon their faces.

Something grabbed her wrist, suddenly, and she spun back to face the archway. A hand, white as fresh snow, held her arm in a death-grip, its fingernails gnarled and cracked. It squeezed, and Lea tried to cry out in pain, but again, no sound escaped her lips. The hand jerked her toward the arch, and she fought against it, to no avail. With a swift yank, she was pulled forward and into the liquid glass. She plunged in, and the icy cold abyss enveloped her.

"Lea!" Thomas yelled as he saw his wife pulled into the archway.

She had barely touched the stained glass when she seemed to be pulled in, lifted off of her feet and into the glass. Thomas ran to the arch and tried to enter in the same fashion, sprinting headfirst into the colorful crystal. It was as solid as stone, and he bounced off of it with all the grace that stone provided.

Ana ran to his side as he hit the floor, clutching his head. His vision blurred, as everything was surrounded by a white halo, and he saw double. Stars danced around his head. Ana tried to help him up, but he waved her away. He was in no shape to stand.

Exra stood before the archway and hesitantly probed the edges with his matchet. Thomas knew it would be of use. The Archway had taken Lea, and it would not return her until it had finished with her. If it returned her, at all.

CHAPTER THIRTEEN

"Hard to port! Show them our aft, Mister Baca!"

The Randy Beast swung about slowly, but not so slow as the Carrion Crow. Pedraza thought the name of the bigger ship too apropos, as they fell into battle with her. Though the Beast flew her battle ensign high, the Carrion Crow had made no defensive move or preemptive strikes before Pedraza ordered the first volley. The captain assumed that they either meant to call the Beast's bluff or were a very inexperienced crew; perhaps both. By the time the men had reloaded, the Crow had prepared its own return volley, showering the Beast and her crew with lead shot and arrows.

Though obviously Eimurial-powered, the Carrion Crow was a sluggish brute, unable to even keep up with the Beast's slow movement. She was steel reinforced, which made for a much more cumbersome vessel, but easily deflected the Randy Beast's fiercest attacks. All it took was a few lucky shots on the part of the Crow to undo all the repair work they had done in the past few days.

The two ships circled each other, the Beast always slightly ahead. They had each fired several rounds of catapult and ballista, and while Pedraza and his crew had so far managed to avoid any serious hits, the best of their strikes were bouncing right off the enemy hulls, doing little to no damage. Pedraza was not sure this was a fight they could win, but without destroying or driving off the larger ship, there was no way to extract the men and women he had left on the island, were they even still alive.

"Shall we retreat, sir?" Baca said as the ship came about.

"Nay, we're just giving her a smaller target." The captain was not sure his answer was entirely true.

He watched another volley of catapult shot ricochet off the hull of the Crow. A ballista bolt lodged itself just above the keel; they would be taking on water, now, but not enough to be a serious threat. The men looked at him, expectantly, and he knew why. They wanted him to pull another stunt like the oil. But this was no fight against strange and invisible magic. They were merely outclassed, and that was not something Pedraza was willing to break the Law for, even if it meant their deaths. Some things were still sacred, even in the face of the afterlife.

A lead sphere hit the rear of the Beast, sending shards of timber flying. Now they were taking on water, as well, only the breach was larger, and they had less room for the water. Perhaps retreat was the prudent action, after all.

A second catapult shot collided with the main mast. Slivers went flying like jagged rain, and the mainsail tumbled to the deck below. The debate about retreat had been close before it had even opened. They were dead in the water.

Pedraza cast a gaze to his crew. His career was finished, he knew that. But these lads all had long lives ahead of them. No need for them to go down with him. The Porters would be on their own, but the Randy Beast could no longer help them, one way or another. Surrender was the only option left.

"Strike the colors, Mister Bustos," he called, surprised at how calm he felt.

"Sir?" Bustos replied, "Are you sure?"

"Aye, Mister Bustos. We're done for. Strike the colors and raise the white."

The crew lowered the battle ensign and raised the white flag of surrender. Every man on the deck laid down his arms and waited for the boarding party that would come to take them prisoner. They may even try to salvage the Beast, but in these waters, they might also simply scuttle the old girl. She was an old but proud ship and had served more than one master better than most.

Suddenly, another volley of catapult shot flew through the air from the Carrion Crow. The cries of alarm rose up across the ship. Two ballista bolts struck true, shivering the hull to the lower decks. The Beast began to list to port as she took on more and more water.

"We surrender!" Bustos yelled, "We surrender, ya briny traitors! Captain, The Law! They cannot attack a ship waving the white!"

"I do not think they care, Mister Bustos," the captain replied. Then, he yelled, "All hands! Abandon ship! To the lifeboats, men! Abandon ship!"

Pedraza ran back to his cabin and stuffed an old cloth sack with the irreplaceable treasures he had collected over the years. Not the gold and jewels, nor even the fancy trappings he had acquired, but the journal and maps of his great grandfather, and all the notes he had gathered throughout his life at sea. A life that may be at an end, even should he survive, but perhaps others may pick up where he had left off.

Another fired shot rocked the ship and almost brought Pedraza to his knees. He ran out of the cabin and back onto the deck. The Beast was listing badly, now, and would be below the sea in little time. The captain waved the remaining men into lifeboats and stood on the tilted bow of his ship.

"Goodbye, old girl," he said. "May Andrella love ya as much as I have."

There was a loud crack, like thunder, that came from the other ship, followed by a plume of black smoke that rose from the far side. An explosion? Did their Eimurial engines erupt as the small ships had? If so, it was by Andrella's grace, as Captain Pedraza was sure they had not done nearly enough damage to the other ship.

There was another explosion, then another, and two more in quick succession. The black smoke was joined by visible flames, engulfing the bow of the larger ship. By all the devils of all the seas, what was happening over there?

Pedraza made his way to the last lifeboat, where Mister Baca waited for him.

"What's happening, Captain?"

"By Illia and Allia I know not, but I'll not question a gift from The Lady. Let's get these men to safety while those lawless bastards are distracted."

With Pedraza in one boat and Bustos in another, they led the surviving crew to the shore of a nearby island, barely large enough to be called such. After an accounting, the crew of the doomed ship watched in awe as the ship they had so recently been defeated by was racked with explosions. The steel reinforced hull cracked like an egg, and the vessel started to sink, billowing the sickly black smoke. Soon, the smoke was so thick that it obscured the other ship, completely, and they were deprived the satisfaction of watching it drift below the calm waters.

"By all the gods, captain," Baca said, "what just happened?"

Before he could answer, someone yelled, "ahoy!" They all strained to see through the smoke. Moments after the Carrion Crow must have dipped beneath the blue, another ship broke through the slowly dissipating smoke. It was smaller even than the departed Randy Beast, and it flew no colors. It was coming fast, under its own power. Pedraza drew his saber, as did any man who still had one. The captain wished he had salvaged his spyglass.

When the ship got close enough, he could see three figures upon its forward bow. One man was dark and looked like an aged fighter. He was a stern figure, bearded in the Eastlands fashion. Pedraza assumed him to be the captain of the mysterious ship. Another man was younger and dressed in the fashion of the Westlands. He looked like a servant of some kind, possibly a ship's steward, though an odd one, if Pedraza had ever seen one.

The third figure was much shorter, and Pedraza would have pegged her for a young boy, but the lass was waving and shouting to the stranded survivors, "ahoy! Ahoy, there!" She reminded him intensely of...but, that couldn't be...

"Mistress Porter?" he called back to her.

The small woman stopped waving and put her hands squarely on her hips.

"We look NOTHING alike!" she yelled.

Madu covered his face with his handkerchief as he looked over the lake of quicksilver. There was no odor, but Amsu knew the high cleric would be familiar with the vapor's effects. They both stood on the lead-coated dock and looked out over the magnificent scene.

Neb er Khalid remained on the shore, several paces away from the lake. Madu gestured for him to join him on the dock, but the sorcerer refused. Amsu could see Madu's ire growing in the face of the supposed disobedience. The old man marched off the dock and up to the desiccated figure. He grabbed the man's robe. Amsu crossed the distance between them in an instant, startling the guardsman who saw him.

"I order you to take us across this lake!" Madu demanded of Neb er Khalid.

The ancient wizard grunted angrily in response, which did little to impress the high cleric. Amsu put his hand on Madu's shoulder, causing the old man to jump, startled. He turned angrily to Amsu.

"What do you think you're doing? Am I to be surrounded by Insubordination?"

Amsu squeezed Madu's shoulder hard enough to make him cry out in pain. The look of confusion, anger, and disbelief was delicious.

"The quicksilver is harmful to him," Amsu said, "crossing it will cause him great pain."

"You...you speak!" Madu explained as Amsu released the cleric's shoulder.

"We must cross this quicksilver, my friend, to make you whole, again," Amsu said to Neb er Khalid, ignoring Madu. "Can you endure?"

Neb er Khalid grunted in acquiescence. He turned to the silver lake, arms outstretched. With noticeable strain, the old Eimurian tensed, as if laboring to lift a heavy weight. Up and up he gestured with his hands. The cavern began a low and steady rumble. The guardsman looked about, anxiously, as rocks tumbled from the ceiling to the lake below. Even Madu looked apprehensive, though he was wise enough to not voice it. Beads of sweat appeared on Ned er Khalid's forehead, tinged with the yellow of iodine. The strain on him must be immense, indeed, Amsu thought.

A pillar of rock protruded from the large body of quicksilver, then another. More and more they appeared, until a clear path across the lake could be seen. When the route was complete, Neb er Khalid collapsed to his knees in pain. Amsu placed a hand on his head, comfortingly.

"Well, done, old friend...well done."

"Come," Madu said, heading for the first new pillar in the lake, "they are still some distance ahead."

"We will let him rest!" Amsu snapped at the cleric, who jumped back. For all his foolish posturing, the man had some sense, after all. Perhaps Amsu would not have to kill him.

"W-what..." the high cleric stammered, "what are you? Who are you?"

"I am nothing more than what you made me, High Cleric. Did you think you could play at forces you barely understood and suffer no ill effects? Your paltry understanding of this world does not have the words to describe what my brethren and I are. What you could become if you but possess the will.

"But," he rounded on Madu, "you have done remarkably well with surprisingly little. Like the first men to steal fire from nature, or the first to bend Eimuria to their command, you have acted with naught but will. I will teach you, High Cleric. Will you be taught? Will you learn what it means to be of the race of Men?"

"Y-yes," Madu answered, head lowered.

"Excellent."

Neb er Khalid had risen, once more, looking no worse for his colossal effort in raising the rocks from the depths. Amsu knew the quicksilver had put an enormous burden on what would have normally been a parlor trick. He nodded at the sorcerer.

"Come, High Cleric, and rejoice. You are about to seize your destiny."

Lea placed her fingers on the keys of the spinet and began playing. It was a song called, All The Flowers Fair And The Ladies They Woo, and it was Phillip's favorite song. Not because of the title or its implications, but how the notes danced and jumped around. It was a difficult and fun song to play. Lea did her best to do the song, and Phillip, justice, but she was not the musician that he was. She had practiced for days to play it, and it was barely passible. Luckily, no one was really listening.

Lea finished playing and noticed that her hands were trembling. She tried to stop them, which only made them shake worse. She put them in her lap and looked about the drawing room. It was filled with people she did not know and who did not know her, or Phillip. Friends and acquaintances of her father's, there to offer condolences. They did not see the girl at the spinet. They did not hear the jaunty song, so out of place at a wake.

"That was beautiful," a voice said, startling her. "He would have loved it."

A young woman with flame red hair sat on the bench next to Lea. It was obvious that she had been crying, and quite a bit. Her eyes were red and bloodshot, and though makeup tried to hide the dark circles under her eyes, to Lea they were plain as day. It was Lucy, Phillip's betrothed. They were to have been married in a month. She wore the engagement ring on a chain around her neck.

"It wasn't very good," Lea replied.

"Nonsense!" Lucy said, putting her arm around Lea. "It was wonderful. I must have listened to Philip play that song a hundred times, and that was just as good as any time he played it."

"You're a terrible liar," Lea said, but she smiled, despite herself.

"It's the feeling, you see," Lucy placed her hands on the keys and began plunking notes, slowly. "Phil missed notes all the time, but no one ever noticed. Do you know why? Because he played with feeling. The song did not just come out of the spinet, but out of him. He made the mistakes part of the song, so they really weren't mistakes, at all."

Lucy began to play faster, and Lea recognized the song as another of Phillip's favorites, The Fairy Circle. Lea knew this one by rote, and joined in, playing the higher notes while Lucy played the lower. It was a much easier song, but still fun to play, and just as out of place as the other. They finished one play-though of the song and immediately went into a second, this time improvising in places that forced the other player to change it up. They giggled as they did so, and it felt wonderful. Lea was beginning to think she may never laugh, again.

When they finished, Lucy kissed Lea on the top of her head, and rested her cheek there. It felt right to Lea. It was the first thing in days to do so.

"I hate all of these people," Lucy said, suddenly. "I hate all of them. Not one of them knew Phillip, loved him. They're here because it would be rude not to be, even for such a small noble house. They're here to save face, and nothing more. I'd send them each to a different Hell if I could."

"I can't cry," Lea said.

"That's all I've done," Lucy relied with a mirthless laugh.

"I've tried, I want to. I even burned my arm with a fire iron," she pulled up the sleeve of her blouse to show Lucy the burn mark, "but I can't. I cry when Jewel takes the last sweet roll, but when I think of Phillip all I feel is a dead pit in my stomach, like a stone. How will he know I loved him if I can't cry?"

"Oh, dear heart, he knew. He knows. You girls meant so much to him. He couldn't wait to make you aunts, although sometimes I think he just wanted...well, never mind that for now. Where is Jewel? Is she still locked in your room?"

"Yes. She won't come out. Mother thinks she is too young to understand, but she knows. She's not as foolish as she pretends to be. I told her that in Esisria it's custom to sit with the deceased until the body is interred, so that the kagh doesn't get lost, and that it's better if it's a relative or loved one, but she said she doesn't want to see him this way."

"We all grieve in our own way," Lucy said, gently rubbing Lea's back.

"Did you know that in Atera and parts of Red Fjord that it's customary to read to the dead, sometimes for as long as a month after internment? In case the spirit is lost or confused or scared. I think that's extremely sweet."

Lucy brushed Lea's hair away from her eyes.

"You remind me so much of him, sometimes," she said, a few tears escaping her eyes.

"I'm sorry!" Lea apologized.

"No! Never. I think it's magnificent. It makes me feel like maybe a part of him is still here." She kissed Lea on the forehead, again, and the two of them sat in silence for a while. A silence that was broken by a crash from across the room as a tray of drinks was knocked out of a servant's hands.

"Cursed!" Lea's father, the Lord Sebastian Barracourt yelled. He threw his own empty glass down, barely missing a minor noble. His fine clothing was askew, his jacket open and disheveled. He was clearly inebriated

"Cursed by the gods! Not only must I endure such poverty in my lifetime, but my only heir is taken by plague? To leave me with what? Not one, but two daughters! Two! And a barren wife. The Barracourt line will end with me!"

He fell to his knees in front of Phillip's casket, weeping. A nobleman Lea had never seen tried awkwardly to comfort him, but he swatted the man's hand away.

"Don't touch me!" He turned his gaze upward and cried, "Why? What have I ever done to deserve such a fate? In a life of hardship, you do this to me? This is the one you take? Are you even there? Do you even care about ones such as we? I denounce you for cursing me thusly!" He threw himself to the ground and continued to weep, though his words were muffled and slurred. Lea could not make them out and was glad for it.

Lucy put her arm around Lea and looked her in the eye.

"He is drunk," she said, "and grieving. He doesn't mean that."

But Lea knew differently. Even at such an early age, she could see that her father had never really loved or cared for her, or Jewel. She did not understand the reasons, the social standings, the politics of court that her lord father had been all but obsessed with. He treated everyone like things. A thing to be won, or thing to be used. A thing to be sold or tossed away. The only exception that Lea had ever seen was her brother, Phillip, who now lay in a casket on a stand in their drawing room, never to wake, again.

"We all grieve in our own way," Lucy repeated as she gently rocked Lea back and forth on the bench. "He doesn't mean it."

But he did mean it, Lea knew. She had not wanted to admit it, but there was no denying it now. And, as much of a drunken fool that he was, he had been right about one thing, something else he taught her, that day:

There were no gods.

The world shifted, like a shimmering pond. Lea was dizzy for a moment, then shook it off. She was standing at the top of the guard tower, looking down at the fort outpost. What had she just been thinking about? It was so long ago, but she felt as if she had been there. At Philip's wake. What an odd time to think about that. And Lucy...Lucy, who had said they would never lose touch, but less than a year later was gone. A sad time in her life, to be sure.

More sad than this, she wondered? She gazed down at Thomas, who was still excited, in spite of everything. Thomas, who had used so much money in tracking this ruin, and who had called in untold favors with the Aelfin to ensure they had accurate information. Undaunted Thomas.

The Aelfin had left nothing but the walls when they left. No weapons, no armor, no artifacts, no artwork...nothing. Not a damned thing. This entire fort may as well be a children's playground. The workers they had hired were still wary; local folklore said this whole area was haunted, but they kept up with Thomas, who still managed to find things for them to do.

She could see Ana and Exra from the tower, as well. They looked to be searching for anything of value, examining outbuildings and barracks with extreme attention to detail and care. Lea know that they would find nothing. She put her back against the wall, slid to floor, buried her head in her knees, and cried.

After a short time, she heard someone climbing the ladder to the guard tower. She quickly wiped her eyes, as if that would hide her tears from anyone, and watched as Thomas peeked his head into the lookout area.

"Lea?"

"Yes, Love," she answered, sniffling.

"What's the matter?"

"What's the matter? Thomas? What's the matter? There's nothing here! Nothing!"

"That's not entirely true, Love," he replied, "the fort is here."

"Thomas, who cares? We knew the fort was here. Everyone knew the fort was here."

"No, everyone suspected..."

"It's the same damned thing, and you know it!" She stood up and looked down at him. It was one of the few times that she could, and she was not going to waste it.

"Just because we were the first people to find nothing doesn't make it any more than nothing. We still don't know why they came here, how they got here, who they brought, why they left...Thomas, we can't even be certain the fort is Aelfin. We have nothing!

"And I'm tired of nothing, Thomas. So very tired. I'm tired of every dig being our last. I'm tired of being laughed at, and I'm tired of almost bankrupting your family's business every time we step out the door. I'm tired of working so hard for so very little in return. I can't do this anymore, Thomas. I just can't."

"Lea..."

"No, Thomas. I know what you're going to say. I know the location of the ruin is worth something to the Aelfin. I know that. But we're scholars, first and foremost. Perhaps we can get positions in university delves or working with salvage teams."

"That's easy fruit to pick," Thomas said, disappointed.

"But it's fruit, Thomas. It's something. It may not be the find of the century, but wouldn't it be better to find something? Anything?" She sat back down.

Thomas climbed the rest of the way into the guardhouse in the tower. He sat with his back against the wall, next to her, and put his hand on her knee.

"Love, I would rather spend the rest of my life failing at the extraordinary than batting at the easy bowls. Not for the money, and not for the fame. To be the first people to set foot in a place that no one has seen in thousands of years? To find a treasure thought lost? To breathe the same air as someone who lived before The Flood? That's why I do this, Love. Sometimes I forget we can even make money doing this.

"But I don't want to do any of those things if you're not with me. If you say you want to run salvage in the Yellow Sea, or open an antique shop in market square, or rescue cats from trees, then that's where I want to be, as well. None of this means anything without you."

"I love you, Thomas," she said, kissing his cheek.

"I love you, too. Now," he said, standing, "if I don't get down there, those men will dawdle to no end."

"What could you possibly have them doing?"

"Well, very soon, I'm going to have them help me fry up those fish we caught. I wouldn't tarry too long, were I you. You know how Ana loves my cooking."

"That's not what she says when you aren't around," she said as he began to climb back down the ladder.

"Lies!" he called back up, "Lies and slander!"

Lea sat there for quite some time, not leaving until the sun began to dip below the horizon. She thought long and hard about what Thomas had said, but she would come to no conclusions, this night. She stood, supposing that she had better get some of that fish before it was gone. Despite her teasing, Thomas really did know how to cook.

Lea shook her head as the world shimmered once more. Her memories seemed so real, today, so vivid. More so even than a dream, like one that sticks with you long after waking. She needed to shake it off and get back to the task at hand. Which was...

Where in the Hundred Hells was she? She had no idea. Nor could she say what she had been doing before her mind wandered off on her.

That happened more and more of late. She revisited the past, and why not? It was so much better, even the horrible parts.

She was in the sitting room, she realized, reading her old journals. No wonder she was daydreaming about the past. It was all her waking mind thought of, so why not her unconscious mind? It would be a lovely thing to think of in her last moments in this world. She looked over to the glass and decanter on the end table. The glass was empty. It was only a matter of time, now.

"So, you're really going through with it?" Thomas said. She looked up to the chair across from hers. Thomas sat there, looking just as he had all those years ago. What would he look like now, she wondered? Just as handsome, probably. Distinguished, no doubt, as only older men looked, even when they were complete fools. Would his hair have turned grey? Or would it have fallen out? She pictured both, his hair mostly gone but with wisps of thin, grey hair flailing about that she would have to keep tame for him, the poor clod.

"You're not him," she said to the man across from her.

"Can you be sure?" he said with a wry smirk.

"Reasonably. Firstly, my Thomas wouldn't taunt me like that. Secondly – and perhaps most importantly - he's quite dead."

"Could I not be his spirit? Escaped from the underworld? Perhaps Arrak allowed me to visit, one last time."

"A ghost? Rather trite, don't you think? You can do better than that."

"Well, if I'm only a figment of your imagination, you only have yourself to blame."

"Fair enough," she conceded. "I'd still rather you leave."

"Most people want company as they exit this life for the next. Perhaps I am a servant of Uru, here to help guide you. Do you not want someone to hold your hand and tell you it will be all right?"

"I will see the real Thomas, soon enough. Or nothing at all, more likely. Either way, you can go."

"Maybe," not-Thomas said mischievously, "I'm part of the archway."

Her head shot up, then. The archway. The gate to that reprehensible city under the sea.

"Yes," the specter said, "perhaps that's it. Perhaps I am part of that place you hate so."

"Why now?" she demanded. "After all these years, you chose this day, this moment, to torment me? For what purpose? Just to see the anger and despair in my eyes as I slip away? No... I don't believe the gods are even that petty."

"Maybe time isn't the straight arrow you believe it to be. You received a vision of the future that day, didn't you? You saw the world as it became, because of what you had done. You saw what The Wretched would make of the world if you continued, but you did, anyway. Why? Because of what I said to you. I said..."

"You said - Thomas said - that no matter what happened, we would face it together."

"That's right," the image of Thomas said. "And then what happened?"

"And then you left me!" Lea spat. "You died! And I had to face those horrors alone!"

"And you hated me for dying, didn't you?"

"Yes! And I hated myself for hating you."

"And now, after all this time, you've decided to end it." He gestured to the empty glass next to her. "Poison? And you called me trite."

"I can't do it, anymore. I can't. The only thing that kept me here this long was the children. And now they are grown, and I just can't stay here. I want to be with you, with Thomas, and this world is a terrible place. I don't have the strength to face it, anymore."

"That day in the Aelfin outpost, the one you were just thinking about," Thomas' double said, "you told me you were giving up, then, as well. But you kept going. Did your courage stretch this far, and no further?"

"Courage?" Lea laughed, almost manically. "I've never had any courage. Spite kept me going. Hate kept me going."

Her head began to swirl, and she was growing tired. The poison was starting to work. It would not be long, now, until she simply slipped into a warm and comforting sleep. And when she woke, it would be...wherever and whatever was after this life. Her head became heavy, and she struggled to hold it up.

"And love?" her faux husband asked.

"Yes, love, too. When faith and hope had abandoned me, there was always love. Fool that I am."

"Some would argue that love is courage."

"Ure-shit. Love is selfish. You give of yourself to feel better. Even if the other person never knows, you still get that warm and fuzzy feeling telling you that you're a good person. You see the look in their eyes, and you puff out your chest and say, 'I did that!' It's all ure-shit."

Lea felt the words slur in her mouth as it became harder and harder to talk. She would have to wrap up this conversation with herself, quickly. Tedious as it was, she did not want to leave anything unsaid, even to a figment of her imagination.

Thomas stood from the chair he had been occupying and walked over to her. He crouched to her and cupped her chin in his hand. She felt him raise her head up so he could look into her eyes. How was that possible? Was her mind accommodating the hallucination? Now, she was not so sure it was all in her mind. She began to cry as she looked into those eyes that she had not seen in close to twenty years. Portraits did his eyes no justice. Gods, how she missed them. It was right that they would be the last thing she saw in this world.

"Tell me, My Lady," he said, "you've seen how it all ends. There is nothing but heartache and sorrow for you in this world, a world ravaged by the actions of evil men. Evil men loosed by your actions. If you could go back and do it all, again, would you? Knowing what you wrought? Knowing you'd have such little time to spend with him? Knowing the fates of your friends? Would you go back, and do it all again?"

"Yes!" she sobbed, "I would! And gladly!"

He leaned in and kissed her, then. She felt his lips against hers and all doubt was swept away. This was Thomas, it had to be. She had not kissed many men in her life, but there was no imitating that combination of awkward and sweet, nor the taste of his lips. It was impossible, but there it was. Her long-dead husband had return to kiss her moments before she took her own life. At least her luck was consistent, she mused.

"I want to stay with you," she said.

"I know," he replied. "I need you to remember what I said, Love. Time is not the straight arrow you believe it to be. We have been here an infinite number of times before, and will return, endlessly. Only you can stop what is to come."

"I don't understand."

"I know," he said, again, sadly. "Goodbye, Lea. I love you."

Lea did not have time to return the sentiment before oblivion took her.

CHAPTER FOURTEEN

Thomas sat on the cold, white stone floor, nursing his head. A rather large lump had appeared there, and it was quite tender to the touch. The raging headache he gave himself was no small matter, either.

Ana and Exra paced about the room, obviously quite impatient and uncomfortable. So far, no one had made any viable suggestions on what to do, next. Attacking the archway was right out of the question to Thomas. Not only did the glass not give at all to Thomas running into it, if they did manage to somehow break it, would that prevent Lea from escaping? No, it was too risky.

Thomas had tried every possible permutation of the Vasik Lex in an attempt to coax the arch open with keywords or phrases. Translating it into Ancient Esisrian, which may have been spoken when the glass was painted, bore no fruit, either. It seemed that its activation was tied to something else. An examination of the stone found nothing of note, and though it could not be moved, there was a hand-width gap between the arch and wall, and it was easy to see there was nothing behind it.

And so, Thomas sat on the floor while his friends paced, all feeling extremely useless. The voice that had been increasingly vocal inside his head had gone quiet the moment they had stepped foot in the temple. He had begged, pleaded with it to give him the answer, a clue, but to no avail. There were times he thought he picked up a feeling, a word from the voice, but it was hard to tell what it was, and so Thomas grudgingly decided it was nothing more than wishful thinking.

With very little warning, the archway swelled and flickered, a dull purr emanating from it. The stained glass seemed to evaporate rapidly, in its place a hole that seemed to lead to another cavern. Thomas leapt to his feet and ran to it. He peered behind the arch to see that the gap and wall were still there. From the back, the archway led nowhere.

"By the gods," Exra said.

"Should we proceed?" asked Ana.

"Well, we've spent the better part of an hour trying to open the damned thing; unless anyone has a better idea, I..." he stopped talking as he heard something from the other side of the gateway. It sounded like crying, soft but near. It sounded like...

"Lea!"

Throwing caution to the sea, Thomas charged into the arch. The area it led to wasn't a cavern, at all, but an open plain of some kind. It was so dark that that it seemed indoors. The only light was from a single moon in the sky, but it looked nothing like the moons he was used to. A few stars peeked through the dense sky. Not many, but enough that Thomas could tell they were not his stars. This place was not in Anthumbra. This was...somewhere else.

Mere paces into this new world he found Lea. She was laying on the ground, facing away from him, and weeping. He ran to her.

"Lea!" he cried, "Are you all right? Are you hurt?"

She Jumped, startled, and tuned to him.

"Thomas!"

He crouched to her, and she sat up. She threw her arms around his neck and squeezed, so tightly that he could hardly breathe.

"Oh, Thomas! I want to stay with you!"

"I'm not going anywhere, Love," he said, slightly confused. "Are you hurt, at all?" he repeated.

"No," she said, pulling back, "no, I'm all right. Oh, Thomas! The archway! It showed me things, horrible things that will happen. Or might happen, I don't know. I'm trying to hold on to it, but it's slipping away, like a nightmare. And you were there, but it wasn't you. And then it was. And Phillip and Lucy...Thomas, we have to stop them. I've seen what becomes of the world if they succeed, and we have to stop them!"

Phillip. Lea almost never spoke of Phillip. It was a time in her life that was so very painful. Whatever experience she had just endured must have been a terrible ordeal. She seemed so determined, and yet, so bewildered.

"Yes, but what do they want? What is their plan? Aside from awakening the Wretched, what is it they intend to do?"

"They want to destroy the world."

The reunited foursome strolled through this new world. It appeared to be a large village, or was, ages ago. After Ana and Exra had passed through the archway, Thomas looked behind the opening on this side. To his astonishment, it was the same as the arch in the white room, where the rear just led back through to the front. It was unsettling, to say the least.

"Perhaps it is the same archway?" Lea posited.

"Occupying space in two separate places? Two separate worlds?" Thomas mused. "The physical sciences are not my strength, but that defies even their most basic rules."

"The gods do not follow the same rules are you and I," Ana stated.

"But it does make sense that they do have a set of rules to follow? And that those rules have some sort of explanation, even if we can't understand it. This whole place defies explanation. We are at least a furlong deep under an island, and yet, there is the sky."

"Are we even on our world, anymore?" Exra asked. "How many worlds were open to the gods? Could this be one of the Hells? Or like Avar?"

"The body is forbidden in the spirit realms, my love," Ana corrected.

"Well, theology aside," Lea said, "There is no denying that we are here, wherever here is. And I daresay we are the first in several centuries to be here. These buildings are in ruins."

She was correct. Most of the buildings in the village were one-story, though two and three-story buildings cropped up here and there. They were spaced apart, with cobblestone walkways and roads placed symmetrically between them, and they all showed signs of decay rather than damage. This was not a place that grew naturally with time, but was designed from the beginning, someone's idea perfection. And yet, here it lay in disrepair and collapse. Paradise abandoned.

They quickly examined several of the buildings as they walked toward what appeared to be the center of the town or village. Most were living quarters, and though they were simple in their design, the materials and construction were unlike anything Thomas had seen, before. Metals were worked seamlessly together to make entire rooms appear to be one piece, furniture and all. Materials blended so effortlessly that Thomas often could not tell where one started and the other ended, and many of the materials used he could not identify, at all.

Some of the buildings had writing on them, but the language was unfamiliar to him. It looked like a variant of Vasik Lex, but much more complex. Large symbols adorned several entrances, perhaps denoting the function of the building, but none of them made sense to Thomas. There were no books or ledgers to be found, no writings to collect for further study. Thomas made hasty notes but knew how incomplete they would be without reference.

At the center of the village stood a large building, at least in relation to the others. It stood taller than three stories but from the outside looked to have vaulted ceilings. It was the one building in the whole of the village that was not crumbling or decaying. Thomas pushed on the double doors, and they opened easily, as if by themselves.

The building was one giant room, a temple, with pews on all sides and an altar in the very center. It was dimly lit by some sort of lamps that hung from the ceiling, most likely Eimurial. How they still functioned after all this time was a mystery. Against the back wall stood another altar, or display of some kind. Thomas walked slowly toward it, wary of what he may find.

"A temple, inside a city, inside a temple? I would not have guessed it," Exra said.

Upon the center altar was a book, and Thomas' heart leapt for a moment. On further inspection, however, there was nothing written in it, at all. Not on the cover, nor any of the pages. The pages, he saw immediately, were almost metallic. In fact, he was sure they were metal of some kind, but to be so thin and flexible was incredible. He carefully picked the book up and put it in his satchel. He half expected a trap to spring out at him, but nothing happened. He released the breath he did not know he was holding.

The far wall turned out to be much more a display case than altar. On a table sat a series of cut-outs; nine slim, cylindrical shapes spaced evenly in a hard, stone-like material that was alien to Thomas. Only one of them contained anything, a vial that was identical to the one Thomas saw in the Esisrian ruin, that day. There was something important about that vial, something he was on the edge of remembering. What was it?

Behind the display was truly a sight to behold. There was a giant yellow crystal, cut with eight sides that came to a point on both the top and bottom. The crystal pulsed with energy, a slight hum emanating with each pulsation. There looked to be something inside the crystal, but it was covered with a sort of frost or ice that obscured the view into it.

Thomas reached up his hand and touched the crystal. It was cold, much colder than the rest of the room. It should have turned the temple into an ice box, but somehow the coldness was contained. Thomas slid his hand down the side, scraping some the frost off. With nothing covering the outside, the crystal was actually quite transparent. Inside the yellow crystal, suspended much like an insect in an ice cube, was a human figure.

It was a woman, her golden hair long and braided. She was naked and somewhat crouched, her arms crossed over her chest and her eyes closed. She was beautiful, Thomas thought, but an odd sort of beauty. Her features were slightly off. Her legs were too long, her features too sharp, her eyes too far apart. Thomas thought it could be a trick of the crystal's refracting, but that did not seem right.

"Is she human?" asked Lea.

"I don't know. I... I don't think so."

"You are correct," a voice came from behind. All four spun around to face a strange party at the entryway to the temple. The leader of the new group appeared to be an old cleric, a high cleric by his robes. Thomas could easily guess from Exra's description who that was, as well as the two men who flanked him. Behind the trio were a number of other men, who appeared to be under-clerics of some kind, and two of the Sightless Sisters, an order known for their martial skills and ruthless obedience to whomever they were assigned.

"Or, at least, half correct. This is Gro-Estrid, daughter of Gol-Adam. And some insignificant mortal mother. She is half-god."

"Madu," Exra practically growled the name, hand on his sword hilt.

"Basaa Khattab. Regardless of what you may think, it is most agreeable to see you again. And your lovely wife. In fact, I believe this worked out much better for all of us, wouldn't you say?"

"Why are you helping them? Helping the Wretched?" Lea asked, fervently. "You know what they are planning? They want to destroy the world!"

"Destroy the world? You silly girl, why would they want to destroy the world? They live here, too. No, they want remake the world. Build a better world. A fair and just world for all mankind. A world not ruled by gods on high, who keep secrets from their vassals, but by men and for men. A perfect world."

"No," said Lea, pleadingly, "I've seen it, the world they make. It's fire and never-ending war. Hundreds of thousands die in the first days. Those of us who survive do so at the whim of the Wretched."

"The Wretched!" Madu cried, dismissively. "A name given by the self-righteous to those who would dare seize what was rightfully theirs."

He was nervous, Thomas noted, incredibly nervous. He was trying to be relaxed and unflappable, but he kept glancing anxiously to the man at his side, the one Exra had called Amsu. Why would this silent servant make him so uneasy? He looked as if he were about to say more, but the man to his other side, the desiccated husk of a man that Exra had identified as Ned er Khalid, one of the Wretched, himself, all but shoved the high cleric to the side and stepped forward.

"You have seen?" he said to Lea, his voice was low and gruff, like rocks tumbling down a cliff. "How have you seen? Who has shown you?"

"This place," Lea replied, clearly afraid, but also clearly not about to back down. "The archway. It showed me what happened if you succeeded."

"No!" the old figure shouted, "it is but one potential future you saw."

"Perhaps," Lea said, holding her own, "but the arch said that we had stood there infinite times before, and would again. Whatever it is you're planning, it fails. Stop this madness before it is too late."

"No!" he shouted, again, and started toward Lea, hands outstretched. "Show me!"

Inside Thomas, something snapped. It started in his stomach, like a dam bursting. A feeling like raw energy washed over him and filled him up like cold, brisk water. Before he knew what he was doing, he stepped between the risen sorcerer and his wife, and raised his hand, defiantly.

"Touch her and die," he said, surprising himself.

The Wretched spent only a moment in shock before the roll of laughter rose from his gullet. It was a truly disgusting sound, gruff and wet. His already withered lips peeled back to reveal black and sharpened teeth, a gruesome and terrible rictus. Still laughing, the corpselike figure advanced on Thomas.

Thomas, still somewhat amazed at what he was doing, took a step forward. Using the palm of his right hand he struck Neb er Khalid in the chest. He felt an energy flow from his center, up his back and though his shoulder, down his arm and to his hand. The man flew back with such force that he knocked several pews over before finally coming to rest mere hands from the far wall.

Far from being the only one stunned, Thomas felt surreal, as if this were all happening to someone else. He took a step back and extended a protective arm to shield Lea. Unnecessary, he knew, but it was instinctual.

In an instant, the man named Amsu crossed the distance between the, and held Thomas by the collar of his shirt.

"Where is it?" the man demanded, "Where is the vial?"

Unbidden, Thomas' eyes darted to his jacket pocket. Is that where the vial was? Why did he think he should know? What was it about that vial that was so important?

Amsu's hand shot to Thomas' jacket pocket. He fished around for only a moment before withdrawing his hand, his finger cut and bleeding. He shoved his hand back in a drew out fragments of glass that had once been in the shape of an amphora. There was no sign of the red and luminescent liquid that had been in it.

"No..." Amsu said softly. "NO!"

Thomas struck with both palms at Amsu, unleashing another furious blow of concentrated energy. The other man flew backwards, but did not immediately let go of Thomas, causing him to lurch forward and tumble to the floor. He pushed himself up to his elbows.

"Get the vial!" he shouted.

"Kill them!" Madu cried in kind, "Don't let them escape!"

All Chaos broke loose. Lea ran to collect the vial from the display stand, with Madu chasing behind her. Exra and Ana assumed offensive fighting positions. They rushed to put themselves between the Ingeleans and the now charging under-clerics and laborers. Thomas pushed himself back to his feet just in time to take a blast of yellow energy to his chest. It knocked him back several paces and he crumpled to the floor, stunned.

Neb er Khalid had returned to his feet and was advancing on Thomas. He was preparing to fire another blast of the raw Eimuria. Thomas rolled to the side just as the yellow beam struck, barely missing him. He could see that Amsu was rising to his feet, as well. They were horribly outmatched and outnumbered.

Lea had made it to the display and snatched the vial from its small niche. The moment she did so, a low hum and rumble could be heard. It seemed to be coming from the crystal, which had begun to smoke or steam. Madu knocked into her, fiercely, causing her to tumble to the floor, and sending the vial skidding along the ground. Thomas turned and thrust his hands forward to throw a blast of Eimuria at the man, but nothing happened.

"Shit," he said, looking at his hands.

Just then he was struck from behind, an Eimurial blow slamming him forward into a waiting pew. He could see the giant crystal that held the woman in stillness. It seemed to be melting. No, evaporating. It had vanished far enough to reveal her head. She looked almost alive, emerging from a translucent cocoon.

"It seems our host is waking up," Amsu said, stepping forward. "Good."

He fired a pulse of Eimuria aimed at the crystal, and Thomas impulsively extended his hand to intercept it. Instead of blowing his hand back as he had expected, however, it actually deflected the stream of Eimuria, harmlessly hitting the wall. *Well, that's interesting,* he thought.

Neb er Khalid and Amsu were now sending blasts toward the crystal with increased frequency, and Thomas was deflecting them as they came. It was draining him, he noted, and he was not sure he could outlast the pair assaulting him. He did not need to defeat them, he thought, just keep them busy long enough for the others to escape with the vial. What happened to him, after, was meaningless.

Madu and Lea wrestled over the vial, and Thomas tried to deflect the Eimurial blows toward him, but could not get a good enough angle, or a clean enough opening. In front of him, he could see that Ana and Exra had eliminated most of the under-prepared Blighted clerics who were no match for the expertly trained pair. The Sightless Sisters hung back and attacked as opportunity presented itself, using the others as fodder to wear down the pair, a strategy that was beginning to bear fruit.

Amsu and Neb er Khalid now stood side to side, and, in a concerted effort, both loosed a continuous stream of energy. Thomas caught the blasts in his hands but could not deflect them away. He tried to hold it, instead, pushing it away from him. He would not be able to hold on to it for long, he knew. It was only a matter of moments before they overwhelmed him.

From behind, Thomas heard a loud smack. Lea landed to his side, her split lip pouring blood. Tears welled in her eyes, but he knew those tears well. They were not from the pain, but from anger. She looked ready to scream obscenities at the man, when her expression changed from one of anger to one of awe. Thomas could not turn his head any further without releasing the Eimuria aimed at him, but he feared he knew what his wife had seen and was terrified by the implications.

Two yellow beams, one to each side of his head, flew past. The heat was intense, and the force pressed against his head, causing his ears to pop. Thomas' assailants were knocked back, and their own Eimurial attacks ended. Thomas dropped to his knees, sweat pouring from his brow, his breath deep and ragged.

Madu ran past in an attempt to flee, but a burst of yellow hit him in the back and he went tumbling forward, sliding across the floor and into a pew, headfirst. Thomas turned his head to see what he had been running from. In all her glory, Gro-Estrid stood over Lea, who looked both in awe and terrified. The ethereal woman's bare feet seemed to just brush against the floor, as if she touched it only to give the appearance of walking. Her long blonde braid wrapped around her naked form, and a look of anger sat upon her face. She was magnificent, Thomas thought.

He reached his hand to Lea, who took it in hers.

"It's all right, Love," he said, "it will be alright."

"Foru sxarar du'a dina gurangar?" the half-god asked. Her voice reverberated in multiple registers, both high and low, and echoed of its own accord. The language was unknown to Thomas, and yet he felt as if he almost understood it.

"Foru sxarar du'a dina gurangar?" she repeated, this time a demand.

"I'm sorry," Thomas said, and her gaze shot from Lea to him, "but I don't understand."

The otherworldly woman tilted her head as if confused, or perhaps surprised.

"Do you fight for your gods?" she asked. Her accent was thick and musical. It took Thomas a moment to realize what she had said.

Thomas shared a look with Lea. He supposed it was technically true that they did, if only in a circumstantial manner. He was not about to debate semantics with a divine being in the middle of a magical battle for his life, however. And, besides, Lea was nodding her head at him, fervently.

"Yes," he said, quickly adding, "My Lady Gro-Estrid."

"Then, rise," she replied, extending a long-fingered hand to each of them, "and fight."

As Thomas and Lea rose to their feet, they could see that Amsu and Neb er Khalid had also regained their footing. Ana and Exra were still fighting, each having taken more than one blow, but still maintained the upper hand against their more numerous opponents.

Amsu approached the prone form of Madu, who was clawing desperately toward him.

"My legs!" he said in a panic, "I cannot move my legs! I cannot feel them!"

Amsu crouched to Madu and took the vial he had recovered from him.

"That is alright, Madu, my friend," he said, taking the cleric's head in his hands. "You no longer need them."

With a twist and a sickening crack, the head of High Cleric Madu faced the wrong direction, his lifeless eyes staring at nothing. Amsu rose from crouching and removed the wax seal from the amphora. He presented it to Neb er Khalid in a reverent manner. The withered form took the vial in his paper-thin hands and raised it to his lips.

"Your phulassein, dear Neb er Khalid. Drink, and be whole, again!"

The corpse-like man poured the red, glowing liquid into his mouth. Almost instantly, the drawn skin began to relax. The pale pallor flushed dark, his features returning to human. His wispy strands of hair grew full, until he had a splendid mane of wavy black hair.

"Now," Amsu said, "you face the wrath of Neb er Khalid, King of The Eternal! A righteous and powerful Exalted, made whole, once again!"

The rejuvenated ancient thrust forth his hands, a red swath of energy bursting from them. Tendrils of orange and yellow swirled around the emanation, crackling like a great fire. Gro-Estrid produced her own blast, yellow, with blue and black dancing about its surface. The two flows met with a brutal clash, sending a visible ripple through the temple and beyond.

Amsu began throwing his own yellow bursts at Thomas, who managed to deflect them, if barely. He suspected that Amsu's goal was merely to keep him occupied while the two Eimurial superpowers clashed. Lea ran to Ana and Exra, helping them fight off the remaining melee fighters. From where Thomas stood, the Sightless Sisters could not be seen. He wondered if he should be relieved or worried.

The heat in the large room was steadily growing, as the clashing of Eimuria swelled, becoming a growing eye where the two forces converged. It seemed to be becoming unstable, tendrils of power branching off like lightning and striking pews, some of which burst into flames as they were hit. Others turned instantly to ash. Thomas did not want to know what would happen when they struck a human body. Nothing good, for certain.

Thomas was tiring fast. He needed to do something, quickly, else he would be overpowered and likely destroyed. He looked around, desperately, for something to use against Amsu, but there was nothing. He could barely stay on his feet as he deflected blast after blast of the raw Eimurial energy. He wished he could send his own bursts back at the man, who showed no signs of tiring or slowing.

The crackling of the pulsing convergence had grown to a cacophonic roar, causing Thomas, and even Amsu, to wince. It began to flicker in an uneven strobe, faster and faster. Suddenly, there was silence, so profound and jarring against the thunderous clamor it had been that it caused everyone to look toward the eye-shaped mass. But the silence lasted only the briefest of moments before the body of energy collapsed in on itself, then, with a deafening boom, exploded.

Thomas felt himself thrown through the air with tremendous force. He was blinded and disoriented, his head spinning, wildly. He had no idea which direction was up or down until he landed with such force that the air was forced from his lungs, and he had to will his body to start breathing, again. Even once he had caught his breath, the world was spinning so fast and forcefully for him that he could not get to his feet no matter how hard he tried.

"Lea!" he cried, "Lea, are you alright?"

"Thomas!" he heard the reply. Thank the gods.

His vision returned to him, slowly, and he saw the temple was all but destroyed. The ceiling and most of the walls were completely gone, and what pews remained were scattered throughout the village. For his part, Thomas had been thrown completely clear of the temple, and was several score of hands away from where the building once stood.

In the courtyard, he saw the ethereal form of Gro-Estrid glide toward the prone Neb er Khalid. She swung her arm around her, and yellow energy formed itself into a whip. She cracked it against the fallen Wretched, who howled in pain. In turn, he put his hand up and a red swirl formed a kind of shield. The half-god cracked her Eimurial whip against it, and it glanced off.

The ground began to quake, and for a moment, Thomas was not sure if it was the ground or him. It took all his willpower to stand without falling over, he was so dizzy. A thunderous cracking sound was heard, and Thomas looked up. The sky...the sky had cracked! Water began pouring in from the sky in a surreal scene.

"Gilafred's ass!" he exclaimed.

Gro-Estrid held her arm straight up, and the whip became a blade, long and sharp. She made to thrust it toward Neb er Khalid when a blast of Eimuria knocked her to the side. It was Amsu, hurling bolt after bolt at the god-like being. He was no match for her, a fact he was no doubt aware of, but he was buying time for the Wretched to regain his footing. Thomas tried to run to intercept the bolts, to deflect them, but he found he could not move in a straight line. Gro-Estrid easily knocked the attacks away but was unable to focus on the real threat while she did so.

There was further cracking from above as additional fissures in the sky erupted, letting more water in. The ground had already begun to collect what could not run off or soak into the ground. Soon, this village would be a lake.

Before Thomas could see from where they came, the Sightless Sisters had ambushed Amsu, attacking from behind and driving their long knives into his back. He cried out in pain and stopped his attacks on Gro-Estrid. He turned his attention to the two silent priestesses, attacking with fists as well as Eimuria, all the while trying to dislodge the blades in his back. Thomas could think of no reason for the sisters to turn on Amsu. Unless perhaps they were pledged to Madu, in which case they would be honor-bound to bring his killer to justice.

With Amsu sufficiently distracted, the half-god was able to turn her full attention back to Neb er Khalid. She glanced up and saw the fissures opening in the sky. Concern on her face, she turned to Thomas.

"Go!" she said, "You must flee this place! Quickly!"

"No!" cried Lea, half running from where she had landed. "We will not leave you!"

Thomas was slightly confused as to why Lea had sudden loyalty to the woman, but her visions granted by the island may have provided her a reason. He would trust her judgement in any case. Whatever her reasons, it caused Gro-Estrid to smile in a benevolent manner, almost lovingly.

"You cannot survive this," she said to Lea, "but I will. You must tell the others what has happened here, today."

"What others?" Lea asked.

The look on Gro-Estrid's face told Thomas everything. She did not know what had happened, about the Upheaval, about the disappearance of the gods. The dawning realization was painful to watch as she pieced together what Lea's words had meant. That she may very well be the last of her kind. But that anguish quickly turned to stone-faced determination.

"Then make today mean something. Go. Go, now!"

The half-god charged at the Wretched, who had finally managed to reorient himself. She grappled him, sending multicolored sparks flying, like an anvil striking hot steel. Multihued lightning danced around the two figures as they engaged in a battle to the death, or worse.

"Go!" Gro-Estrid yelled, one last time as a giant rupture formed in the domed sky above.

"Oh, shit!" Lea cried as water poured in faster than ever.

Thomas grabbed her by the elbow and ran, still dizzy, but able to head in a straight line. More or less. Ana and Exra followed, their erstwhile opponents occupied with Amsu. They ran through the village, the flood waters chasing behind them. Thomas could see the archway ahead, but the opening was black as pitch rather than the white of the room they had come from. Did that mean it led to a different place, now? Did they have a choice in either case?

With the water on their heels like a giant wave, the unspoken consensus was to use the arch, regardless of what might be on the other side. Thomas dove through with Lea, Ana and Exra just behind them. It felt like splashing into a pool of oil, thick and viscous. His instinct was to cough the substance out of his lungs, but he found he could breathe normally. He found he was no longer holding Lea's arm and tried to call her name, but the thick ooze allowed nothing out.

Damn this arch! he thought as he floated in the inky blackness.

CHAPTER FIFTEEN

Lea stood in the blackness of nothing. Stood was not quite the right word, as there was nothing beneath her. She could see herself in the deep blackness, which made no sense. There was no light, no shadow, no substance. It was unnerving, to say the least. There was no sound, as well, a deep silence that she found unnatural.

"Damn this arch!" she said aloud, mostly just to hear something.

"Damn me?" Came a reply in Thomas' voice.

Lea turned around somehow to see him walking toward her. Walking on that nothing.

"You're not him," she said.

"I believe you said that before."

"Stop the games. I'm tired of them. Just tell me what you want."

"Some things can't be conveyed in words, even if there were words for them."

"Games and riddles. Now I know you're not him, he doesn't have the head for them."

"Maybe I'm him, and something more. Both changed by the other, something more than we were, separately."

"If so, you've become annoying. Why waste my time so? Don't we both have better things to do?"

"Time is all but meaningless, here," he said, looking around. "It can't be wasted or bought. If I were as selfish as I wanted to be, I'd keep you here, forever. Believe me, it's tempting."

He looked sad, forlorn, and Lea was inclined to believe him for a moment.

"Each time we meet like this I pray it will be the last, and yet...I don't want that."

"What is this place?" she asked.

"A place out of time. A world between the worlds."

"That's not much of an answer."

"I know," he said with a sad smile, "but it's the best I can do, now."

"Did we do it? Did we stop them? I suspect that we'd not be having this conversation if we had."

"You were always so much more clever than me...No. Not yet."

"You said we had done this an infinite number of times before. Do we never learn from our mistakes? Are we doomed to just repeat ourselves like a broken wax cylinder? Skipping back to the beginning? Is that not one of the Hundred Hells?"

"There is an end to all of this, I promise, Love."

"Neb er Khalid said the future you showed me was just one potential future. Is that true?"

"Yes," Thomas said, "but it is the most likely. Think of time like a ship. If you're heading for rocks, it's much easier to avoid them if you start steering, early. The closer you get, the harder it is to turn away. But eddies and currents and winds can pull and push you toward them. You must fight both the wind and the sea for control of the ship. It's no easy task."

"Then it's possible to save your life?"

"No," he replied, sadly. "That's the one thing that can't be changed."

"I don't understand," Lea said, frustrated. "If you die, how are you here? How does this 'skipping' start? Why am I caught in it? Are there more like this, like me? How do we end it? If things can be changed, why not just tell me what to do? Or how to save you? I hate this, Thomas!"

She felt the tears of frustration in her eyes and tuned her head away from him. He grabbed her face with his hands and turned it back, kissing her deeply. It was that kiss, his kiss. It made her angrier, some-how, that she thought it really was Thomas. Because the Thomas she knew would never aggravate her, so. But it was still his kiss, and she returned it, despite herself. Damn him.

"I wish I had all the answers," he said, finally pulling back, "but I don't."

"Can you tell me nothing?" she pleaded.

"Just this: there's one thing you've never been able to do, no matter how many times we stand in this place. Even when you know you must."

"What is that?" she asked with trepidation.

"You must let me go. When it is time. You must let me go."

"Will I see you again?"

"You'll see me in just a moment," he said, smiling that sly smirk of his.

"You know what I mean, you horse's ass!"

"I knew you were going to say that."

In the blink of an eye, he was gone, and she found herself stepping out of the archway and into the white room. Thomas stepped out just behind her, almost knocking her over. She pulled him out of the way as Ana and Exra materialized from the black of the arch. As Exra emerged fully, blackness rippled and was replaced by the stained glass that was there, before.

The ground was shaking, and water was seeping through tiny cracks in the ceiling and walls, beginning to pool on the floor. Nothing else was coming though the archway, but it appeared they were still not out of danger.

"Well, that was an odd experience," Thomas said, looking at Lea. "Love, are you alright?" He wiped tears away from her eyes with his thumb.

"Yes," she lied, "just much brighter of a sudden."

"Of course," Thomas replied sympathetically. "Oh, look...the writing is different!" He pointed to the stained glass of the arch.

"No time, my friend," Exra said.

"We are still in peril," finished Ana.

"Yes, of course. Let's go!"

They raced down the cavern and to the lake of quicksilver. There was a new path of stone that looked to have been raised from the bottom on the lake, itself. Thomas shrugged at Exra and started moving as swiftly as he could across the raised stones, forgoing the boat. It was much faster, but the water entering the cavern was beginning to pool on top of the quicksilver and was threatening to cover the raised walkway. The four companions reached the far shore of the lake and continued to the lift that had brought them so far down.

They stepped into the circular lift area. The water had reached shin depth for everyone save Lea, for whom it was past her knees. The four of them turned to each other, each with a look of expectant confusion.

"Well, now what?" Lea asked.

The floor jerked beneath them, knocking Lea to the ground, and soaking her backside. Everyone else managed to keep their balance, of course. The flatform rose slowly, much too slowly for Lea's comfort. The water began to drain from the bottom, though Lea imagined that it was rising below them almost as fast as they were. After an excruciatingly long accent, the lift finally came to rest in the mural covered room of the surface temple.

They ran from the ancient building, Thomas complaining the whole time about samples and notes, and fled into the jungle. The race back to the shore was much easier than the trek in, save for the quaking of the ground. Everyone but Exra fell at least once along the way.

When they reached the mound of discarded possessions, Thomas' disappointment increased tenfold. He began shoving random objects into his pockets and bag, and soon was lagging behind the rest of the group.

"Thomas," said Lea, "we have had enough fun with history, today. We must go!"

With no small amount of grumbling, he complied, finally climbing down the pile, encumbered with his loot. The sea had receded to the base of the giant pile, and small waves lapped against their ankles as they ran. The ground was quickly turning to mud, their boots sticking more with each step toward the shore.

They reached the landing site and scanned the horizon. The Randy Beast was nowhere to be seen. Had Captain Pedraza abandoned them? Had they been destroyed by the Blighted? What would happen to them if they were marooned here? The island was sinking, but even if it did not go all the way beneath the water, there was still the matter of food and shelter. And gods forbid, any remaining Deathless guardians. Should they try to make it to another island and hope it was less perilous? Lea's head spun with questions.

From around the bend in the shore, a small boat came into view. It was being rowed by at least eight men, and at its bow stood a figure, hand to their brow, scanning. They saw the four companions almost as soon as they came into view, and began waving wildly, losing their balance, and almost tumbling into the sea. They regained their footing and cupped their hands to their mouth.

"Ahoy!" came the high-pitched voice, "Ahoy, there!"

"By all that is sacred," Lea said, putting her head in her hands.

"It can't be," Thomas said.

"Any port in a storm, I hear," Ana said, laughing.

The small boat came closer, and soon a larger ship could be seen behind it, and farther out from the island. It was definitely not the Beast, Lea saw, but was larger, and somehow more industrial in design. It had no sails and moved under its own power. The flat-bottomed dinghy rowed right up to the stranded companions and stopped.

"Fancy meeting you all, here" Jewel said with an infuriating grin.

Thomas stood on the bow with his arm around Lea as they watched the island disappear. It was sinking, and Lea could tell that Thomas was saddened by the loss. She, for one, was glad to be rid of the place. There was nothing there but pain. Let another generation of delvers dig it up, she thought.

Thomas had also been understandably silent since learning of Petyr's passing. The cousins had never been close, but he was still kin, and from what Lea knew of him, a good man. Jewel was uncharacteristically serious when she told of his heroism. It was his sacrifice that had driven her and Lyle to come after them, she said, so Lea supposed she had Petyr to thank for the rescue.

Lyle had been instrumental in the ordeal, as well, using Porter Mercantile contacts to eventually hunt down the Tanrin Eli and follow them through The Storm and to the Garden. She looked to where he and Jewel stood, not far from herself and Thomas. Jewel held Lyle's arm and rested her head on his shoulder. He kissed the top of her head, and she squeezed his arm, a genuine and girlish smile on her face.

Interesting, thought Lea. It would not last, but the gods knew that they both deserved the time it gave them. Then, again, Lea had certainly seen stranger things these past days. Maybe there was something there, after all.

The island finally vanished below the water, and Thomas turned away, heading toward the cabin they had been given. They all could use the rest, Lea knew, but for some reason she found herself not tired. Her body ached for sleep, certainly, but her mind was a whirlwind of activity. Every answer gave way to more questions. She wanted to tell Thomas of her experience in the archway, but somehow every time she tried to bring it up, she did not know how to start.

As she walked across the deck of the ship to join her husband, she was greeted by nearly every member of the household. It seemed that all but a few had joined Lyle and Jewel, and those who remained behind had to be convinced that someone needed to guard the estate in everyone else's absence. They were all surprisingly sweet, offering condolences and expressing relief that she and Thomas were alive. She hugged each and every one of them, an act that took many of them by surprise. It seemed that they were just as awkward with her as she was with them. Well, no more, she decided. They were her family, now, as much as Jewel and Thomas, and Ana and Exra. She would make sure they knew it, with no doubts.

As the last well-wisher departed and she climbed below deck, she found her eyes had grown very heavy, amazingly fast. Yes, a good night's sleep would do wonders for her body and spirit. She opened the cabin door and disrobed as she crossed the floor to the bunk. She crawled into bed with Thomas and held him tight against her. She was asleep before her head hit the pillow.

Neb er Khalid set Amsu on the shore of the small body of land that could ostensibly be called an island. He struck the man in chest, once, with a sharp blow, expelling a large amount of seawater. Amsu started coughing, ridding his lungs of the last of the salty brine. He rolled to his side and continued to cough.

"He has taken your pagagh, bother," Neb er Khalid said, water still pouring off his black locks of hair. The aesthetically perfect man offered Amsu his hand, and he took it, rising to his feet.

"Then I will rip it from his still-beating heart," Amsu replied.

"It will not be easy. He has merged with it. It would easier to find another."

"No. He is still weak, and it is mine. Bad enough to be trapped in this body; I will have my own heart back."

"The other phulassein were missing," Neb er Khalid continued, "have the others arisen? Their bagh still lie in Esisria."

"I don't know, my friend, but there is one who does."

"Who?"

"The one who set us on this game. We were all of us played, endiha. We must find who pulls the strings and cut them."

"Could it be him?" Neb er Khalid said, the fear evident on his face.

"Most likely," Amsu said casually, "and unless I'm very wrong, he will be expecting us."

Gro-Estrid's bare feet slid along the surface of the sea, her long toes dipping and dragging in the water. How long had she been away from this world? Already she could see the changes. Where once had stood a glorious city, a monument to the majesty of the gods, there was but a small port, its tiny ships moving in and out like insects in a hive.

She paused, hovering above the water. It would not do to rush into this new world and demand answers, especially if what that human woman had said were true: "what others?" The words haunted Gro-

Estrid to her core. Could she really be the last? Did the gods – did her father – abandon her here? Or were they dead? Impossible. Only gods can kill gods, which would mean there was at least someone else, besides her. They could not all be gone. She would not accept that answer.

With a flick of her wrists, her long braid untangled and began to shorten, until her hair hung just below her chin. It darkened, changing from the bright yellow it had been to a deep and dark brown. Her arms and legs shortened, along with her fingers and toes. Her eyes became smaller and changed from their natural brilliant blue to a murky hazel.

A plain and tan colored cloth wrapped around her body, forming nondescript skirts and a blouse. A hood covered her head, and a scarf wrapped itself around her face, covering everything but her eyes. Sandals appeared to wrap themselves around her feet.

She took one final look behind her where the ruined Garden had once been, and moved forward, gliding across the water and toward this new world.

Sisters Mandisa and Olabisi rowed side by side in silence. Nothing needed to be said, even if their vows had allowed it. They were anathema, now, pariah. Denounced, they were forbidden to return to the Temple. They had been tasked with the life of High Cleric Madu and had failed. That he was a vile and reprehensible man who had made them do unspeakable things was irrelevant. They had failed in their duty.

They had removed their veils, as custom demanded, revealing the ritual scars and tattoos that marked them for what they were. Anyone who saw them would know them for Denounced and would know they were undertaking the Labor of Absolution, a thought that made battle-hardened warriors cower in fear. A Denounced Sister undertaking her Labor would do anything to complete it, and only feared failure.

Whatever this Amsu had become, his life was forfeit. Mandisa and Olabisi would travel to the ends of Anthumbra to find him and kill him if that is what it took. It was now their sole purpose for existence. The two looked at each other in understanding and continued their slow row toward land, each stroke fueling them like the drums of a battle march.

"It is not fair," Ana said, the words echoing out of the bucket her head was in, "how are you not seasick, anymore?"

"I don't know," replied Thomas, sincerely. "I'm sorry. I wish I could help you."

"It is not your fault," she said, "but I still hate you."

His new sea-legs was the least of the changes to her husband, Lea thought. They had not talked about how he was able to manipulate the Eimurial attacks. Everyone had been too afraid of the implications and pretending nothing had changed was easier for the moment. It would not always be so, Lea knew. The conversation would have to happen, sooner than later, and she was not looking forward to it. Right now, she just wanted to enjoy having escaped with their lives.

Lea, Thomas, Ana, and Exra sat around a large galley table with Jewel, Lyle, Captain Pedraza, and Mister Bustos. They had all exchanged their versions of the events of the last few days. Lea did not share her experiences in the archway, however. Provided they did not immediately have her committed, those were personal, and she was not sure what effect they would have on everyone. Besides, she was still sorting them out in her own mind.

She was most interested in the tales of the battles at sea off the shore of the island. Pedraza using oil, and then Jewel and the Tanrin Eli using blasting gel in navel combat was pure insanity. But the Eimurial cannons, as they had decided to refer to them, warranted the extreme measures in Lea's opinion. Of course, it was not her career that had been ended by them.

"None of the crew will take action against the captain," Bustos was saying, "but many have resigned their commission with him. They say what was done was justified, but they can't serve with someone who breaks the Law."

"That seems awfully hypocritical of them," said Thomas, "and un-grateful. Surely, they see that you saved their lives?"

"Aye," answered Pedraza, "but ya have to understand, lad. The Law is a religion unto itself. Even knowing I did what needed done, the guilt gnaws at me. You don't unlearn a lifetime of belief so easily. Not going to the Guild is far more 'grateful' than I could have hoped for."

"Still..." Thomas said.

"It's all moot anyway, lad...I've no ship, anymore. Looks like I'll be a land-legged shore-dweller like the rest of ya, now. I've been a captain too long to take a job as bosun under some greenhorn."

"Well, about that," Thomas said, mischievously. "I've been going over your great-grandfather's notes and I think there's more temples like this one, hidden at sea. He was remarkably close to uncovering the whereabouts of some unbelievable finds. How would you feel about picking up where he left off?"

"You have a ship, do ya?" Pedraza said with a gleam in his eye.

"I own a mercantile business, Captain, I have several ships. But a vessel for exploration? No. I'd have to commission one. I'd like you to oversee its design and construction. You can even name her."

"Ah hahaha!" Pedraza exclaimed, "The Randy Beast shall sail, again!"

"I've been meaning to ask, Captain," said Lea, "why the name? It struck me as a bit.... unconventional."

"I named her after my grandmother," Pedraza said with forlorn sincerity.

"I can't tell if he's joking or not," Exra said.

"I never joke about my grandmother."

The table erupted in laughter. It felt good to laugh again, Lea thought. It had been too long. They continued talking and laughing for several hours. The Storm had dissipated for the first time in living memory when the Garden sank beneath the sea, and the waters were calm. They ate, joked, shared stories, and drank a large amount of ale. For a fleeting time, everything seemed normal.

"They were called what?" Lyle was asking.

"Deathless," Thomas said, "the undead guardians of the Garden."

"That's what I mean!" Jewel said, clearly inebriated, "Undead! What does that even mean? It makes no sense. Either you are or you aren't, right? If you are un-dead, doesn't that just mean 'alive?'"

"Yes," Lyle said, "why not 'un-alive?'"

"Look, that's just how it translated, I didn't make the damned things!" Thomas said, laughing.

"How about, 'mostly dead?'" suggested Jewel.

"Non-dead?" said Lyle.

"Re-alive?" from Jewel.

"You'll have to ask the gods!" Thomas said.

"Oh, and that," started Pedraza, "half-gods...there can't be such a thing, can there?"

"If I hadn't seen her, myself," said Exra, "I'd not believe it."

Pedraza exhaled forcefully, causing his lips to flap, spitting ale and saliva everywhere.

"Andrella's grace!" he said.

"You!" Jewel shouted unexpectedly, pointing to Lyle. She jumped up, abruptly, and barely kept from toppling over. "Take me to bed!"

Lyle's eyes shot wide, and he swallowed hard. He looked to Thomas and Lea like a moonstruck fawn.

"You'd better do as she says, Lyle," said Lea, "stubbornness runs in the family."

"You heard the woman," said Thomas. "Go on, I'll see you in the morning, Lyle."

"Y-yes, My Lady," said Lyle to Jewel, adjusting his collar. He grabbed her by the elbow, somewhat more forcefully than he had perhaps intended. He led the younger Barracourt sister out of the galley.

"Did that just happen?" Exra asked, shocked.

"Indeed, it did," replied Ana, "and it is going to happen, again. Come, husband. Take me to bed." She extended her elbow for Exra to take. He did so, then clasped his other hand on Thomas' shoulder.

"Duty calls, my friend."

The Esisrian couple left the galley on the heels of Jewel and Lyle.

"Well," said Pedraza, "let no man say that Captain Neto Pedraza doesn't know when to retreat. Come, Mister Bustos; are ya ready to be a famous explorer and fight half-gods?"

"Aye, sir."

The two sailors stumbled out of the galley, leaving Lea and Thomas alone. They sat together for a moment in silence, the illusion of normality shattered. Thomas reached over and took Lea's hand in his and kissed the back of it. She smiled and lay her head on his chest.

"What do we do, now?" she asked. It was such an open-ended question, but she still could not bring herself to ask the more specific queries.

"Now? We go home," he said.

"And then?"

"I don't know, Love. Take stock of what we have, and what's happened?"

"I can't help but feel we've done something terrible, or at least that we let something terrible happen because of what we've done. We have to make it right, Thomas. We have to."

"I know the temple gave you visions of the future, and I know that you'll talk about them when you're ready. We can only do the best we can with what we're given. I don't know what tomorrow will bring, Love, or the day after. But, no matter what comes, no matter how terrible things seem, I know that it will be all right. Because we will be together. No matter what happens, Lea, I promise you that we will face it, together."

"I know, Thomas. I know."

Epilogue

The man who called himself Blackmoore put the wire missive down. His contacts in the Tanrin Eli had confirmed everything. It was all as he planned. Finally. After more than four hundred years he had finally set his plans in motion. Impatient man that he was, he had expected to have to wait longer to find the perfect combination, but the Ingeleans had done everything perfectly. His agents could not have infiltrated the Garden without them.

The loss of High Cleric Madu was disappointing, but not unexpected. His former followers were nothing if not predictable. Pawns like Madu were common enough. He had plenty more waiting in the wings.

With the first part of his machinations underway, he could finally dispose of this disgusting guise. Pretending to be this corpulent leech was sickening. Necessary, he knew, but sickening. His next mask was far more entertaining. Especially considering Neb er Khalid and his abomination companion were sure to try to find him.

He walked to the window of the drawing room in the manor he had usurped for this charade. The sun shone down on the landscape, a picturesque scene as far as the eye could see. The world humanity had built in his absence.

He would burn it all to the ground.

ABOUT THE AUTHOR

Erik Pouch is a native of the West Michigan area who resides in Chattanooga, Tennessee. There, he writes novels and short stories, acts in films and television, makes music and short videos, and herds cats. He also plays far too many video games, board games, and tabletop RPGs. His favorite food is anything spicy.